THE COMANDANTE'S GIFT

Frank Gallo

Granada Publishing Services

The Comandante's Gift
Second Printing

ISBN: 978-0-692-01682-4

This book is dedicated to the

Memory of

Victor Sevilla Soto, a Contra combatant,

Killed in Chontales Department, 1989

ACKNOWLEDGEMENT

Quite a few years ago, a writers' group was formed in Granada, Nicaragua, with weekly meetings at the "Maverick Coffee House and Reading Lounge," a meeting place popular with tourists and expatriates, now sadly gone. Through attendance at these meetings, and with the generous support and encouragement of my fellow members, I developed the first outline of a historically-based storyline that took place during the Sandinista-Contra conflict. Previously I had lived in Costa Rica about fifty miles south of Ollie North's CIA Point West airstrip, had seen its remnants from the air on one occasion, and I became hooked on the history of the Nicaraguan conflict. My first draft was sent to degreed creative writer Karen Cox, a friend. Karen suggested that major structural revisions needed to be made. I made them. The book languished for some time, despite the insistence from friends that I get on with it and publish it. I received a great deal of help from several others who read the final draft – Bill Marshall, Jane Kizlauskas Long and others. Captain Vern foster, a retired United pilot with thousands of hours in the DC-3 (same as C-47) was kind to review the chapters that dealt with the C-47, the Maule M-7, and the Cessna 206. Trish Shapiro, a publishing specialist, completed the numerous technical steps needed to prepare the manuscript for publication in Kindle, Nook and soft cover versions. Jacquie Gallo, an accomplished artist, was kind enough to produce the map for the book. The help and encouragement of my wife Vanita, both as a sounding board and also as one intimately familiar with Costa Rica and Nicaragua, was invaluable. The second edition was necessary to correct some typos of both English and Spanish words, to correct usage of some Spanish words, and clarify some cultural observations, some of which were differences between Costa Rica and Nicaragua. I am deeply indebted to Augustin LLanes, owner of the wonderful Montecristo River Lodge (www.montecristoriverlodge.com) on the Río San Juan for his very complete reading of the first edition, pointing out errors in Spanish spelling, incorrect usage and suggestions for changes that would align the story to actual conditions as they were in the time period that the book's story takes place. For instance, in the latter part of the book, the first edition had the rescue party leaving Los Chiles, Costa Rica by way of Río Claro (should have been Río Frio) to the west of Los Chiles, but Augustin pointed out that the river entrance into Lake Nicaragua and the mouth of the Río San Juan was heavily guarded by the Sandinista army at the time that the story takes place. Augustin said the better route to the Río San Juan would have been the Rio Medio Queso to the east of Los Chiles, less guarded and a shorter distance to the Río San Juan. Even now this river is somewhat of a clandestine route. This change was made. In early 2014 I was able to visit the Montecristo River Lodge, and experienced the run down the Río San Juan by panga, somewhat as the fictional characters in the book experienced. I was able to kayak up the Río Sábalos that the rescue party used. Augustin holds a FAA Commercial pilot's license and multi-engine rating, and was able to critically read the book with a pilot's viewpoint as well. While the book is historical fiction, my intent was to provide the framework that while it did not happen, it could have happened as narrated.

-FG

HONDURAS

1 Guatemala City
2 Tegucigalpa
3 San José

MEXICO
BELIZE
GUATEMALA
7
HONDURAS
2
EL SALVADOR
NICARAGUA
COSTA RICA
3
PANAMA

ESTELI • • JINOTEGA
• MATAGALPA

NICARAGUA

Lago
de Managua

• COMALAPA

MANAGUA • • SONOJAL
• JUIGALPA
MASAYA • • PUERTO DIAZ
GRANADA • Isletas

Laguna Calera
Isla de Zapatera

PACIFIC
OCEAN

Isla de
Ometepe

RIVAS • Lago de
Nicaragua

Río Sábalos

SAN JUAN del SUR •

Río San Juan

POINT WEST • LOS
CHILES

COSTA RICA

• LIBERIA

PROLOGUE

Nicaragua is an astonishing country of volcanoes, expansive lakes, wide rivers, numerous Pacific and Caribbean beaches, mountains dotted with rows of coffee, and plains with cattle and cowboys. It is also a country that has suffered serious political turmoil and armed conflict. Its people are warm, hospitable, courteous and independent. But they will rise up in anger when their way of life, their culture, their well-being, their individual freedom is threatened.

Beginning in 1936 the Somoza family took control of Nicaragua. In that year, Anastasio Somoza Garcia, then Commander of the National Guard, seized power. He was followed first by his son Luis, then by son Anastasio Somoza Debayle. The 1972 earthquake that devastated Managua was followed immediately by an outpouring of international relief aid. Much of the aid went into the Somoza family coffers. This particular event galvanized stronger opposition to the dictatorship.

The FSLN (Sandinista Front for National Liberation) was born in 1961 with a Marxist foundation and political philosophy. Support for the FSLN became more wide-based, not for its political aim, but in spite of that objective. In 1978 Pedro

Joaquin Chamorro, the editor of *La Prensa,* was assassinated. The newspaper had been highly critical of the Somoza rule, and the murder was widely attributed to Somoza. The assassination created a martyr for the opposition to the dictatorship. Businessmen, trade unions, non-aligned conservatives and liberals joined with the FSLN in an armed insurrection. The Somoza dynasty was over by July 1979.

The FSLN and supporters formed a five person ruling junta, composed of three Sandinistas and two outside the party. The Sandinistas consolidated their power in the true communist tradition, organizing along the Cuban model with Cuban hands-on direction. Trade unions and rural worker organizations were mandated for Sandinista control. Strikes were barred. Sandinista Defense Committees were established in every neighborhood, the eyes and ears of the government. The Sandinistas assumed total control of the army, electoral council, and judiciary. The two non-Sandinista members of the ruling junta resigned after only one year.

As the repression and control of citizens' lives grew – price controls, enforced cooperatives, favorable treatment of Sandinista party members, etc. – the emergence of the counter-revolutionary Contra movement began. At first many of the ex-National Guard were in the forefront of the Contra movement which began along the Honduran-Nicaraguan border. As the Contra forces grew and leadership was centralized, the ex-National Guard element was largely replaced.

With the growth of a Cuban-inspired revolution in Central America, Soviet military supplies arriving weekly in Nicaragua, and the transshipment of military supplies to the revolutionaries in El Salvador through Nicaragua, the U.S. became alarmed. Support for the Contras in terms of dollars and military equipment was authorized by the U.S. Congress. Air bases in El

Salvador, Honduras, and later Costa Rica became the aerial re-supply bases for the Contra forces operating within Nicaragua.

By 1988 the economy of Nicaragua was collapsing and aid to the Sandinistas from Russia and other Soviet-bloc countries was becoming unreliable. The U.S. Congress had refused to pass a bill that would continue military aid to the Contras, and these factors plus international pressure for the two factions to reach an accord resulted in the Sapoá agreement. The agreement provided for a cease fire, the acceptance of a disarmament plan by the Contras, with Sandinista guarantees of return of exiles without penalty, freedom of expression, peaceful dissent, and non-interference in the political process of returning to a democratic form of government, including free elections.

The accord was enacted slowly, as the cease fire was broken on occasion, and the Sandinistas cracked down on the opposition at times, but the economy continued to deteriorate and military aid to both sides was disappearing. In 1989, Daniel Ortega, confident that he would win the presidential election, set the election date for February 25, 1989. A number of anti-Sandinista candidates emerged, and it became clear that Ortega would win the election unless one candidate was chosen to represent the opposition. That candidate was Violeta Chamorro, widow of the martyred *La Prensa* publisher, and herself a Sandinista junta member in the first year of Sandinista rule until she left the party.

The Sandinista political machine was well funded and Ortega appeared in huge and well-planned and well orchestrated rallies. Hundreds of Sandinista political volunteers ranged throughout the country to promote their candidate. Thousands of spectators were brought into the rallies in long convoys of buses and trucks. In contrast, Chamorro's appearances were much less publicized and not particularly well attended, and her campaign funds were only a fraction of that available to Daniel Ortega. Her defeat and Ortega's win seemed inevitable. But when the votes were counted, Ortega was soundly defeated, garnering only 42% of the vote to Chamorro's 55%, to nearly everyone's surprise.

The success of the Contra counter-revolution is evident. It forced concessions from the FSLN, and perhaps most importantly, resulted in the first free elections.

This story is based on the times and many events in Nicaragua during the 1980's. Much of what is described is based on historical fact, e.g., there was a Point West air strip in the Guanacaste Province of Costa Rica on the Santa Elena Peninsula; a C-123 was shot down in Nicaragua by a missile on the same date and same location used in this story. On the other hand, the story itself and the characters portrayed are fictional.

CHAPTER 1—MISSION ABORT

There it was again. The tiniest change in vibration and sound in the "Gooney Bird", military jargon for the C-47, the equivalent of the DC-3, not noted for its quietness. Marc looked over at Guillermo "Bill" Baltodano, in the right pilot's seat. Bill, short, muscular and dressed in his usual camouflage pants and white t-shirt, was scanning the forest below, looking for the tell-tale flash of a shoulder-fired heat-seeking ground-to-air missile, supplied to Nicaragua's Sandinistas by the Russians. SAM-7's were the Sandinistas' favorite and most reliable anti-aircraft weapon. They were still 20 minutes away from the drop zone as they neared the eastern shore of Lake Nicaragua. The C-47 had departed the Point West airstrip in nearby Costa Rica in the late afternoon to make this dangerous daylight drop to a Contra force desperately in need of supplies. The crew of last night's re-supply drop was not able to identify the drop zone and had returned to the base with its full load.

Marc noted both engines were at normal power, 31 inches of manifold pressure, propellers set at 2150 RPM, cylinder head temperatures normal. Then he saw it. Oil pressure on the right engine, generally referred to as the Number 2 engine, was down to 60 psi. That was 30 psi below normal operating, and it was fluctuating 2 to 3 psi. The oil temperature was at the maximum of 170 degrees.

"Bill!   Take a look at Number 2's oil pressure and temperature. Think we got a problem. How's it look outside?"

"Uh oh.   We've got some oil streaming back along the cowling. Got a leak somewhere."

Marc made a quick decision. "I'm going to reduce power to 27 inches on Number 2. This looks like an abort to me. We better cut back across the lake. It should be about 45 minutes back to Point West. Clyde, you on?"

Clyde Cummings, the barrel-chested loadmaster of few words back in the cabin answered. "Yep, I hear you. We've got nearly 7,000 pounds of guns, ammo, rations, and medical supplies back here. I don't suppose you want to dump them in the lake?"

"No, no way," Marc responded. "But if we lose Number 2, I sure don't want to attempt to single-engine into Point West with this load. We don't dare land at the Llano Grande Airport at Liberia. That would really stir up a hornet's nest. If we keep the engine, we'll land with the load. Otherwise, let's just kick the stuff out on downwind at the last moment. We're going to crank it around now and head back."

Bill's eyes were locked on to the gauges now. "Marc, Number 2 oil pressure is down to 40 psi, and the oil temperature is above red line. It's up to 195 degrees. We're going to trash the engine if we don't shut it down."

"I think you're right, partner. I'm shutting her down." Marc increased power on the left engine to 41 inches of manifold pressure and increased RPM to 2550 to compensate for the loss of power when the right engine was shut down. He pulled the right mixture control to Idle Cutoff, pushed the feather button, turned number two fuel selector and fuel pump off, closed the cowl flap, pulled the throttle to "Off". He and Bill exchanged a quick glance as Marc turned the ignition switch and generator switches for the engine off.

"Hydraulic pump selector valve on number one," Bill said, reaching behind and moving the selector handle to the left engine hydraulic pump. Bill helped to neutralize the yaw to the right by pressing his foot on the left rudder pedal with Marc. Marc began trimming out the yaw with the rudder trim wheel as the old C-47 fishtailed awkwardly and its speed slowed. They worked as a silent team. Both were veterans of past emergencies, simulated and real.

"Bill, let's skirt the south side of the Solentiname Islands. I hear there's almost no Sandinista presence there. From what Intel says, we can easily stay out of AK-47 range. Then we can head for El Tigre. That's more or less Contra territory. That land is so heavily mined that the Sandy's avoid it. So it should be safe from El Tigre back direct to Point West. We'll have to skirt north of the Santa Elena Mountains on our westerly heading. We want to keep to a left traffic pattern north of the airstrip, so we don't have to turn into our dead engine. You know what they say, 'Turn into a dead engine and that's the last turn you'll make.' Then we'll circle around and come back east heading to the strip. Clyde, you're going to have to get as much of that load out the door as possible when we're on downwind."

"Got it, Cap," Clyde replied. "Say when, and give me as much warning as you can. I'm going to loosen up the first pallets right now, so don't do anything crazy."

"You can bet your life I'll try not to," Marc grunted, trimming the slowing aircraft which was now at maximum continuous allowable power on its left engine.

Above the roar of the left engine at maximum power, Marc shouted "Bill, open the cowl flaps full. Let's see if we can stabilize Number one's cylinder head temperature. If not, we may have to dump our load over the lake after all. Sure don't want to get in a bind and dump it on the Interamerican Highway."

"Roger that," Bill's face was tight. He had already given Point West Control a heads up on frequency 122.75: one engine shut down, no supply drop, mission abort, but there was no acknowledgement. He called Cascabel Uno on frequency 120.55 in the clear, advising on the Contra task force common frequency that this afternoon's supply drop was cancelled. Bill was sure the Sandinista Radar and Communications site at Peñas Blancas just north of the Costa Rica-Nicaragua border picked up the transmission. They seemed to know everything before it happened anyway. There was no time for encryption. Marc and Bill knew the CIA radio on Cacao Peak, on the Guanacaste Cordillero east of the Interamerican Highway, would also intercept the message. The CIA station would encode it, and send a more detailed message to Cascabel Uno. They'd use a specific frequency denoted by day and time of day to confuse and deny Sandinista intelligence receivers. The conversations would be over before the Sandy's located the frequency.

"Bill, how do things look to you? There are the Solentiname Islands on the nose, about ten miles out."

"Looking good so far. We're doing about 125 miles per hour groundspeed with the trade winds at our back. I figure we should be in the pattern in 40 minutes or so." Bill's voice sounded strained over the interphone, his Spanish accent more pronounced than normal.

Low on the western horizon, the evening sun spilt a glorious orange for the tourists on Guanacaste's Pacific Coast beaches. Silent again, the pilot and co-pilot looked for El Tigre at the south end of Lake Nicaragua. They could see the mountains of the Santa Elena Peninsula to the west south west, with home base just to the south of the middle part of the range.

"Clyde, we're almost to El Tigre. How's it going back there?" Marc asked.

"I can get at least half the pallets out the cargo door in 5 minutes. If you give me about 15 minutes before we get in the pattern, I can get all 10 pallets out. The pallet beacons will activate as soon as the pilot chute opens. Those pallets are going to be scattered all over hell's half acre. Hope they don't ask me to go four wheeling to help find them."

"Not our problem," Marc said. "I'll just be glad to get them back to where they can be recovered. The next C-123 re-supply shipment from Ilopongo won't be till Tuesday next week. The supplies we're dumping will probably be back in the air on their way to the good guys day after tomorrow."

"Okay Cap, just let me know when."

"Roger that," Marc replied. "Bill, let's try home base again."

"Point West, Point West, Mariposa One here," Bill called on 118.5, the Point West control frequency.

"Go ahead Mariposa One," came the reply.

"We are ten east of Point Charlie at 1,500 feet. Number 2 engine is shut down, we have aborted the mission. We should be on a wide left downwind to runway 9 in about 35 minutes. We still have our load. We'll begin kicking it out when abeam you, with homing beacons activated."

"Point West copies. Wind is zero nine zero, right down the runway, at 15 knots."

"Roger that," came Bill's reply to Point West. "That's a break," he said over the interphone. Marc said nothing and simply nodded. He was sweating profusely, both from the physical exertion of keeping the bird straight and level and the heat of the Guanacaste air even at 1,500 feet.

Crossing the southern border of Lake Nicaragua, Marc steered them over the little coastal village of El Tigre, also known as Point Charlie to the air crews. The old Gooney Bird labored along on its overworked Pratt and Whitney R1830, the cylinder head temperature at 400 degrees, only 25 degrees less than red line and creeping slowly toward the red arc of the instrument gauge.

"....ap, I've got the first five pallets untied and ready to send down the rollers to the cargo door," Clyde called. He had cut off the first part of his transmission by talking before his interphone switch was depressed. Marc knew that the usually laid back Clyde was now under a lot of stress in the cargo hold wrestling with the supply pallets. Damn, we should have a second loadmaster on these flights, he thought to himself.

"Clyde, we've left the Lake and crossed El Tigre and we're abeam Cerro El Hacha. That puts us about 15 miles to Point West as the crow flies. I'll be giving you the green jump light in about 7 minutes. Bill, we have to keep this altitude till we cross the Santa Elena mountain range. At 1,500 feet that gives us about 800 feet ground clearance. We can turn from a wide downwind to a base leg where the north-south gap is in the mountain range. Let's hold the landing gear till we've got the strip made, and go quarter flaps just before touchdown. I'm going to give home base a position report. Take the controls for a bit."

"I have the controls," Bill replied.

"Point West Control, Mariposa One here. We're on a 240 degree heading, on the north side of the Santa Elena range, at 1,500 feet, so we don't have you in sight. We'll begin dropping our load in a couple of minutes, and call you when we're on a base leg crossing the gap to the northwest of you."

"Roger, Mariposa One. Standing by."

The 5,500 foot dirt airstrip of Point West which lay in the narrow Potrero Grande Valley was only three miles away over the mountain range. They would not see the air strip until they turned left 90 degrees and flew though the gap on a base leg to final approach. The sun had already set, plunging rapidly in the last minute. No green flash this time either, Marc reflected, amused that such a trivial thought would come to mind at a time like this.

"Clyde, in about one minute."

"Okay Cap."

"Bill, when the radio compass needle shows we're abeam the field, hit the jump switch. Clyde should be able to get all the pallets down the cargo rollers and out the door in fifteen minutes. Wish we had one more guy back there."

"Roger. Right now we're almost abeam the Point West low frequency beacon. We're so close the needle is going to swing fast."

Within a matter of seconds, Bill called out over the interphone "90 degrees abeam!" He lifted the safety cover on the overhead console and switched the jump button to "on".

"Okay Clyde, start pushing them out," Marc ordered.

Clyde had already removed the pallet tie downs. He then rolled each one down the cabin floor rollers to the door, and then on the transverse rollers out the door. Parachute straps connected to the overhead cable activated the chutes once the pallets were out the door. It was the same system paratroopers use. Marc and Bill felt the trim change fore and aft as each pallet was rolled out.

"Marc, we're 30 degrees past the radio beacon now. We should be about a mile from the gap.

A sudden violent movement caused the C-47 to wallow to the left. Marc fought for control.

"Clyde, what's happening back there?" No answer.

"Clyde, for God's sake, what's going on?" Marc asked again. And again there was no answer.

"Bill, get back in the cabin quick. I'm going to have to pull the power off a bit on the left engine. I can't control the left turn that we get at maximum power. I have full right rudder in now."

Marc started a slow descent and lowered the right wing to maintain heading. The airspeed had dropped to 90 miles per hour, only 8 miles per hour above stall speed. The Santa Elena Mountains were very close now. Any more left turn and they would either barely cross the gap in the mountain range or worse.

Bill unbuckled his seat belt and shoulder harness, clambered between the two seats, and struggled aft, around four pallets that were in line. Clyde was between the cargo door and a pallet, hacking a parachute strap with a hunting knife. Bill yelled at Clyde, who couldn't hear with the noise of the air beating on the cargo door opening. Clyde was bent over, facing the door, as he slashed at the straps of a chute that was partially deployed and streaming out the door. Bill could see that the pallet was jammed against the side of the right latched door.

"What happened?" he yelled in Clyde's ear.

"Damned parachute strap for the pallet got snagged, deployed the pilot chute before the pallet was out."

Both knew time was precious and conversation near impossible in the deafening noise in the doorway. Together they straightened out the pallet packed with boxes marked "RPG-79 Grenades." Going to make a hell of a noise when it hits, Bill thought to himself, as they pushed it out the door without its parachute.

"Clyde," Bill yelled in the loadmaster's ear, "Don't think there's any more time to get the rest of the pallets out. Cinch'em down, we should be turning base leg through the gap in a minute or so."

Bill climbed back in his seat, buckled, and saw the question on Marc's face.

"Parachute deployed before the pallet got out. Clyde cut it away. He's securing the remaining four pallets. That leaves us about 2,800 pounds."

"Okay," Marc replied. "That was a close one. But we're not home yet. We're coming up on the gap now. We lost 300 feet when the parachute deployed, so we're barely going to clear the gap. I'm going up to 48 inches for a few minutes so we can regain some altitude. Hope the engine can take it. We need both the altitude and airspeed."

Without prompting, Bill called the strip.

"Point West Control, Mariposa One turning left base through the gap."

"Roger," Point West responded. "We don't have you in sight. Runway lights are on, runway is clear."

"Mariposa One copy," Bill answered.

Turning left into the operating engine in as wide an arc as possible, Marc aimed the C-47 for the middle of the gap.

"Bill, let's get rid of some of this fuel. Time the dump for two minutes. We can dump 600 gallons per minute. That will lighten us up by 1,200 pounds."

"Roger that," Bill replied, unbuckled and got out of his seat, then knelt on the floor behind the pilots' seats. He opened the access door to the fuel dump valves and pulled the T-handle on the left to "OPEN". This lowered the dump chute and opened the dump valves. He timed two minutes on his watch, then pulled the right T-handle to close the valves. He closed the access door and returned to his seat.

"Looks like about 200 gallons remaining," Marc said, pointing to the fuel gauges.

The trade winds were flowing over the gap from the north, giving the tired gooney bird lift like a glider.

"Need all the help we can get," Marc said, pointing to the vertical speed indicator that registered a 500 foot per minute climb, otherwise unbelievable for an engine-out approach. Crossing the gap, and flying south into the Potrero Grande Valley, the downdraft came on the lee side of the gap as the two pilots expected. They were now clear of the higher terrain, and Marc began a gentle turn to the left to fly east up the valley.

"All stowed in the back," Clyde said on the interphone, and came forward. He quickly unfolded the jump seat just aft of the pilots' seats, and belted himself in.

Marc glanced back at Clyde and nodded. Now the really hard work begins, he thought. The situation was not good; single engine, almost dark, dirt strip, a steep hill to the left of the runway, and the Río Potrero Grande to the right. To top it off, 2,800 pounds of cargo on board, much of it explosive.

Mariposa One turned left 90 degrees to a long slow final, now heading back to the east into the wind. Normally by now Marc would be slowly reducing power, and trimming nose up as airspeed decreased. But this was a much different approach. The differential power from only one engine, the brute torque force of the Pratt and Whitney R1830 on the left wing fought against the two pilots trying to maintain directional stability. The added 2,800 pounds of cargo was a recipe for disaster.

Here, Marc thought, is when all the training, experience, and judgment accumulated over the years has to pay off.

"Call it out when you see it," Marc instructed his co-pilot.

"Think I can see the lights on the south side of the strip," Bill responded. He could see the glimmer of the low power temporary lights that were set along the south side only of the 5,500 foot dirt strip. Night landings on the northern bank of the Río Potrero Grande were not relished by the pilots here.

"Marc, it's about 10 degrees to your left, a mile and a half out," Bill said on intercom. Depressing his mike button, he made an advisory position report.

"Point West Control, Mariposa One a mile and a half out, have the strip in sight." Bill switched on the landing lights.

"Roger, have you in sight, winds now zero eight zero at eleven."

"Mariposa One."

"I'm easing off on the power, Bill, but stay on the rudders with me. No go-around on this one, so let's make it good."

"Roger that," Bill answered. "Are you ready for the gear?"

"We better wait. I remember what my old flight instructor said. 'When on one engine, when the gear goes down, the airplane goes down.' I'm pulling back to 30 inches and 2550 RPM. Go ahead and give me half flaps. At 1,000 feet above ground, put the gear down."

"Half flaps," Bill responded. Marc pulled the power back to 24 inches manifold pressure and set up a rate of descent of 500 feet per minute and airspeed of 95 miles per hour.

At 1,000 feet altitude on final approach, Bill put the gear handle down. Two green lights came on indicating the gear was down and locked.

Directional control was now much easier with the throttle reduced on number one engine. Mariposa One continued down the glide path to a smooth touchdown on the gravel runway of Point West.

The old C-47 came to a stop at the end of the strip. A Landcruiser pulling a tow bar left the operations shack in a swirl of dust and headed for the C-47.

Marc shut down number one engine.

"They say any good landing is one you walk away from," Marc said, visibly slumping in his seat. His shirt, like Bill's, was soaked through with perspiration.

"Yeah, I think I've heard that before," Bill said.

"Tough way to make a living," Clyde offered. "Thought we might not make it when the chute deployed early."

"Now I know why you loadmasters carry a hunting knife on your belt," Bill said.

"Let's get out of here," Marc said, as two Landcruisers pulled up to the parked C-47.

CHAPTER 2—POINT WEST AIRSTRIP-1986

"Typical, but damned good," Marc said aloud as he wolfed down a breakfast of gallo pinto, the Costa Rican black beans and rice dish that every restaurant in the country labeled "tipico". The mess rancho at Point West was a simple affair. A long tile roof was supported by eight posts on each side. A concrete slab floor, a propane stove, and several picnic tables were serviced by two local cooks.

"Heard you had quite a time yesterday," a tall lanky man in his mid-fifties said as he walked into the rancho.

"Hi Jimmy," Marc replied to Jimmy Shackleton, who was handed a mug of strong coffee by one of the cooks as he sat down across from Marc.

"Gracias," he offered to the short, rotund cook everyone knew affectionately as "Gordita".

"Con mucho gusto," she replied, the Costa Rican version of "you're welcome" accompanied with her usual smile.

Marc reviewed yesterday's events as briefly as he could. Having told the story several times, he was now getting bored with it.

"What're you doing here, man? After a day like that I'd be in San José on R&R," Jimmy said.

"Well, first of all I was too tired to even go into Liberia to the crew house. Besides that, Bradlee said he wanted to talk to me this afternoon." Marc exaggerated the "lee" in Bradlee. Brad McGowan did not like to be called Bradlee. Calling him "Mac" would likewise draw a frosty stare.

"I wonder what the spooks are up to now," Jimmy said.

"I dunno. Guess I'll find out. If you Ops and Intel guys talked more to each other, you would probably know," Marc shook his head. "Brad asked me how comfortable I was in the Maule. I told him I had lots of recent single engine time in light aircraft. I had a Cessna 182 in the States, which I sold a couple of months before I came down here. The Maule and the 182 are very similar in size and handling characteristics. They both have about the same horsepower, the 182 has tri-cycle gear, but the Maule is a tail dragger and a much better bush plane. If you remember, I flew the Maule a couple of times last month, checking out the beaches around the peninsula. It´s a good stick and rudder bird with no surprises."

"We have a third one coming in, you know. A private donation by the CEO of a Colorado beer company that I'm under orders not to name, but you can guess."

"Yeah, I heard that through the grapevine. That'll give us three for the low and slow intel flights north of the border," Marc said.

"Tell you what. I´m heading for Liberia now, I'll be back tomorrow morning. If Brad McGowan doesn´t have you tied down, let´s drive down the Río Potrero Grande to Playa Nancite."

"Sounds good. I'm staying here tonight. I'll call you by radio telephone if Brad has me scheduled for something and I can't go."

"Good enough. Catch you later then," Jimmy said, as he unraveled his long legs from the picnic table and walked back to the operations shack.

Marc sat alone at the table. Gordita walked up and poured another cup of coffee without being asked. Three mechanics were at the far end of the rancho eating their breakfasts. Carla, the other cook, as skinny as Gordita was fat, hurried back and forth to their table with extra helpings of fried eggs, tortillas and gallo pinto.

Marc sipped his coffee slowly, and realized he was bone tired, even after the night's sleep. Stress, he decided. The rooms in the tin roofed barracks had screened windows, but there had been little evening breeze. His small floor fan had hardly moved the hot sticky air. He saw Jimmy leave the Ops shack and get into an old Land Cruiser. The diesel engine turned over several times, finally fired, and the Land Cruiser pulled onto the dirt road alongside the runway. It left a cloud of dust billowing behind, mixing with the trail of acrid black diesel exhaust. Marc watched as the vehicle accelerated on the washboard road leading away from Point West to the Interamerican Highway.

There was very little activity at the airstrip. It was too early for the C-123 re-supply flight from Ilopango. That would arrive in a couple of hours. Marc looked out on the dirt airstrip, which ran east and west on a natural plain for a mile in the narrow Potrero Grande Valley. The valley itself was framed by two narrow parallel ridges on either side; the ridges were bare except for stunted scrub trees and low bushes. The lack of vegetation attested to the dry Guanacaste climate that provided sparse rainfall over the year. The wind blew in hot gusts down the valley. The Rio Potrero Grande, more a trickle than a river at this time of year, lay in the middle of the valley. A series of levees rose from the banks of the river to the north protecting the airstrip which lay between the river and the northern ridge of mountains.

Two C-47's were tied down toward the eastern end of the strip on the north side, in a cleared dirt area. The two Maule aircraft were under individual shelters with zinc sheeted roofs to give protection from the sun. These were next to the Operations shack. Referred to in official documents as the Operations Center, it was always generally referred to as "Ops" by Jimmy and the others. A large bodega, a warehouse of heavy steel siding, was even further away, on the far side of the C-47 parking area. When the C-123's arrived, their cargo was unloaded and stored in the bodega. Pallets to be dropped by the C-47's were made up of the munitions, weapons, food supplies, clothing, boots, medical supplies, and other items requested for drops to operating Contra units.

"Marc, can you come over to Ops now?" It was Brad's voice. The growl over the Motorola handheld startled Marc out of his exhaustion.

"Yep, on my way, Brad," Marc answered. He got up from the table, blew a kiss to Gordita, and walked over to the Ops shack.

"What's up, Brad?" Marc asked. He pulled a metal folding chair away from a table that was covered with a variety of UHF, low frequency and two HF radios. A mass of cables behind the radios fell to the floor in mind-boggling disarray. Brad, of medium build with close cropped hair who appeared younger than one in his early sixties, was sitting behind an old gray metal desk on the other side of the room. The only other office furniture in the one room shack was two gray metal file cabinets and a radio telephone on a small unpainted wooden table. A handmade sign on the wall read "Udall Resources." Marc dragged the chair over the red clay tile floor to Brad's desk and sat down.

"Marc, you had a hell of a time yesterday. You guys did a great job saving the payload. All of it was recovered intact except the ammo pallet that went without a chute. That pallet was scattered over two acres. It's not worth retrieving," Brad said, peering at Marc over reading glasses perched on the end of his nose.

Marc decided to go along with the small talk. McGowan was a CIA operative, not one of the operations officers that handled the day-to-day scheduling of aircraft, pilots, and maintenance for the two C-47's and two Maule M-7's at Point West. The Ops guys provided the assets, and the spooks, the Agency guys, tasked the missions to be flown. Brad and his clandestine "company" coordinated the Contra supply flights from Honduras, El Salvador, and the relatively new Point West on the Contra southern flank. But the lines between the two functions often were very blurry.

"Yeah, it got a little hairy," Marc said.

"I talked to the maintenance guys. An oil pump is being flown in from Ilopango today. The bird should be ready day after tomorrow."

"Glad to hear that. We need to make up that lost re-supply flight. I feel for those guys on the ground," Marc said.

"Me too. But I guess you're wondering what I really wanted to talk to you about. Marc, you flew the Maule last month a couple of times. How did you like it?"

"A good honest bird, Brad. Responsive, fun to fly."

"I have a special mission. It involves taking a passenger north and dropping him off at an airstrip on the east side of Lake Nicaragua. Our intel is that the airstrip is not guarded. Although you would be tracked by Sandy radar, they would have no idea what you were doing. They certainly wouldn't expect you to be landing. A minute or two on the ground, and then you'd be off. If you're down low over the water, the Sandy's shouldn't even know you landed. They would see it more as a mapping or some other sort of intel flight, or maybe even a drop. Interested?"

"What time of day? Do you have a picture of the airstrip?" Marc asked.

"First light, day after tomorrow. We have pictures. It's about 2,000 feet, and no obstructions."

"Who is my passenger?"

"Can't tell you in any detail. Goes by the name Fernando. The nature of his trip is something you shouldn't know, for his safety and yours. We'll launch the other Maule at the same time. The two of you will split up over the lake, he will head for Ometepe Island, then turn towards Rivas, and beat it for home."

"My better judgment says "say no", but I'm a sucker for intrigue," Marc said.

Brad pulled a folder out of the top drawer of the closest file cabinet and handed it to Marc.

"The route of flight is marked on the chart, and there's a good photo of the airstrip. You'll have to study it here in the office. You can make some diagrams or drawings on paper to take with you, but none of this material can leave the office."

"Okay, let me look over the folder."

Marc pulled the folder over to his side of the desk, opened it, and studied the ONC K-25 chart that detailed terrain and features at a scale of 1:1,000,000.

"No sectionals, Brad, with more detail?" Marc asked.

"Nope. Sorry. None for this part of the world. There are aerial photos in the green binder that give a good visual of the Sonojal strip, and its location inshore of the lake. The photos are only six weeks old. There is one satellite shot in there that shows the prominent landmarks you can use to find the strip."

The route marked on the map with a heavy black line showed an almost direct heading from Point West across the southern end of the Lake. It extended to a point 10 miles west of the San Miguelito airstrip on the eastern shore - 20 kilometers north of San Carlos. Then the line turned abruptly to the North Northwest, first following the Lake's shoreline until abeam the Sonojal airstrip. It then turned directly inland to the east for 12 miles to Sonojal.

"Brad, any Sandy activity at San Miguelito, or on the shore going north? Like La Flor, San Bartolo, Cañas Gordas, La Garita?"

"No, our intel assets keep a good watch. The Contras have roving Special Forces patrols. They keep the Sandy's from putting any copter and observation planes on those strips. They tried setting up a temporary chopper base at Cañas Gordas to cover the Boaco and Chontales regions about six months ago. They were only there a week when one of our Contra Tiger Teams hit them. Two MI-25's destroyed and several Sandinistas KIA. They haven't tried it since."

"Okay. The way the route is laid out, it's 127 nautical miles to Sonojal. The Maule M-7 cruises at 125 knots True Air Speed, add five minutes for climb, and that makes about an hour, five to get there. The return route shows heading east passing north of Juigalpa. More friendly territory. I like that. From there a turn to the south, we cross the Río San Juan east of San Carlos, into Costa Rican territory, then straight back to Point West.

That's another 163 nautical, one and a half hours. It's all figured no-wind, but it should even out. That totals two and a half hours. I figure four hours of fuel, and I'm adding an extra 20 minute pad of flight time for Mom and the family. That's a comfortable reserve. When's the launch, and how much gear will my passenger have?"

"Figure 6:00 a.m. departure. That's the same as zero six hundred to you fly guys. We're talking day after tomorrow. Your passenger will have no more than a small duffle bag and brief case," Brad said.

"Who's going in the other Maule?" Marc asked.

"Joe Parks said he'd play decoy for you. He's in Liberia now, said he won't be up here till 4:00 a.m. that morning. I warned him not to be late. He should stay over tomorrow night. I guess he's in love with a little Tica from Liberia. Joe has already briefed and studied the ops order. He'll fly along with you. You're the lead. When you pass north of the Solentiname Islands, he'll turn northwest and head directly for Ometepe Island. That's when you hit the deck and keep on course towards San Miguelito. Same rule as always on these flights. No personal ID, no radio contact except in an emergency and then the day's authentication code will come from me. I'll be here to see you guys off and give you the current codes then. Any questions?"

"No, sounds simple enough. That's what worries me. I'm going back to the quarters to read a little Clive Cussler. Tomorrow morning Jimmy and I are going to drive down to Playa Nancite. I'll be back by mid-afternoon in case anything changes."

"Okay. I've got to get ready for the re-supply flight from Ilopango. I asked them to bring us some Salvadoran export-quality filets in a cooler. If they didn't forget, Gordita and Carla will be barbecuing steak tonight."

"I'll look forward to that, Brad. See you," Marc said as he got up and walked to the doorway.

It was barely light when a flock of parrots swarmed to the gnarled guanacaste tree outside Marc's window. Squawking calls sounded like loud bickering of a bunch of young unruly school kids. Two times the flock flew off. Marc would close his eyes, and within minutes they would return to the tree, noisier than ever. Further sleep was impossible. Marc got up and headed for the central barracks washroom. Returning quickly, he donned a pair of snugly fitted jeans that didn't require a belt, and a Banana Republic t-shirt. He headed for the mess shack where he was welcomed by a smiling Gordita. By his second cup of coffee, the sun was peeking into the eastern end of the Potrero Grande Valley. It was a cool morning, the best time of day in Guanacaste. He heard the grinding of gears before he saw Jimmy's white Land Cruiser come into view at the east end of the landing strip. Jimmy drove down the center of the strip, a cloud of white dust marking his progress. The Land Cruiser veered off, headed straight for the Mess shack. At the last moment Jimmy jammed on the brakes. The old vehicle shuddered to a stop less than ten feet from one of the posts holding up the roof. Jimmy jumped out and walked over to Marc's table.

"Buenos Dias, Amigo. Listo?" Jimmy said.

"Buenos Dias. Sí, listo, ready, as soon as I finish my coffee. You have a hell of a lot more confidence in that old bucket of bolts than I do. You going to have breakfast?"

"No, had it already. I stopped at the Bramadero Restaurant in Liberia." Jimmy replied.

"Well, I'm done. May have to unload some of this coffee on the way," he said, as they walked over to the Land Cruiser.

"Tico Cadillac," Marc grunted, as he swung into the right seat.

"Yeah. The old Land Cruisers are virtually indestructible, probably the most durable vehicle ever made. Which explains why they're all over Costa Rica," Jimmy replied, cranking the engine. It fired after several revolutions, and then a large cloud of black diesel erupted briefly from the exhaust pipe. They drove off, the engine clanking noisily as they left the level valley floor and began the descent to Playa Nancite. They had to ford the shallow Río Potrero Grande as they followed its course to the west.

"If it were a month or two later, after the rains start, we wouldn't be able to ford the river like this," Jimmy said, as if reading Marc's mind.

Down and down they descended, out of sight of the barren Santa Elena Mountains, leaving the heavy fields of jaragua grass and entering the thick humid old forest. As they neared the mangrove swamps bordering the coast line, the morning birds demanded their attention. Noisy, squawking parrots argued, herons took off from the higher branches of hundred foot trees. They could hear the occasional barking of nearby howler monkeys.

"We'll skirt some extensive mangrove swamps before we get to the beach," Jimmy said. Within minutes the road took them alongside an estuary of red mangrove, each tree a solitary island, held aloft by large mature roots that grew down into the water.

"Lots more birds down here than up in the Valley. Quite a few parrots. I'm on the lookout for Macaws. Never seen one in the wild," Marc said.

Marc was startled when they burst out of heavy growth onto the white sand of a mile-long deserted beach. Rocky points a mile distant guarded the beach at each end.

"To the south is Bahia Potrero Grande," Jimmy said, pointing. "Great surfing there. Witches Rock, just offshore, is a world class surfing spot with some of the best breaks in Costa Rica. Some of our California guys drive down here with surfboards and spend the day when they have time off."

Marc was stunned. Up close the beach was much more beautiful and expansive than it had seemed from the Maule.

"What are the islands to the west?" Marc asked.

"The first is Isla Colorado, and in the distance are the Bat Islands, or in Spanish, the Islas Murciélagos. The winds really kick up out there, 60 knots would not be unusual this time of year. The C-123's pass over here on a base leg to a final approach to the airstrip. They fly a bigger pattern than you guys in the gooney birds. The turbulence can be from moderate to severe for a few minutes. Scares the hell out of the crews who've never flown in here before."

Jimmy backed the Land Cruiser off the beach and parked it under a plumeria tree, also known as the frangipangi. It was in full bloom and filled the air with an orange blossom fragrance. The tree's white five-petal flowers were surrounded by little clusters of waxy green leaves. Marc and Jimmy walked out on the beach, now wide at mid-tide.

"Look here, Marc. You can see part of the tracks of an Olive Ridley turtle. Last night she came up on the beach to lay her eggs. We can follow the tracks up higher on the beach. Here you can see the depression," Jimmy said, pointing to a swale that looked to be about four feet wide. "This is the hole she dug to deposit her eggs. It takes the turtle four to five hours to dig the hole. Then it takes her maybe 30 or 40 minutes to drop the eggs one by one in the hole, and more time to cover it up. She's exhausted by then, of course. But she makes her way back to the ocean, not to return until next year. This beach is the nesting ground for thousands of Olive Ridley turtles that come back to this particular beach every year."

"Pretty amazing. Look there, Jimmy. Looks like a dog digging in the sand," Marc said, pointing to the south end of the beach. Jimmy turned and looked, took his baseball cap off and held it up to block the mid-morning sun.

"That's a coyote, Marc. It's digging up turtle eggs. It's a wonder any of the turtles survive. The Tico poachers dig the eggs up like the coyotes and sell them for their supposed aphrodisiac qualities. When the turtles hatch, they make a run for the water. Lots of them are caught by the birds before they can reach the safety of the surf. Once in the water, they're fish food. Let's walk down the beach."

Marc walked the tide line, looking at shells. Jimmy waded calf high in the surf. He had hung his canvas sneakers tied together around his neck. Marc moved higher on the beach, exploring the low scrub just beyond the beach.

"Keep your eyes open, Marc," Jimmy yelled. "When I was down here a couple of months ago with two naturalists from the University of Pennsylvania, they pointed out jaguar tracks."

Marc immediately veered back toward the beach. "That's enough to convince me," he said. "I saw a couple of jaguars at an animal refuge south of Liberia. Those cats are big and powerful."

"Yeah. They're the most powerful cat in the Americas. They can weigh 250 pounds or more and reach six feet in length.

Furthermore, they don't seem to be afraid of man's scent. These naturalists said jaguars can follow you as you walk through the Santa Elena dry forest and you'll never know they are there. Most foreigners think the big cats live up in the cordillera, the whole range from Orosi Volcano south to Panama, but the tropical forest lowlands is really their habitat. It's pretty interesting. The Penn naturalists spend every summer here studying the flora and fauna. They say the Santa Elena dry forest is the largest mostly intact of its kind in Central America."

"Yep. Wild country. Glad we came down here. But I'm ready for one of those Imperial cervezas you brought in the cooler."

"Good idea. This sun will fry you if you're not careful. Let's find some shade," Jimmy said. They sat under a plumeria tree, sipping their beer and munching on Gordita's ham sandwiches. They talked little, content to enjoy the exotic tropical beach and the refreshing offshore breeze in their faces.

"Let's call it a day," Marc finally said, and stood and stretched. "I've got an early morning "go" tomorrow."

"What is it," Jimmy asked.

"Sort of unusual. A Maule mission, passenger drop off."

"By chute, I hope," Jimmy said.

"Nope. Land, kick him out, and go."

"Be careful on that one. Leaves a lot of weight on the intell. And it's not always that great."

"Yeah, I know. If it doesn't look right, I won't land. I'll have to admit, I'm a little uneasy about it."

"Let's get back to the base then. You may want a little more mission study," Jimmy said.

"It's pretty simple. That's what I told Bradlee. I also told him that's what scares me. The simple ones can turn to shit fast, usually when you're least prepared."

The Land Cruiser crawled up the two track trail in first gear. They surprised a group of howler monkeys, the dominant male bellowing his outrage. At last they left the dense dry forest. The mountain ranges of Santa Elena reappeared. Marc grabbed two Imperials out of the cooler, popped one open for Jimmy, then one for himself. They rode in silence back to Point West, savoring the cerveza and the natural wonders the Peninsula bestowed upon adventurers.

Jimmy dropped Marc off at the Ops office and headed for Liberia. As Marc walked in, Brad was at his desk with Walkman headphones on, reading an edition of the Miami Herald.

"Anything new, Brad?"

"Hi Marc, what did you say?" Brad asked, slipping the headphones off.

"Is it still a go?"

"Affirmative. All set. Marc, the Ops Duty officer said the maintenance guys have pre-flighted both Maules. They're ready.

"Good. I'm heading over to the mess now. Did the steaks arrive and are there any left?"

"Yeah, the Ilopongo boys came through. Gordita has steak, baked potatoes, frijoles, and ensalada on the menu. What more can you ask? Enjoy. See you in the morning."

"Vaya! Vaya!," Gordita yelled as she ran to the center table and chased Charlie the coatimundi out of the eating area. Charlie was well known to the men of Point West. They had evidence that the coatimundi opened screen doors and snatched various items from their rooms. As this newest scene unfolded, Gordita walked back to the cooking area as Charlie ran around the far end of the shack and came back to the other side of the picnic table. He hopped up on the bench. Gordita turned around just in time to see the coati grab the napkin holder.

"Vaya, Vaya," she yelled, and ran as fast as her short fat legs would allow.

Charlie leapt to the ground and ran to the far end of the shack. Gordita picked up the napkin holder and scattered napkins, muttering "animal malo, animal, malo."

Marc could see Charlie outside the shack, just waiting till Gordita was back in the open kitchen area, and trying not to laugh as the little coati played his game.

"Cute little rascal," he said to Bill Marshall, another retired Air Force pilot who was Ops Duty Officer of the day. Bill had just sat down across from him.

"Yes. And smart too. I remember a few months ago when we had a high powered NSA guy from Washington visiting here. Coat and tie yet. Nobody would say what his name was. Very hush hush. Charlie went over and bit him on the ankle."

Marc laughed, broke off a piece of bread and offered it to Charlie. Charlie was still determined to play his game with Gordita and headed for the center table again. The coati took the bread, sat down at Marc's feet, held the bread in his finger-like front paws, and nibbled.

"Marc, you got an early one tomorrow, I see," Bill said.

"Yeah. Think I'll turn in early. Buenos noches."

"Buenos noches, Marc."

CHAPTER 3—THE MISSIONARY

The old yellow school bus with "Rappahannock School District" painted on its side in faded black letters lurched through a series of potholes stretching from one side of the road to the other. The driver shifted down to first gear, the gears grinding angrily in protest as the well-worn clutch gave evidence it was near life's end. The passengers were thrown to the left and to the right in successive waves. Those in the outer seats fought to keep from sliding off. Many were holding packages and bags from the Managua markets, but were contained by the passengers forced to stand in the aisles of the crowded bus.

Ellen was lucky. She had traveled from Comalapa to Managua several times for the Mission's quarterly meetings. She knew to get to the Managua east-side bus terminal well before the 6:00 a.m. departure if she wanted to avoid standing during the four hour trip.

Ellen always joked that the Assembly of God Mission Headquarters had the feel of a motel. "U" shaped and one-story, it enclosed an empty swimming pool in the center. There were several offices, a dozen bedrooms, a dining area and kitchen that served those who lived in Managua and those deployed out in the country's departments. Its location was less than a mile from the up-scale Las Colinas barrio on the eastern side of Managua. But Mission Headquarters had seen better days, and was in need of paint, gardening, and physical repairs. The quarterly meeting at the Assembly of God's church mission headquarters provided little in the way of material help to the nurse missionaries who had come in from the outlying regions. There were several meetings. Subjects such as security, dealing with the current political situation, budget allocations, and analysis of trends in illnesses such as dengue, cholera, typhoid, malaria and hepatitis, were all current health issues in this and the other Central American countries. Some medical supplies were parceled out to Ellen and her fellow mission nurses. She had received a two month supply of antibiotics and some tetanus and typhoid serum, though hardly enough for a month. Those supplies were in a box tied down on the bus' roof carrier. That space was shared with baskets, burlap bags of commodities and foodstuffs, including half a dozen old bicycles. It seemed the roof carried as much as the interior of the bus, and oftentimes there would be several youths perched on top as well.

"Chicken bus," Ellen thought ruefully. Only there were no chickens on this bus. They would have gone one-way to Managua for sale in the market, providing their owners some hard earned cash with which to buy necessities which would be carried back home. Ellen didn't know if the Nicaraguans knew the term "chicken bus." It was a common term the gringos used for the old yellow school buses driven down from the States to serve as the primary form of local and regional transportation within the country. Chickens, pigs, and other animals were quite common, sharing the crowded space with the endlessly patient passengers.

Ellen leaned against the window. Thankfully all the upper sliding windows were open, allowing the breeze to cleanse the packed bus. It had been good to see Bob Stevens again, she mused. She was aware that Bob had already been at the Church's health clinic in Chinandega for three years. It was unlikely he would stay in-country more than one more year. Bob had become a close friend though their time together had been infrequent and their relationship was one of good friends, though for the first time Bob had suggested it could be more. Last night at the buffet dinner hosted by the Church's health clinic administrator, Bob had told her his plans. He intended to return to the States, get his Master's Degree in public health nursing, and then strike out again for another third world assignment, perhaps Panama. Would she be interested in joining him, he had asked.

The bus went around a curve, forcing the large lady sharing the seat into Ellen.

"Disculpe, Senorita," she apologized, and Ellen smiled in return. Her thoughts again shifted to Bob. She was quite surprised that Bob's offer had left her unsettled. It had sounded positive to be back in the States. She was not sure she was ready to follow that with a sojourn to another third world country. But that wasn't what bothered her, and it surprised her. She always anticipated meeting Bob at the quarterly meetings. They talked, joked, and strolled about the city in their free time as if they were there for a light-hearted holiday. It was a release from the oft-times hum-drum life she led in Comalapa. That life was filled with stress. There were so many patients, so little medications available, so few hours for the demands that were made but could not be met. Nevertheless, Bob's offer had come as a surprise, and, she reflected, not a particularly welcome surprise. This morning, when both left the

Mission for their stations, Ellen to Mercado Ivan Montenegro where buses departed for eastern cities, and Bob to Mercado Israel Lewites, the departure point for buses to the north, they had a few minutes to talk. Neither one mentioned the discussion of the night before. Ellen wondered if that left it settled or unsettled.

Yesterday's other surprise she remembered well; the unexpected visitor who arrived in mid-afternoon at the Mission's building to see her. Ellen had met Byron Smith six months prior when Bob Stevens asked her if she would like to lunch at the Hotel Inter-Continental with he and a friend. Byron was with the U.S. Embassy, Bob had told her, and was interested in the Mission program. Without hesitation Ellen had said yes. It would be quite a treat for one who just got by on the small monthly church stipend. Byron had picked up the bill, and it became clear that it was he, not Bob, who had initiated the meeting. Bob and Byron were far from bosom buddies, she had decided. Nevertheless, there were three hours of delightful and interesting conversation and a wonderful lunch.

Ellen's reverie was interrupted as the driver suddenly brought the bus to a shuddering stop. Ellen had just seen the road sign that announced they were entering the little village of San Benito. That meant the Sandinista Army post there would be conducting a routine search of the bus. Ellen's seat mate got off at this stop with several other passengers, with a "Buen viaje, señorita" to Ellen, and Ellen responded "Gracias". Only one soldier of the three standing outside boarded the bus, an AK-47 slung over his shoulders. He walked half-way to the back of the bus thoroughly disinterested in this bit of work. He gave a second look at Ellen that said he recognized her as a foreigner, and then turned and got off the bus. Another 100 meters further, a dozen or so passengers got off. This was the first official stop of the so-called "express" bus. Ellen would be too late for the connecting bus from the main highway east up into the hills to Comalapa. She knew Jorge would be at the highway to meet her.

The bus turned off the highway leading to Matagalpa onto the Carretera Rama, the two-lane highway to the river port town of Rama that offered boat passage to the Caribbean. Within 30 minutes the bus was at the Comalapa road intersection. Ellen saw her medical assistant Jorge, the son of a Juigalpa pharmacist, lying in the back of the single-axle pony cart at the side of the road. Jorge stood at no more than five foot five, was dark skinned with slicked back straight hair. He was incredibly strong for his size, an attribute of the young men of the campo. The pony cart was typical not only of rural transportation but also was common in the cities like Managua. Gasoline was in short supply, most of it going to the Sandinista Army.

The bus driver's assistant climbed the ladder attached to the back of the bus, retrieved Ellen's box of supplies, and handed them to Jorge. With her supplies loaded in the back of the cart, Ellen and Jorge climbed up on the flat-board seat of the cart. Jorge guided the pony across the highway and they began the gradual ascent on the rutted gravel road to Comalapa village. Though Jorge spoke fairly good English, and Ellen fairly good Spanish, they conversed little after greeting each other. Ellen felt too tired to make the effort at polite conversation, and Jorge, a quiet and earnest young man, seemed to understand.

The cart stopped at Ellen's small house on the outskirts of the little village of Comalapa. It was only a three minute walk to the small Assembly of God Mission health clinic. She had electricity and a well, both luxuries in this remote cattle-country settlement. Ellen asked Jorge to take the medical supplies to the clinic, thanked him and bade him goodnight. Though it was only 6:30 p.m., it was already dark and Ellen munched on a cold tamale, washed up from a basin, and changed for bed. She had brought a three month old *Newsweek* magazine from Managua, which was considered a treasure in the remote Chontales Department. She fought to keep her eyes open as she read the magazine. She was saved further effort when the unpredictable electricity cut off. Exhausted, Ellen fell into a deep slumber until wakened by the village roosters at 4:30 a.m.

Still there was no electricity, but a candle and her small propane burner were all she needed to start the day. The smell of percolating coffee eased her to life. The clinic opened at 7:30 a.m., and Ellen was there 20 minutes early. She entered the large one room building, with its heavily waxed red concrete floor. There were 10 wooden chairs neatly lined up against the wall, Jorge's desk where he interviewed patients, and Ellen's station which was curtained off. There was already a line of a dozen villagers and nearby neighbors, mostly women with children and old men and women. Ellen readied her medical table in the curtained enclosure of the clinic when a loud commotion erupted outside. She looked outside and saw Jorge trying to calm down an excited, somewhat frantic mother at the doorway. The young girl was holding a squalling baby in one arm and the hand of a two year old on the other side. One of the child-mothers, Ellen noted, as she turned away from her elderly patient seated on a chair by her examination table. The conversation between the child-mother, no more than 16 or 17, and Jorge reached staccato proportions, and Ellen could not understand.

"Tranquilo, por favor," Ellen said in a firm but gentle voice. "Jorge, what is the problem?" she asked.

"La señora no quiere esperar en la fila," Jorge said. Ellen could see that the young girl was very upset. Tears were running down her brown cheeks as she looked past Jorge to Ellen. Nicaraguans were generally very courteous. The girl's refusal to wait in line for her turn to see Ellen spoke of her desperation.

Ellen gently dismissed the old gentleman seated next to her with his sweat-stained white straw hat in his lap, and asked him to wait on one of the wooden chairs lined up against the wall. She told Jorge to bring in the mother and her children. Without hesitation the young mother put the crying baby in Ellen's arms. Ellen could feel the fever wracking the infant, but worse, could see the latent signs of hemorrhagic dengue. As she put the infant on the exam table, there was evidence of blood at the nostrils and on the child's gums. She had never seen an actual case of hemorrhagic dengue, but the symptoms had been discussed at the Assembly quarterly meetings. It was said this worrisome disease was becoming increasingly common. There was no vaccine, Ellen knew, and no specific medications that were used to treat it. Ellen also knew it was unusual for an infant or young child to have such severe complications, and guessed the child was infected several days ago. The immediate danger was dehydration, and Ellen used one of her precious intravenous saline solution bags for immediate treatment.

"Jorge, we need to get the baby and her mother to Juigalpa for emergency treatment. The baby is very much in danger of circulatory failure. Go to Ramon's house, and see if he will drive them to Juigalpa. Tell him I will pay him for the trip."

Jorge quickly left to find Ramon, while Ellen held the squirming baby on the table. The young mother stood by, now quiet and hopeful that Ellen would save the infant. Ellen felt the weight of that trust, misplaced she knew, for there was very little that could be done for the infant other than hydration and hope its immune system would kick in hard. Ellen heard Ramon's truck pull up to the door, and Jorge ran into the clinic.

"Take them to Dr. Mendoza," Ellen instructed. "He will know what to do. Jorge, you go with them. Take the saline bottle. I can't afford to send another one, there are only three left in the clinic."

As Jorge left the clinic, Ellen looked out to the front, and saw that the line of patients had doubled. She heaved a heavy sigh, and called "Señor" as she beckoned to the old gentleman she was treating before the commotion began. Within two hours, Jorge returned, with a sad look on his face.

"Doctora," he said, as he often called her, "La niña murió." He had reverted to Spanish to tell the sad news of the baby's death.

Ellen sat in her chair next to a middle aged woman perched on the examination table. Tears began to flow down her cheeks. She said nothing for a moment, and stared at Jorge.

"Jorge, I forgot to tell you that a truck will come from Managua with some supplies." Then she turned back to her patient and fastened a blood pressure cuff on the woman's arm.

CHAPTER 4—THE MATAGALPINA

The bus engine roared to life and departure was at hand when a young blonde blue-eyed woman in her twenties squeezed through the closing doors, holding her small knapsack in front of her. The driver gunned the engine and the old yellow school bus lurched out of the bus depot at Managua's Mercado Ivan Montenegro that served the country's eastern cities' routes. The pony-tailed blonde dressed in jeans pants, white T-shirt, and jeans vest threaded her way through the standing passengers that filled the aisle-way, with an occasional "disculpe" uttered in the clear and polished tonal quality of the country's upper educated class. She continued her way, weaving amongst the standing passengers and their boxes and bags on the floor until she reached the wide seat at the very rear of the bus. Two middle-aged men who sat near the center of the seat immediately parted in unison to open up a space for her to sit. She thanked them with a "Gracias", both nodded in return without comment.

Her blue eyes scanned the other bus passengers who were suffering the physical demands of the early hour departure with stoicism as they faced several hours of bad roads in a crowded bus that would grow warmer and more uncomfortable with the rising of the sun.

There were at least three Sandinista soldiers on board, without weapons, she noted. They were obviously on leave enroute to their homes somewhere to the east. Among the campesinos she saw a brunette, an attractive gringa, sitting in a window seat on the left side three rows in front of her. Not a "sandalista", she guessed, as the scruffy Sandinista-sympathetic internationalistas who had flooded Nicaragua were called. Probably a missionary, she supposed, which was unusual. The missionary women were not noted for their looks. There were two young Germans only two seats in front of her on the right side of the bus. They had turned around to ogle her. She was sure they were some of the adventurous members of the communist-oriented East German brigade, known as the Brigada Alemana. She could easily overhear their conversation in German, as they giggled and laughed like two school girls. She gathered from their conversation they were on their way to the river port town of Rama, the end of this eastern route. At Rama they would catch a boat to Corn Island for a holiday week on the beach. She was annoyed at the attention, but did not show it and feigned indifference. On the other hand, the two men on either side of her gave the young men stern looks, which seemed to diminish their interest.

The bus' back wheels dropped into frequent potholes on the main highway as it traveled towards Tipitapa, sending those in the back of the bus bouncing off their seats. Nevertheless the blonde became immersed in her own thoughts. The sounds and smells of the bus and passengers retreated from her consciousness. She did not like courier duty. It was not usually assigned to someone of her position, but the blow to be struck was so significant that it could only be released to a few individuals. That she was entrusted with the information, having had to commit it to memory, was recognition of her post in the organization. And of course there were her follow-on duties that would be very important to this mission. But it was dangerous to be in Managua. She felt eyes were on her all the time. There were Sandinista spies all over the country, and many in Managua. The young blonde was accustomed to admiring glances from men and even women because of her natural beauty, and that drew attention that was unwelcome in these circumstances. She would deliver her message to her contact in Libertad. That had struck her as ironic, for that little town was the birthplace of Sandinista leader Daniel Ortega. But nowadays it was more of a no-man's land, as much in control by the Contra's as the Sandinistas. The Sandinistas could only hold that part of the country by major force, which they could not spare. Any small guard detachment could be, and had been, overrun quickly by highly mobile Contra strike forces.

As the bus approached the San Benito army checkpoint just northeast of the town of Tipitapa, the brakes suddenly squealed and the standing passengers struggled to maintain their balance as the driver brought the bus to a shuddering halt. There was some grumbling by the passengers. They knew that the driver covered the same route day after day, month after month, and the stop at the checkpoint was no surprise.

A Sandinista soldier boarded the bus, and the Blonde's right hand reached into her open knapsack. The passengers' eyes were focused on the checkpoint soldier with the AK-47 slung over his shoulder, maneuvering his way down the aisle as a few passengers were trying to leave at this stop with their belongings. It was not noticed that the two men on either side of the blonde had slipped U.S. Colt .38 revolvers out of ankle holsters and placed them in their laps under the day's issue of

La Barricada, the Sandinista newspaper. The soldier gave up his effort half way down the aisle, turned, and walked back to the front of the bus and out the door. The .38's were back in their ankle holsters so quickly no one noticed. Both men picked up their newspapers and continued to read.

The blonde visibly relaxed and zipped her knapsack shut. She studied the back of a woman's head near the middle of the bus that seemed somehow familiar. The bus started moving, but would go no more than a hundred meters to the official bus stop. There passengers would connect to Sébaco, Matagalpa, and Jinotega to the north. Her bus would turn shortly onto the Carretera Rama and head southeasterly. As the bus stopped, an older lady in her early sixties, her light brown hair streaked with gray tied in a bun at the nape of her neck, rose from her seat and struggled to control two bulging cloth bags. She turned and looked directly to the back of the bus at the young blonde, who then recognized her Aunt Helga. Helga neither spoke nor showed facial signs of recognition, though her eyes told the blonde all is well. Helga would be taking the connecting bus, the blonde knew, heading north to Matagalpa and the finca that adjoined that of her parents. She stifled the impulse to jump up, run down the aisle and stop Aunt Helga and give her a hug. But that could not be. Helga turned for one brief glance and the blonde smiled as much as she dared. Aunt Helga would soon be in the wonderful mountain town of Matagalpa, where the blonde was born and raised. Now, at least, her parents would know she was alive and safe. For that she was grateful.

How it had all changed, she thought, in such a few years. She should have returned from Germany with a medical degree, settled in her hometown of Matagalpa, and had a practice with Enrique. Enrique had abandoned his studies in Germany to help defend his family's property rights in Nueva Segovia. Murder by the Sandinistas was his reward. Distraught and buried in sorrow, she left medical school and returned to Nicaragua. She found little comfort or solace when she visited Enrique's family in Ocotal. Their shared grief became a heavy burden, and she returned to Finca Kupper and her family. She had not liked the Sandinista regime as it changed from a revolutionary movement to a police state with communism competing with Catholicism as the national religion. She had seemed far removed from these worries as she pursued her medical studies. But with Enrique's death she was no longer a distant observer, but rather a determined opponent.

She was particularly close to Uncle Herman, Aunt Helga's husband. Her uncle was a second cousin to Jorge Salazar, the outspoken and martyred anti-Sandinista Matagalpan murdered by the Sandinistas. Uncle Herman had been very cautious, very secretive about his contacts with Jorge's followers, but finally he and his niece discussed the underground resistance that had formed and was growing throughout the country. Her Uncle Herman had tried to discourage her from undertaking an active role in the local underground resistance. He had said if she wanted to join the Contra movement, he could arrange it. With her two years of medical school she would be invaluable and safe at one the Contra base camp medical clinics in Honduras. As she remembered this, the blonde permitted herself a bit of an inward smile. How surprised dear Uncle Herman would be now if he knew just how dangerous the mission was that was assigned to her.

Uncle Herman had arranged it all. The young woman returned to Enrique's parents' home at their finca near Ocotal for a visit. She had spent a week there. Then she went with Enrique's father to visit a farm to the north, near Jalapa, closer yet to the Honduran border. Enrique's father returned to

Ocotal alone. The blonde was escorted by a team of 20 contra commandos to the Honduran border. That had been a two day trek through pine forests and over the tops of misty mountains. The nights were cold, and the fear of Sandinista ambushes caused them to detour at times from cattle trails into the forest to make their way. The squad leader, Mauricio, at first was concerned that she would not be able to maintain the squad's steady pace. But he had not reckoned with the stamina of a girl who though barely weighing 50 kilos, had been raised in the mountains and could hike with the best of them.

Once in Honduras, the blonde was driven by Jeep to Danlí, where she spent the night in a small hotel. By the next day she was in Tegucigalpa, finding the Holiday Inn a luxurious change. She learned that Uncle Herman was an important person in the Frente Democratic Nicaragua. Her duties with the FDN were to be much more than as a pseudo medical doctor. That need had been filled by exile Nica medical doctors who came from Miami, New Orleans, Los Angeles, and the Washington D.C. areas. While there was a power struggle for control of the FDN, with associated intrigues, she was seen as an impartial participant whom all sides trusted. Her first assignment had been to meet with the Miskito Indian resistance. She and a bodyguard team of five were sent to eastern Honduras by helicopter to a landing zone across the Río Coco from Biliwaskama. There she met with the Miskito Indian resistance leaders, and became the key FDN contact and negotiator from then on. An abortive meeting was scheduled once on the Nicaraguan side of the river. The blonde had held her own with the bodyguard team in a firefight against a Sandinista militia company. Backed to the river and outnumbered, the small band fought bravely with a half dozen Miskito Indians at their side. Suddenly new firing had erupted. The Sandinista ambush was broken, as a company size Contra force hit them from behind. The Contras were led by a red-haired gringo dressed in jungle fatigues and wearing a Miami Dolphins ball cap. He had introduced himself simply as Peter. The force dissolved back into the forest as quickly as it had appeared. As a result of this incident she had gained much respect among the fighting elements of the FDN.

Her reverie was broken as one of the young Germans turned and spoke to her in halting Spanish interspersed with German in a teasing and rude manner. The man to her right rebuked the young man with a sneering "Bárbaro". Whether or not the young man understood he was being called a barbarian, he turned back around in his seat and laughed with his companion.

At last the bus arrived in Juiglapa, and the blonde and the two men stood up to get off as did several other passengers. Passing the two teenagers, the blonde leaned down and said "Ich kann Euch manches beibringen Ihr frechen Bengels" in perfect German. Both of the youths looked up in astonishment. They had been told they were rude clowns who should be taught a thing or two. Their mouths hung open but no words came out.

Without acknowledgment of each other, the blonde and the two men walked over to a dirty old brown Landcruiser, where a driver was waiting. As they climbed in, the blonde turned around to the two men and said "Bien hecho, mis amigos." She thought she should add "so far, so good" to her "well done," but that seemed to tempt fate. The tall and lanky driver, Luis, dressed in jeans and straw cowboy hat, drove them straight out of town towards Libertad. They arrived within two hours. Libertad was a dusty, unimpressive town. They continued through the town and started a climb up the hills overlooking the town. Their destination was a large farmhouse sitting on the top of a hill. There they could look down on Libertad and see any approaching vehicle or person. A good choice, she acknowledged. Now to deliver the plan and wait. The task force commander should be here tomorrow. Then he would have his job, a diversionary attack to draw troops from Managua. And then, if things go right, she will have her own demanding task that the plan required.

All was in order. Her East German press credentials and passport had been carefully prepared. She spoke fluent and flawless German. Her beauty was an additional passport of accessibility in the Nicaraguan macho society. The Lada parked inside the steel plate gated parking area with diplomatic plates and miniature East German flags mounted on each front fender would not be questioned. She would meet Fernando and then they would be off to Managua.

The blonde looked out over Libertad as she stood on the porch of the hilltop ranch house. The sun had fallen below the horizon in a matter of seconds. The quiet calm of the evening had enveloped her, but she was unable to shake a foreboding that had arisen.

Luis, more than a driver, came out on the porch.

"All is ready, Adriana."

CHAPTER 5–A COVERT FLIGHT NORTH

Marc awoke to his alarm at 5:00 a.m., followed almost immediately by a pounding on the door.

"Marc, Five a.m." It was the voice of Brian Smith, the Ops duty officer of the day.

"Thanks, Smitty. I'm up." Marc flung the sheet to the foot of the bed, swung his feet to the cold cement floor, reached over to the bedside table and turned off the alarm. His rest had been fitful. Despite the floor fan, the room had seemed never to cool off. He felt better after he'd showered down at the central bathroom. As he shaved he could hear the whirl of the Maules' starters. The engines coughed to life almost immediately. The engine rpm's increased and decreased as the mechanics checked mixture, prop governor, carburetor heat, and magnetos. Finally they shut the engines down.

Back in his room, Marc dressed in blue jeans and a grey cotton short sleeve shirt. He strapped on a shoulder holster for the .38 Special he always carried on missions. Next he slipped an old bayonet scabbard onto his belt. The dagger-like bayonet held a fine cutting edge that only the best hunting knives could equal. He was surprised to see that it was already 5:25 a.m., and hurried over to the mess rancho. Brad had said 6:00 a.m., and Marc knew he didn't have much time for breakfast.

Brad was already sitting with a steaming cup of black coffee. He sat huddled with Joe Parks at the far end of the rancho away from the cooking area, an aeronautical map spread between the two.

"Didn't hear you drive up in that old bucket of bolts," Marc said, as he walked up to the table, catching Joe's eye.

"That old Datsun pickup will never quit, Marc. Not pretty to look at, but I've got a mechanic in Liberia who keeps it running."

"Have a seat, Marc," Brad said. He waved Marc to sit down on the other side of him, so that he would be in the middle of the two pilots.

"Both birds were pre-flighted this morning and are ready to go. No squawks on either one. Your passenger is on his way, Marc. And Marc, the girls won't come over here to the table unless they're called. They see the maps out and know we're briefing a mission."

Mac stood up, and yelled to Gordita. "Dos huevos, gallo pinto, y tocineta, por favor, Gordita." Marc was normally a light breakfast eater, but some inner voice urged him to add two eggs and bacon to his customary gallo pinto this morning.

Gordita nodded, and asked "Café, Señor Marc.?"

"Of course, claro que sí, señorita" Marc answered, knowing full well Gordita with several children at home was far removed from being a señorita.

Marc sat down, and looked at the map, the same one he had seen at the Ops office two days before. Point-to-point lines marked the route the two Maule's would fly, another point that marked where they would split up. He again noted the individual routes that each would subsequently follow.

"I'll go over the routes, and you guys let me know if you see any problem or conflict. Our radar site up on Orosi already has the info, so any changes will have to be minor."

Gordita walked to within 10 feet of the table with a cup of coffee. Brad folded the map, and Marc waved her to the table.

"Gracias, Gordita."

"Con mucho gusto," she said as she walked away, averting her eyes from the table top.

"Okay. Let's review the mission," Brad said, as he spread out the map. Call signs are Firebird One and Two. Marc, you're number One, naturally. You both will maintain radio silence. The call signs are only to be used in the case of an emergency or until you are back in friendly territory. Monitor tactical frequency 123.7. The Orosi Radar station will use the call sign Scarlet. They'll give any emergency advisories on 123.7, such as possible intercept by the Sandy's or an abort call. Here are your authentication codes for the day. Takeoff time is delayed till 6:25. I've got 5:47 now. You will take off in formation, with Number Two maintaining close formation so the radar track will only show one blip. Marc, use IFF code 0535. Joe, you use 0540, but keep yours in standby mode until you split up, then go active. Of course, squawk 7700 in case of emergency. We have you planned at 1,500 feet until three miles before breakup point. At that time you both descend in formation to 300 feet over the lake, and split up at the breakup point."

"Brad, you haven't mentioned any abort criteria," Joe said.

"Just the usual. Obviously any major degradation of engine performance, electrical failure, and fuel system malfunction. If either of you aborts, that is reason to call in the clear using your call sign. If Firebird One aborts, Joe, you head directly back to Point West. If Joe aborts, Marc, you are to continue regardless of where in the mission Joe aborts. Your passenger's mission depends on his arrival at Sonojal this morning. There will be no backup flights if this one fails. I can tell you that the project has been approved and authorized at the highest Washington levels. Any clarification needed?"

Both Joe and Marc shook their heads "no".

"Okay. Let's continue. You can see on the chart the breakup point is 5 miles offshore of San Miguelito airport. Start your descent three miles prior to that. At the breakup point Joe turns to a heading of 279 degrees. Visually, that's the southeastern shore of Ometepe Island on your nose. Marc, you will turn to a heading of 325 degrees, paralleling the eastern shoreline, staying five miles off shore. Joe will continue towards Ometepe, and turn to a heading direct for Point West 10 miles before the Island. Any intercept threat would be most likely out of Rivas. If our guys at Orosi Radar spot a likely intercept from Rivas or elsewhere, they will call out in the blind, "Firebird One or Two, bogey bearing so many degrees and distance. You abort, hit the deck, and head for the closest Costa Rican border. Marc, your route keeps you offshore till abeam Sonojal. Then turn right to a heading of 067 degrees, direct to the airstrip, land, dump your passenger, and get out of there. Winds this morning are the usual. Out of the northeast at 10 knots, so you can land straight-in. Here's your passenger now, Marc."

A black Mercedes four-door, vintage 1950's, with headlights on, sped towards them. It followed the northern side of the runway, and pulled up to the mess rancho. A tall lanky man, Latin in complexion with a trim mustache and wavy salt and pepper hair, got out of the back seat. Good looking guy, like a Hollywood character actor in the Cesar Romero mould, Marc thought to himself.

"Hola, Fernando," Brad said, and got up from the bench and walked over to greet the new arrival.

"Hi, old man," Fernando answered, grinning widely as they clasped hands. Although Fernando's speech was unmistakably American, Marc noted there was a hint of a Spanish accent. The driver of the Mercedes had retrieved a knapsack and attaché case from the trunk of the Mercedes and handed them to Fernando. The driver was apparently a no-nonsense guy, Marc surmised. He looked about 50, mostly bald, and carried over two hundred pounds on a solid frame of medium height. Under his sleeveless denim jacket Marc could see a holstered .45. He was sure this guy knew how to use it.

"Gracias, Donaldo," Fernando said, taking the knapsack and attaché case. Donaldo nodded, said nothing, and immediately walked back to the Mercedes and drove off.

"One of our best men," Fernando said to no one in particular. Marc was sure "our" meant the Agency staff at the Embassy in San José.

Brad introduced Fernando to Marc and Joe, led them back to the picnic table, and called for a cup of coffee for Fernando.

"Fernando, obviously you've already been briefed in San José on the full mission. For our part of the mission, we've been told there are no alternates planned. If a landing can't be made at Sonojal, it's a mission abort. You and Marc will return to Point West.

"We must not let that happen. The success of my mission could shorten this war we have with the Sandinistas."

"I understand, Fernando. You will not find a more experienced or competent pilot than Marc. You'll be in good hands. We have about 15 more minutes. Have another cup of coffee if you wish."

Marc stood up, reached into his right pocket, and pulled out a very small automatic in a holster. He raised his right trouser leg, and with his foot up on the picnic bench, bent down and strapped on the ankle holster. He slipped the automatic into it.

"That's a nice little automatic, Marc," Brad said.

"Yeah. It's a .25 caliber Browning automatic. Only four inches long, less than an inch wide, and weights less than ten ounces. I bought it in the States at Eglin Air Force Base when I was there for gun ship training. Then when I got to Saigon I had this holster made. When I was flying a mission, I just put the little automatic in the upper left arm zipper pocket of the flight suit, where most guys put their pack of cigarettes. It's not heavy firepower, but the clip holds six cartridges. With one more in the chamber it gives me a fighting chance. In Saigon I was always on guard for the Viet Cong assassination squads that roamed around the city on motorcycles and scooters. We should have been wearing a pair of six guns John Wayne style. On these missions I also carry a .38 caliber revolver that was standard for all the aircrews when we flew in Vietnam. Joe, let's go check on the birds. Fernando, see you in a few minutes."

When Fernando and Brad walked up, Marc and Joe had finished the pre-flight check of their aircraft, which were parked side-by-side.

"All set, Fernando," Marc said. "We can put your attaché case and backpack in the rear seat, but we won't strap them in. Shouldn't be bumpy this early in the morning. That way when we land at Sonojal, you can grab them and get out pronto. I can land this bird in 500 feet, and get off in 300 feet, so it won't be necessary to back taxi. Once you're out, I'll be on my way."

Daylight was already filtering down the valley, though the sun had not yet climbed over the cordillera range to the east. Both Marc and Fernando were strapped in, belt and shoulder harnesses secure, and headsets on. Marc methodically went through the Before Starting Engine portion of the aircraft checklist and then looked over to his right where Joe's aircraft was parked. Joe was looking at Marc and gave a thumbs up. Marc raised his right hand, right forefinger in the air, and made a circling motion, the no-radio signal to start engines. Marc pushed the mixture control all the way in, cracked the throttle one quarter, turned the master switch on, rotated the start switch from "off" past right and left magneto positions to "start". In one turn of the propeller the engine roared to life.

"Oil pressure," Marc announced automatically over the intercom. He pulled the throttle back to 1,000 rpm, switched both radios on and the IFF to standby.

"We don't need to do an engine run-up, Fernando. The mechanics did that this morning. I have good cylinder head temperature and oil temperature. We're ready to go if you are."

"You're the boss," Fernando replied over the intercom, which was voice-actuated and did not require the use of a press-to-talk button.

As Marc looked over to his right, Joe was looking at him. Marc made a forward motion with his right arm, and began his taxi. Joe fell in trail behind Marc as they taxied west to the end of Runway 9. Marc lined up on the runway, and Joe pulled alongside to his right and slightly behind, with a wingtip separation of about 10 feet. Marc quickly ran through the Before Takeoff checklist, turned the IFF to "On", and looked at Joe, who nodded. Marc threw his head back, and then forward, released the brakes and added power. Joe followed the no-radio signal for the formation takeoff, began his take-off roll at the same time, maintaining his position slightly behind and to the right. The two aircraft in formation broke ground in less than 1,000 feet.

"We're on our way, Amigo," Marc said.

"Yes, so far, so good," Fernando replied.

"Joe is going to hang in pretty close, so we look like one target on radar. We're going to level at 1,500 feet. I've picked up a heading for the Solentiname Islands. From there we will head on almost the same course to San Miguelito airfield. The breakup with Joe is five miles short of San Miguelito. Then we head northwest along the lakeshore. I know you've been well briefed on the route. We will cruise at 130 knots after we level off. Have you done any flying, Fernanndo?"

"Some. Got my private pilot's license years ago in Florida. Then before the Bay of Pigs I was sent to Honduras and trained as a B-25 co-pilot. However, I got another assignment before the invasion, and missed out on that."

"That may be your good fortune. Do you still fly?" Marc asked

"No, for two reasons. First, it would be hard for me to stay proficient in my line of work. And second, remaining anonymous is important. It's hard to be anonymous when you're flying around as a pilot."

"I see your point. We're leveling off now." Marc made a sideways motion with his right hand, palm down, for Joe to see, indicating they were leveling at 1,500 feet. Joe was maintaining his position just to the right and slightly behind, his left wing tip not more than 10 feet from the right wingtip of Marc's Maule.

"Well, as a pilot you can appreciate the Maule which is one of the most versatile small aircraft made. One unique characteristic I'll show you now. You probably noticed that we took off with 24 degrees of flaps down. Once we got airborne and started our climb, they were retracted, of course. But now that we're at cruise altitude, there's a flap position that gives a negative seven degrees. In that position, the flaps are slightly above the wings, and that improves cruise speed. We can get

130 knots cruise with the flaps in the negative 7 degree position."

"Good. The faster we get to Sonojal the better. I can see the south end of the Lake now."

The two Maules flew on in tight formation, passing over the Solentinames, and on towards San Miguelito airfield.

"We're coming up on our descent point, Fernando." Marc made a descending motion with the flat of his right hand for Joe to see. Then he began a shallow descent of 300 feet per minute, leaving the throttle untouched. The airspeed increased to 140 knots, entering the yellow arc on the airspeed indicator as Marc began easing the throttle back.

"Time to head up the lake," Marc said. He began a gentle left turn and, passing 400 feet, began his level off for 300 feet indicated on his altimeter. He raised his right hand, waved a goodbye to Joe, who was now to take up his own navigation towards Ometepe Island. Marc reached down and turned his IFF to standby.

"So far, so good, Fernando. No traffic on our tactical frequency. You can help me identify landmarks as we fly north. I've never seen the Sonojal airstrip, only studied SR-71 aerial photos of it."

"Okay. I think I can see the north end of the lake already. The point at Cañas Gordas should be easy to spot, and La Pelona point beyond is pretty distinctive."

"I agree," Marc said. "It's only about 12 miles from Punta Pelona to our turning point inland. About 5 minutes after Pelona we turn east, and should be able to pick out the airstrip. As you can see on the map, it's only five miles inland, to the right of a small river, which is to the right of a paved road. To be honest, I don't like being this close to the north end of the lake where all the military activity is. I'll be glad to get in and get out ASAP.

"And I'll be glad to be on my way. Thanks in advance for the lift."

"You bet. There's Puntas Gordas on the right, about 8 or 10 miles."

"Firebird Two, Firebird Two. This is Scarlet. Abort! Abort! Authenticate Uniform Foxtrot Kilo. Bogey at 11 O'clock, 18 miles."

"Oh oh. Joe's getting an intercept," Marc said.

"Firebird Two, Firebird Two, do you read Scarlet?" Marc was just about to break radio silence, and call Joe when he responded.

"Scarlet, Firebird Two, copy abort."

"Firebird Two, bogey at 15 miles, angels two."

"Firebird Two, roger."

"Fernando, I would bet Joe is down on the waves by now at max manifold pressure. I would guess that the bogey is one or more MI-25 helicopters on a radar directed intercept. They have a "look down" radar search capability. But not sure they could pick up Joe down on the water."

"He should make it to the Costa Rica border before they can get within rocket range, don't you think?" Fernando asked.

"Probably, though the Sandinistas don't always respect the border. Our Contras on the southern front do have shoulder fired anti-aircraft missiles, and the Sandinista helicopter pilots know that." Marc was about to elaborate when the Orosi radar station called even more urgently.

"Firebird Two, Firebird Two, one bogey at your 6 o'clock at ten miles, one bogey at your 4 o'clock at 13 miles."

"Firebird Two, understand," Joe replied, his voice calm as usual.

"Punta Gordas off at our Three O'clock, Fernando. Think I can see Pelona from here."

"Yes, I can see it out there at one O'clock. I think Joe has attracted all the attention of the Sandinista Air Force. Good for us, and hopefully not too bad for him."

"He should be close enough to make it across the frontera," Marc said. Again he was interrupted by Scarlet.

"Firebird Two, one bogey nine miles at 6'oclock, one at 11 miles at 4 o'clock."

"Firebird Two, roger."

"Firebird Two, Scarlet here. We show you 12 miles to the border."

"Firebird Two, Firebird Two, heads up. We show a missile launch."

"Firebird Two, Scarlet here. Do you copy?"

"Firebird Two, this is Scarlet. We have lost you. Ident."

The calls continued, without a response from Firebird Two. Fernando looked at Marc, who had a worried frown.

"Marc, do you guys have any kind of protection against air-to-air or ground-fired missiles?"

"Like flares? Nope, evasive action is our only protection. Hopefully Joe is down so low over the water and taking evasive action that he doesn't have time to answer Scarlet. Coming abeam Pelona. Get ready, Fernando. Keep a lookout as soon as I turn inland and help me pick out the Sonojal airstrip."

"There it is, Marc, at two o'clock."

Marc squinted into the sun, and finally saw the brown east-west oriented dirt strip, outlined by platano fields on the north, south, and western sides, with pasture on the eastern end of the runway.

"Good eyes, Fernando."

Marc began a slow right turn, pulled the throttle back, and applied half flaps as the speed slowed to 60 knots. The Maule descended rapidly towards the tree tops that bordered the cane field west of the strip. Flaps were increased to 45 degrees. Marc pulled back on the stick bringing the nose up as the airspeed decreased towards the stall speed of 43 knots in the quick flare. The plane skimmed the low trees at the end of the strip and dropped heavily in a full stall. Marc pulled the stick full aft into his stomach, and applied the brakes as hard as he dared.

Then he saw it.

"Hold on," he yelled to Fernando, whose unease throughout the landing sequence was obvious as he had been uncharacteristically quiet. Two hundred feet in front of the quickly decelerating Maule was a narrow ditch cut directly across the airstrip. Marc jammed the throttle forward, hoping to regain enough speed to hop the ditch. The engine coughed momentarily from the sudden influx of full throttle fuel dumped into the carburetor. Then the power caught and acceleration began, but too late.

The two main wheels caught the edge of the ditch. The craft flipped over, continuing down the dirt strip on its back for a short distance before skidding to a stop. "Let's get out of here before the bird blows up," Marc shouted to Fernando, as he reached up, unsnapped his seat belt, and fell heavily to the cabin's headliner. Marc looked up at his passenger, hanging upside down from his seat, unconscious. Marc reached up, unsnapped the seat belt, and tried to ease Fernando's fall. Kicking the deformed left door, Marc crawled out, dragging Fernando. His eyes would not focus, and he could feel the warm ooze of blood down the right side of his face. Then there was nothing.

CHAPTER 6—A SURPRISING ALLY

"Can you hear me?" a soft female voice asked in English. Marc struggled to open his eyes and tried to remember where he was. "Can you hear me?" the voice repeated, in a distinct southern drawl.

"Yes. Where am I? Who're you? Where's Fernando?" Marc replied, as he opened his eyes and tried to focus them on the surroundings of the small room he was in. Then he saw her. A brunette, rather petite, brown eyes, not more than 5 foot 5 inches, and quite attractive.

"You're in the small village of Comalapa, 20 kilometers from the old agricultural landing strip where you crashed. Three of our boys from here were moving cattle nearby, saw the crash, and brought you here to the village in an ox cart. Your friend was dead and they left his body at the crash site so it will appear he was the pilot and only occupant of the plane. I'm Ellen Hutchins, a public health missionary nurse with the Assembly of God ministry here in Nicaragua. The locals call it Asamblea de Dios. This house was donated to the church by a wealthy rancher who lives in Juigalpa for use by the missionaries who come here. He owns many hectares of ranchland, and is a devout Assembly of God parishioner, and may be of help. This was used as a ranch house years ago and that is the reason it is set apart from the village, which gives some security for the moment. I am sorry about your friend. I believe his neck was broken during the crash. The airplane burned after you got out of it. Now that I have answered your questions, can you tell me who you are? I assume you are flying for the Contras. It is very dangerous here for you, and for us as well. Here in the Chontales Department and Boaco to the north much of the population is sympathetic to the Contras, but there are many State Security agents in the little villages. The people here are very careful."

Marc was quiet for a moment. "You can call me Marc. The less I tell you about myself and what I do, the better it is for you. I guess it's obvious that I'm flying for the Contras. I remember getting out of the plane after the crash, and pulling Fernando out, but nothing more. I don't remember that there was a fire. Fernando was carrying a backpack. Did your boys find that?"

"Yes. All the items that were in your passenger's pockets have been put in the backpack. There is a laptop computer as well as clothing and other items in the backpack. Oh! And a large amount of dollars and Nicaraguan córdobas. I hope that the Sandinistas will believe that your passenger was the pilot and the only occupant of the airplane. But, I am sure they are looking for anyone else who might have been on the plane. I need to get you out of here as soon as possible to a safer place. For now, get as much rest as possible. We will leave early in the morning."

An insistent shaking awoke Marc out of a fitful sleep. He had nightmares of unavoidable airplane crashes which he was helpless to prevent, sitting at the controls more as a spectator than pilot.

"You only have a few minutes to eat," Ellen said in a hushed voice. He sat up on the edge of the cot trying to shake the grogginess and soreness away. It was still dark outside. She handed him a plate of steaming gallo pinto, the same breakfast dish of beans and rice he had found typical in Costa Rica. Here it was made with red beans instead of black and had two fried eggs on top.

"Thanks, Ellen," he said, using her name for the first time. He gulped down the rice and beans.

"Marc, here's some tea. You may not like the taste, but it will be good for you. It will help heal your bruised body."

"What is it?" Marc asked as he took the brown ceramic mug Ellen held out to him.

"It's tea made from the zorillo plant. I believe in the medicinal qualities of many of the plants that the campesinos use for healing. I have seen them work. The zorillo plant has been used since Mayan times for many purposes. It's used today as an anti-coagulant, to heal stomach and skin infections, for cramps, toothaches, arthritis, nervous system disorders, and as an anti-cancer medicine. Oh, and also for snake bite."

"Right now I feel like I have the symptoms of every one." Marc took the mug, smelled it, and grimaced as he slowly drank the tea.

"It has the taste and odor of garlic," Marc said, as he handed the empty mug to Ellen.

"It has many of the same chemical properties, Marc. The plant has little star-shaped flowers and looks quite innocent. You are a good patient. Would you like some more?"

"No thanks. I remember that my grandfather believed in garlic as a medicine. When he had a cold, he would wear a clove of garlic on a string around his neck. A remedy from the old country, I suppose. Now what are we going to do?"

"We're going to hide you in a cave at El Quizaltepe Mountain for a few days. It's about 20 kilometers northeast of here. There are Contra supporters in our village. They can make contact with elements of the Contra's Jorge Salazar Task Force, which is operating both in the Chontales and Boaco Departments with local sympathy and support. But I guess you know that anyway. The Task Force should be able to get you safely out. Meanwhile, we need to hide you and El Quizaltepe was the best place I could think of. We need to be on our way."

Outside a horse cart rolled to a stop by the front door, and there were some hurried whispered voices. Ellen appeared at the door. She motioned Marc to follow, with her finger to her lips. "Get in the back and lie down," she whispered as she put her hand on his shoulder. She handed him Fernando's backpack. Ellen and two young muchachos covered him with clumps of long grass.

The cart rolled out of the small village on what Marc supposed was an ox cart trail. To any observer it would look like they were on the way out to collect firewood with a load of grass to feed the little pony. Ellen's small house sat apart from the others. It was at least 500 feet from the nearest village home. They shouldn't be drawing any undue attention, he thought hopefully.

Each jolt of the cart brought a flash of pain as the deep bruises from yesterday's crash made their presence known. Marc could hear the hoofs of another horse riding behind. He assumed it must be Ellen. After what seemed to be more than an hour the cart stopped.

"Marc, have a drink of water," Ellen said, pulling away the grass clumps covering his face. It was just before dawn. Marc accepted the well used two liter plastic Coca Cola bottle. He could look back to see the cart had been climbing. There were small clusters of lights below marking small farming villages.

"Thanks. How much longer do you figure?"

"Two hours or so, I think. It's slow going with the horse cart, but there has been almost no one on this trail. In any case, people around here know me. I tend to the sick in the nearby villages and some public health work. If they spot me it will not cause any particular suspicion." She knocked on the side of the cart with a knuckle for good luck. Marc smiled.

"Cecilio, no mas descansar. Vámonos!" Ellen said, telling Cecilio he had enough rest and clapped her hands lightly for emphasis.

The cart lurched forward as the tip of Cecilio's switch touched the pony's back. They continued the long climb to El Quizaltepe. Marc had time to contemplate as he lay in the bed of the cart covered in grass. He was still weak, groggy, sore. He had put his life in the hands of this young woman he knew nothing about. As the cart bumped on the rocky path, he dozed off, but awakened when the cart suddenly stopped. The two muchachos, Cecilio and Efraim, brushed away the grass covering him. He sat up in pure amazement.

"Holy Cow! When you said cave, Ellen, you meant cave! I could have hidden the Maule in here." Marc was staring at a cave entrance that measured about 250 feet high, almost 100 feet wide, and went as far back as he could see.

"I've only been here once before," Ellen said. "It's off the beaten track. But let's get the backpack out, the food and water for you. Then we'll all eat what is going to be your favorite food, I'm afraid; gallo pinto and tortillas. I want the boys to start back to the village as soon as they eat. They are totally trustworthy, and no fans of the Sandinistas. But they are putting themselves in danger helping you and it worries me."

The boys had taken most of the cut grass piled high in the cart and thrown it on the ground. Your bed is going to be a bit primitive. The boys will carry the cut grass to the back of the cave, put plastic sheeting on top. With a blanket that will be your bed. We are at about 2,000 feet here, and it will be much cooler than you might expect."

"Ellen, the bed will be fine. I've slept on worse. I just hope that the pony and your horse don't eat up my mattress," he said in mock seriousness, looking at the two animals grazing on the pile of cut grass.

Ellen pretended to ignore his comment. But she couldn't suppress a slight smile, the first in the short time he had known her. Marc reflected on how good that smile made him feel, and forgave himself the dumb joke.

Efraim had started a very small fire some ways back in the cave. He heated gallo pinto in a frying pan while Cecilio prepared Marc's bed. The bed was well out of sight in the rear of the cave. The four of them sat on rocks at the cave entrance. They slowly ate the warmed-over gallo pinto, cold tortillas, and cabbage salad on metal plates. They washed their food down with slugs of water from the old plastic cola bottles.

After a few rapid instructions in Spanish from Ellen, the boys made ready to leave. They walked up to Marc with formality, bid him adios, and shook his hand in turn.

There was an awkward silence as Ellen and Marc watched the cart depart for Comalapa. They sat down on a large flat rock at the entrance to the cave. From there they could see a vista of the eastern shore of Lake Nicaragua. It was Ellen who broke that silence.

"We need to agree on a plan to get you out of here. The sooner, the better. There are just too many informers around, too many eyes and ears. I know who to talk to in the village. They can make contact with the Contras to get you south and across the border into Costa Rica."

"What do you think my chances would be of heading out myself, hiking down the east side of the lake? When I got to San Carlos, I could steal a boat and cross the San Juan River to Costa Rica? I'm an old Air Force pilot, and we were trained in escape and evasion. This should be a heck of a lot easier than Vietnam."

Ellen's eyes scanned the vista. "You might make it and you might not. There are a lot of Sandinista Army patrols, militia patrols, and some irregulars that are wandering around in attempts to ambush the Contras. Of course the Contras are trying to ambush the Sandinistas. There are mine fields along the border. I think your chances would be much better with a Contra escort. Here's an unpleasant thought." She turned to him. "If you are caught by the Sandinistas, they will have ways to persuade you to tell who has helped you since the crash. That's something we both have to think about, Marc."

First a smile, or almost a smile, and now she is finally using my name. Marc considered it a breakthrough.

"I have to go along with your thinking. In the meantime, I have my own cave, in fact my own small mountain. I should be able to see anyone coming up the hill. And I can climb up a bit and see even better."

"Marc, I'm leaving you enough gallo pinto and tortillas in plastic containers for a day. Keep them in the back of the cave where it's cooler. You have matches and a pan to heat them in. You have bottles of water. I am sure you know to make only a very small fire. Don't make one at night. I'm sorry we can't do better."

"Like I said, Ellen, I'll get along fine. Don't worry, or at least don't worry too much."

"I can't help worrying about all of us. I'm going to start back down the hill at dusk. There won't be anyone outside to see me by the time I get near the village. No one will wonder where I've been. I'll leave in an hour or so. As you know, it gets dark before 6:00 p.m. here, the benefit of being at the lower latitudes near the equator. Tell me what you can about yourself. None of the Contra spy stuff, of course. Where you're from, are you married, kids, that kind of thing."

"I'll give you the short version," Marc said, "so we'll have time for your story. I am 47 years old, born in Fairborn, Ohio. My dad was an aeronautical engineer at Wright-Patterson Air Force Base across the highway from Fairborn. Quite naturally I went to Ohio State, did the R.O.T.C. thing, was commissioned upon graduation, and went to flying school. I spent a few years in B-47's, then B-52's. I got very tired of the Strategic Air Command alert duty. We spent about a third of our time behind a fence in an alert facility. The bombers were all fueled, armed, and ready to go to Russia. I volunteered for AC-47 gunship training and Vietnam duty - the only way I could get out of bombers. I retired after 20 years as a Lt. Colonel. After that, I flew for a commuter airline in the right seat of a Beech 1900, hated it. Now I'm flying for the Contras as a contract pilot. As for the future? I don't have a plan; I'm just flying for a living. Aviation is my way of life. I've been at it for a long time now, so it's in my blood, I guess. How's that for short and sweet?"

"It was so short and sweet you forgot to say if you were married with kids."

Frank Gallo

"Was, not am. Met my wife my last year of college. She was a year behind me. We got married when I graduated from flight school and got my wings. While I was off in Vietnam flying Puff the Magic Dragon gunships, she was entertaining one of the single bomber pilots back at the base. We had no kids. I heard they have two."

"A bit bitter?"

"A bit."

"Girlfriend?"

"Nothing serious. Now that we're on true confessions, it's your turn. Do you want me to guess?" Marc asked.

"If you want."

"Okay, I'll give it a shot. You are from Georgia, maybe Alabama. You're close to 30, plus or minus 2, I'd say. Your father is a minister. You go to church every Sunday. You went to nursing school right out of high school. You've never been married. You aren't hardened enough. You get your satisfaction in life working with poor, disadvantaged people. You're obviously very good at languages. You must be pretty self-reliant and independent to be out in the boondocks on your own. How did I do?"

"I'll let you be the judge of that," Ellen said, with an impish glance. "I was born in McAllen, Texas. My father was a professional rodeo rider and my mother an accountant. They have a large ranch 25 miles outside of McAllen. I went to Texas A&M on a scholarship, with a Bachelor's and Master's degree in Public Health Nursing. I met and married my husband in my senior year. After I got my postgraduate degree, we moved to Denver and built a house in the mountains. After 10 years, my husband Ben, an engineer, was terminated at Martin-Marietta due to reorganization. He took a job in Atlanta. I stayed on in my job with the State of Colorado Health Sciences Center for the time being till he was settled, could find a house, and we could sell the mountain property. Then one evening I got a call from him. He said not to plan on coming to Atlanta. He had met someone else and wanted a divorce. We had no kids. I floundered a bit. Then through my church I was offered this missionary post, the chance to forgive and forget. Well, forget anyway."

"How long have you been here?"

"I've been here almost two years. But I won't be here much longer. The Sandinistas have ordered all of the missionaries out of the rural areas where there are Contras. They say it's for our safety but I think they also believe we may be aiding the Contras."

"And are you?" Marc asked.

"That would be a dangerous thing to do."

Marc let that answer slide by.

Ellen continued. "You know, when I came here almost two years ago and got my in-country briefing in Managua, it seemed like the Sandinistas were trying to help the poor people. They had succeeded a bit. But the nurse I replaced here was very bitter about the Sandinistas. After about a year, I'm beginning to see why. When the Sandinistas came to power there was supposed to be freedom from the tyranny of Somoza. But instead the Sandinistas had their own form of tyranny. They shut down the opposition press, namely *La Prensa.* They also imposed restrictions on leaders of the Catholic Church, and created neighborhood intelligence centers in the Cuban fashion. The promised free elections were impossible. Those who had businesses and land saw them confiscated, and tenants lost land that was given to cooperatives. The party formed along strong Marxist/Leninist lines after the revolution succeeded. Many of the rural Sandinista officials felt anyone who owned a small finca or farm, a truck, or a pulpería which is a small store, was an enemy of the State. People were persecuted. When property titles were finally given to some farmers for land that had been expropriated, it was largely due to the pressure of the Contra war. The farmers found out that those titles could not be sold or inherited. While the campesinos wanted the clinics, schools, and good prices for their harvests, their culture and customs did not accept the collective way of farming. They didn't agree to being told what to grow, how to grow it, where to sell it and the price they could charge. Many farmers abandoned their land and went to find the Contras. Families that had given aid to the Sandinistas when they were fighting Somoza then began giving aid to the Contras fighting the Sandinistas. I remember meeting a humble old man north of my village on the road to Boaco Viejo. He was in ragged clothes, with no shoes. He had his shotgun tied with a hemp rope instead of a leather strap. He was walking to join the Contras. It will always remain a vivid picture in my mind."

"I can understand why it would."

"Marc, did you know your passenger Fernando well?"

"No, I met him for the first time a few minutes before we left Point West in Costa Rica. Seemed like a nice guy. He said nothing about his mission. I was asked if I would volunteer to fly him into that little landing strip. In the military they say don't volunteer for anything. Guess I didn't learn that very well."

"So you don't have any idea what his mission was, then?"

"No, and I guess that was intentional. No need to know, as they say. I would like to look through that backpack now, though. I'll get it and be back in a minute, with a bottle of water.

Marc returned with the black canvas backpack that was trimmed in dark brown leather. He handed the bottle of water to Ellen.

"Well, let's see what we have here." Marc pulled out what appeared to be a laptop computer case.

"I've seen one of these before," he said, as he opened the computer case. "This is a KL-43. I was shown one about a week ago in our operations shack at the airstrip. It's an encoding machine to be used when making a telephone call. I think we can safely say that Fernando was on some clandestine mission. Look at the dollars! There must be about $10,000 in U.S. dollars alone, I would think, without counting. I really don't see anything in the way of personal papers that Fernando was carrying, except this passport. Marc handed the passport to Ellen. He continued rummaging in the backpack. Here is a Xerox copy of an article about Fidel Castro's arrival in Managua next week. It's from the Sandinista newspaper *Barricada*."

"Marc, this is a Cuban passport."

"Aha, the plot thickens. Wish I could somehow get word back to Point West that Fernando was killed in the crash. He must've been on an important assignment."

"It's about time for me to get my horse and return to Comalapa," Ellen said.

"Oh," Marc said, "Before you go, you haven't finished your life story. Is there a boyfriend in the picture now?"

"No, not really. At the Dallas Missionary Training Center I met a very nice man my age, a pilot like you."

"Oh? A missionary pilot? That has always sounded interesting to me, but not as a way to make a living."

"Well, Dale and I dated for the two months we were at the Training Center. Of course I came to Nicaragua and he went to the Marshall Islands. He flew island hopping missions, carrying passengers and supplies for the missionaries based on various islands. We had exchanged a few letters through the central office in the States. Then one time when I went to a quarterly mission meeting in Managua, there was a letter there for me from Dale's mother. I had never met her. As soon as I saw the letter I knew something had happened to Dale. His mother said he was on an emergency medical evacuation flight to one of the islands, and attempted to land in the middle of a thunderstorm. The plane crashed in the ocean short of the runway."

"That's tough, Ellen. I'm sorry."

"Up north of Chinandega there is a missionary, Bob Stevens, also a Texan. He's a nice guy, and we get together in Managua when we're at quarterly meetings. We're just friends.

There hasn't been enough time to develop a relationship. A pretty dismal love life, you could say." Ellen sighed with a wry smile.

"Doesn't sound too different from mine."

"I need to leave before it gets any later. I have my sick call at 7:00 a.m."

"Sick call? Sounds like the military."

"Yes, I suppose it does. I'll have a line of a dozen people by 7:00 each morning outside the clinic. One or two afternoons during the week I visit the schools in Comalapa, Camoapa, and some of the other small villages. I also travel to each of the nearby villages two or three times a month for a clinic in the morning, and give immunizations when I have supplies on hand. One of my problems is that the electricity is erratic here. My little fridge does not hold the cold well when the power is off. So I dare only store serums I receive from Managua for a short time. When they arrive, I go out to the outlying villages and give the immunization injections immediately."

"Sounds like it keeps you pretty busy."

"There's no social life here. It's difficult for a foreigner to really become an integral part of the local community. They may like me; I think they do. They accept me. But the cultural gap is just too wide. I have a wonderful garden around my small house. That is my recreation. I always bring back books when I return from my Managua meetings.

Tomorrow afternoon I will return. Fortunately I'm away often treating some sick or injured person. Being out of the village won't raise any suspicions. I'll talk to one or two of the principal Contra supporters in the village. We can devise a plan to get you safely back to Costa Rica."

"Is it difficult to know who you can talk to safely? How can you tell who're Sandinistas and who're the opposition?"

"I find that the openly Sandinista supporters and quiet sympathizers of their cause are more stand-offish. I can tell their political leanings easily, but that doesn't stop them from visiting my clinic. I'm sure there are many more who oppose the Sandinistas, but they're careful in voicing their opposition. The innuendos are there, purposefully for me to pick up. I know who I can trust. Well, I must be on my way."

"Ellen, be careful on the way down," Marc said, putting his arm around her and squeezing. Ellen and Marc walked over to Ellen's horse. She cinched the belly strap of the simple campesino saddle. The saddle was little more than a leather mat with stirrups, set on top of a roughly woven blanket.

"You be careful yourself," Ellen said, then gave Marc a peck on the cheek. She mounted the horse, and began her descent on the rocky trail towards Comalapa through the early evening twilight.

The sun had set in a fiery orange glow, reflecting up against scattered cumulus clouds. The dim lights of small homes on the distant slopes below began to appear. Marc sat on the large rock that served as a veranda at the cave entrance. His thoughts were interrupted by the flapping of bat wings as hundreds of bats departed the cave in their erratic flight paths. Marc made his way to the pallet in the back of the cave and, exhausted, fell asleep immediately.

In the morning, Marc awoke with a start, for a moment unsure of where he was. Efraim had pointed out the location of a spring 200 feet from the cave entrance. Marc splashed himself awake with the cold, clear water that surged out of a crevice in the rock into a small pool. He returned to the cave, and made a small fire to heat the gallo pinto for breakfast. He folded a tortilla over a stick, and held it over a corner of the fire as the gallo pinto warmed. He ate in the total quietness of the cave, aware of a light, mysterious breeze that always seemed to be present.

The field radio crackled. Tomás, the operator, slipped on his headset, pulled out a small notebook and pad and began writing furiously. When the transmission ended, he sat on a log at the edge of the forest clearing with a codebook balanced on his left knee and notebook on his right. He began to decipher the message.

"Comandante," Tomás called to Pete. The tall red head gringo wearing Tiger jungle fatigues and a Miami Dolphins ball cap looked up from the topographical map he was studying.

"Sí?" he questioned.

"Un mensaje muy importante."

Pete got up and strode quickly across the clearing. It was the bivouac of the moment, a fire pit in the center with hammocks strung around in a circle. Pete knew that for Tomás all messages were important. But they were deep in central Nicaragua now, and every precaution was necessary.

Tomás handed the decoded message to Pete, who was known as Comandante Delfin, in tribute to the Dolphin's cap that was his trademark.

For Tiger Team Bravo only. Proceed to area 10 kilometers east of Comalapa for support of important FDN directed mission. More to follow. Separate instructions will be sent within 12 hours to the 4,000 contra forces located within the 25,000 square kilometers of the Department of Chontales, Río San Juan, and Zelaya. Expect further instructions when in position near Comalapa. So advise.

"Omar, salimos ahorita," Pete yelled to his second in command, who was holding the topo map. The tone of Pete's voice told Omar of the urgency to strike camp immediately. Instructions were shouted. Those napping rolled out of their hammocks, perimeter guards were called in, and packs were quickly assembled. Within 15 minutes the Tiger Team was double-timing south.

Marc spent the day exploring the base of the mountain. The mountain itself was no more than a huge monolithic rock perched at the top of terrain that rose from all quadrants. He found several springs, and a spring fed pool in the shade of guapinol, cenizaro, and guanacaste trees. He climbed some of the lower rocky reaches of the mountain, but thought better of going higher for the view. In the afternoon, time passed slowly as he awaited Ellen's return, sunning himself on the rock at the cave entrance as the sun made its way west.

He heard the singing before he saw her. It was a simple tune, a happy song that seemed to relieve the tension of being a fugitive in a war torn country. Ellen came into view, the sun low on the horizon behind her, her shoulder-length brunette hair pulled back in a pony tail.

"Hi there," she shouted to Marc.

"Hi yourself, cowgirl. I can tell you're from Texas the way you ride that thoroughbred."

"Yeah. Thoroughbred. Sure," Ellen responded, laughing. "Remember who you're talking to, the daughter of a rodeo cowboy."

"I did enjoy your singing."

"Just a little church tune. You know, one of those melodies that run through your head subconsciously. The members of our little church in Comalapa like to sing hymns. A good part of our two services each week are hymnals."

"Do you conduct the service?"

"Heavens no! We have a Nicaraguan pastor. I'm here to minister to health needs. I attend the services when I can to show support. How was your day on the mountain?"

Marc recounted his adventures, and then Ellen opened a knapsack she had brought.

"Here's some fresh pork and some tomatoes. Let's get a fire started, and you can have something besides gallo pinto for a change."

They prepared their supper over the small fire in the back of the cave. Each took a stainless steel plate loaded with barbecued pork, tomato slices, and rice out to the rock. They ate as the sun set over Lake Nicaragua.

"That's a beautiful sight. I do love Lago Colcibolca."

"What did you say?" Marc asked.

"You know, Lake Colcibolca. That's the old Indian name for Lake Nicaragua. The name is used commonly even now by Nicaraguans."

"Hadn't heard that. By the way, lots of bats flew out of the cave this time last night."

"I hope they weren't vampire bats," Ellen said, raising her eyebrows.

"Of course you aren't serious. Trying to scare me?"

"Actually, Marc, there are vampire bats in this region. They are especially bothersome to horses and cattle. The vampire bat will swoop down and land in a pasture. Then it scampers on its hind legs and thumbs over to a sleeping cow or horse, climbs onto the back and bites a hole in the skin with sharp incisors. As a rule the animal will not even feel it. The vampire then sucks the blood. Its saliva contains a coagulant to stop the bleeding after it gets done feeding. The bat will return the next night. Or another vampire bat will feed on the same bite. It's a real problem for ranchers in Nicaragua."

"And I thought vampire bats were only in the movies."

"Here in the tropics we deal with different health problems. In the past week I have treated one patient for Chagas disease and another for leishmaniasis or what they call here leprosy of the mountain. Chagas disease is caused by the kissing bug, which is really the chupasangre bug. It's known to bite a sleeping person on the lips, and it passes a parasite during the bite or kiss. It's deadly when the parasite gets into the muscle."

"You're beginning to worry me, Ellen. I'm not sure I want to know about the other disease."

"Well, the other, leishmaniasis, is also caused by a bug bite. But it's a very tiny mite-like bug, and the infection can cause an ulcer of the flesh right down to the bone. That's the reason it's called Leprosy of the Mountain."

"Sounds pretty ugly."

"It can get that way. Both my patients will have to go to Managua for treatment. I don't like to talk about such uncomfortable things. But it gives you an idea of life in rural Nicaragua."

"You're a mighty brave lady."

"No more than anyone who was born here and suffers many hardships. Yet they are a gentle people who work hard, always smile, and are content to enjoy life with their families."

"Looks like we have a storm brewing," Marc said, looking up at the darkening sky. "You can see the thunderhead growing rapidly right on top of us. Lots of orographic lifting; the wind pushing the warm air up over the mountain."

"I don't want to get caught in a downpour on the rocky trail. It's difficult enough for the horse."

"Ellen, you might want to bring him in the cave. We sure have plenty of room. I can already hear the rumble coming out of that cloud."

Ellen got up and led the horse into the cave. Then she returned to the rock veranda. It was near dark, and a white bolt of lightning lit up the sky. It was followed by a loud boom of thunder that shook the ground beneath them. Ellen moved closer to Marc and shivered.

"It's so dry; our farmers need the rain, so I'm glad. But it seems a rather violent thunderstorm," she said.

"I guess that's because it parked itself right on top of our mountain. It doesn't look like it wants to move."

A few scattered raindrops fell and then suddenly a deluge. Marc and Ellen ran into the cave, laughing at their narrow escape from the sudden downpour.

"Let's see. My living room is bare, also dining room and family room. We're going to have to sit either in the bedroom or on dirt," Marc said.

"I choose the bedroom," Ellen said, "if you can call that mound of hay a bed."

"I slept like a baby on it," Marc said. "Do you want to give your horse part of my mattress?"

"No, he's okay. He found good grass over by the spring."

Ellen and Marc sat on the bed. The ever present soft breeze in the cave had turned much cooler. Marc grabbed the blanket at the foot of the bed and put it around them. Ellen snuggled closer for warmth.

"If this doesn't let up soon, Marc, I'll have to stay here tonight and leave early in the morning. It would be too dangerous to try to go down to the village tonight."

"In that case, I'll pray to the rain gods to keep it coming," Marc said, looking up at the cave ceiling in mock prayer.

Ellen jabbed him in the ribs, and Marc laughed.

"Tell me more about yourself," Marc said.

"You first," Ellen replied.

"We might as well lie down and talk, more comfortable than sitting," Marc said.

Both lay on the pallet, facing each other. A flash of lightning would occasionally light the interior of the cave for an instant. The mood was enhanced by the flickering of dying embers in the cooking fire. It gained momentary life from puffs of the breeze that ran softly through the cave as it sought a hidden outlet somewhere in the rear. The small talk ended as Marc experimented with kisses on Ellen's hand, cheek, and neck.

She responded with a kiss right on his mouth. At that moment a tremendous thunderclap exploded.

"Some kiss," Marc said.

"Shut up, Yankee," she replied, and kissed him again.

Marc awoke, and looked over at Ellen. Her eyes were open, and she smiled. Marc put his arm around her, and they lay quietly.

"I hate to go, Marc, but I must. I can be down to the village before my 7:00 a.m. sick call if I leave now."

Ellen slipped on her jeans and blouse. She filled her canteen at the spring and washed her face with a kerchief. Still inside the cave, Marc had started a small cooking fire. He worked at heating two tortillas on a long stick.

"Cooking," Ellen said with a smile.

"Yes, one of my specialties. I just learned how to heat the tortillas. These are for you to eat on the way down."

"Thanks. I'll be back in late afternoon. Hopefully I'll have some good news on how and when you can return to Costa Rica. Meanwhile, don't do any serious climbing. I'm not equipped to repair broken bones."

"You be careful too," he replied, and he looked steadily into her eyes. She held his gaze for a long moment. Then without further comment, Ellen saddled the horse and started the trek downhill. She turned in the saddle and with a wide smile blew a kiss with a dramatic wave of the hand as Marc watched from the cave entrance. He would remember that look, that blown kiss, and the immediate sense of loss he felt as she disappeared down the trail.

Marc heated the new batch of gallo pinto Ellen had brought. He was not really tired of it. Ellen had brought a little bottle of salsa picante which spiced it up nicely. Tasty and satisfying, he told himself. For the rest of the morning he hiked around the mountain until the sun was overhead. Back in the coolness of his cave, he ate some of the pork that was left from the night before. Then he went to his pallet for an afternoon nap.

CHAPTER 7—CAPTURED

"Arriba! Arriba!" The voice shouted.

Marc opened his eyes to find the muzzle of an AK-47 six inches from his nose. Three soldiers in olive drab uniforms and fatigue caps were standing around him. They motioned with their hands for him to stand up. As he arose warily, the muzzle of the AK-47 followed, remaining inches from his face.

"Americano, verdad?" one soldier asked.

"No comprendo," Marc said the first reply that came to mind.

"Americano," the soldier answered angrily.

"Vamanos, manos arriba," he said, and raised Marc's arms in the air to explain what he meant.

Two other soldiers at the mouth of the cave turned around and pointed their AK-47s at Marc. His hands were then tied behind his back. Two of the soldiers searched the back of the cave and found the black canvas knapsack with leather trim that Marc had hidden in a niche. Not good that they have the KL-43, he noted critically. He should have destroyed it before now.

Hands tied, Marc stumbled out of the cave into the morning sunlight. Two Sandinista soldiers at the nearby spring looked up in surprise. Talking excitedly, these soldiers approached to look him over.

One of the seven clearly appeared to be the senior in command. He walked calmly over to Marc, seeming neither agitated nor angry. He appeared much older than all the others. His uniform was cleaner and neater. He was clean shaven and of fair complexion. His hair was cut short, unlike his compañeros who to the man sported scraggly mustaches, goatees, and hair spilling out from beneath their fatigue caps. As the tall soldier neared, Marc could see captain's insignia on his cap. The Captain appeared to be in his mid-thirties, older by many years than his subordinates. On the left shoulder of his shirt was an emblem that read "Fuerzas Armadas Revolucionarias."

"Americano?" he asked.

"No, Canadian journalist," Marc replied, finding a possible cover story.

"I think you are an American pilot, señor," the leader said in good English. "We have been looking for you, and now we have found you, quite easily I must say. Our intelligence sources are very good. The people here in Chontales support the revolution."

Marc almost said "That's not what I heard," but thought better of it.

"It appears you have had help from someone who lives nearby. Is that not true?"

"No, I just stumbled on this cave. It seemed a good place to hide," Marc responded. He dropped any pretext that he was not the American pilot they were looking for. It was too obvious.

"So you have received no help? But you have cooking pots, a little bit of food, blankets. Where did they come from?"

Marc was silent. This was not a game he was going to win.

"Well," the leader said, "We shall take you to our headquarters where the questions will be even more difficult. There are always ways to get the correct answers. Usually when suspects spend a few days at our cells in El Chipote prison, they become very cooperative."

"Comandante," one of the soldiers addressed the Captain, and handed him Fernando's backpack. The Captain pulled out the KL-43. He opened the case.

"I see you have a code machine. Very unusual for a pilot, but not for a spy. Did you fly from Ilopongo in San Salvador, Santa Elena in Costa Rica, or Aguacate in Honduras?"

Marc did not answer.

"We will waste no time here. I am sure there will be better answers at El Chipote. Of course you will be treated harshly as a spy. Your headquarters may not even know you are alive. That makes your position very serious, is it not so?" The Captain said it with a smile that Marc realized was fraught with malicious intent. Marc could only hope that Ellen would know that he had been captured by the Sandinistas and that she would run. He was not sure what torture methods the Sandinistas would use. But he had no illusions.

As he talked, the Comandante Captain found the Cuban passport with Fernando's picture and the stash of dollars and córdobas. Marc's foreboding deepened, for he knew he should have destroyed all the contents of the backpack or buried them in the cave.

"A Cubano. Very interesting. I don't know this friend of yours."

Then it hit Marc. Cuban intelligence officers were deployed throughout the Sandinista Army. Just his luck! This guy was one. He could see the Nicaraguans were deferential but not in a friendly way with the Cuban. One young female soldier who stepped up to take the backpack appeared to be the Captain's personal staff, so to speak.

"We will return to the truck, and arrange your transportation to Managua," the Captain said.

The soldiers walked single file down the trail, assault rifles at the ready. Marc was in the middle. The Cuban and his female soldier brought up the rear. She was not one to mess with, Marc thought, as she seemed very comfortable with the AK-47 she was carrying. The Cuban, on the other hand, had only a holstered pistol. Bringing up the rear keeps the Comandante out of the frontal assault of an ambush, Marc surmised.

After a kilometer march downhill, the group arrived at a parked army truck, an EFI East German model used by the Sandinista Army. The driver was lying down on one of the two bench seats in back. Harsh words from the Captain roused him and he became the target of a short verbal lashing. Marc, hands tied, was physically lifted into the back of the truck by four soldiers. The Comandante climbed into the wide seat in the front cab. His female bodyguard squeezed in alongside with her assault rifle. The right side of the cab roof had a round gunner's hatch that opened to the rear. Another soldier climbed into the cab. He stood so that at chest high he could man the light machine gun mounted on the roof. The driver started the engine, and the truck began its trip down a road that was little more than an improved ox cart path. A cloud of smelly black diesel fumes left a trail behind. On each side in the back of the truck there were two benches. Marc was in the middle on the right side, two Sandinista soldiers on each side of him. Three soldiers faced him on the opposite bench. The soldier on his right uncapped his canteen, and offered Marc a drink. Marc nodded.

The canteen was held to Marc's lips, and he drank in huge gulps, dehydrated from the walk down the trail. Water spilled over his face and onto his shirt, a welcome shower.

"Gracias," Marc said.

"De nada, señor piloto," the soldier responded, not unfriendly.

Marc felt himself an object of curiosity. The soldiers bantered back and forth, looking at him from time to time. He didn't know if they were talking about him or not. The truck, strongly sprung, reacted to each large rock and each deep rut with a spine wrenching jolt. At times Marc thought he was going to get thrown off his seat. He steadied himself by grasping the back of his seat with his tied hands.

The truck entered a little village which Marc realized was Comalapa. It was not yet time for Ellen to have started up the mountain. He wondered and worried when the truck stopped at the western edge of the village. There was a small building ten feet from the road, a Sandinista Army puesto or post. Two soldiers remained seated on a bench in front of the building. They waved to the troops in the back of the truck, while a sergeant sauntered over to the truck. When the Captain got out of the truck the sergeant stood erect. The two soldiers on the bench jumped up and stood at attention.

The Captain said a few words to the sergeant, who walked behind the truck.

"El gringo," the sergeant said to no one in particular, with a smirk. Marc ignored him, again thinking of Ellen who must be nearby. He worried that an informer in the village might have revealed Ellen's part in Marc's escape and evasion. All but two of the soldiers in the back of the truck got out to stretch. Some lit cigarettes; others relieved themselves at the side of the road with indifference. The Captain, followed by his female bodyguard, walked to the side of the truck.

"And how are you feeling?" he asked.

"So so," Marc answered, deciding the less he said the better.

"You are going to be a present to Comandante Fidel, who arrives in Managua tomorrow for the seventh anniversary celebration of the revolution. He likes to make a point about America's imperialism in Latin America."

Marc said nothing. He began to imagine that he could be a propaganda showpiece, in the fashion of the American prisoners in North Vietnam.

The Captain ordered the truck loaded up and it drove off slowly, as the driver shifted up through a long series of gears. The road led to the Carretera Rama, the paved road that connects the Caribbean river port town of Rama to Managua. Once on the paved road, it was only 80 miles to the west to Managua. Their gravel road passed through some densely forested areas, which opened up occasionally to tilled fields and pastures. The Sandinista soldiers had quieted down. Several had their eyes closed and appeared to be dozing, despite the high whine of the truck gears.

Marc was already trying to plan his story for the interrogation that he had been promised. He was quite sure the Sandinista radar had followed his flight after takeoff from Point West. The radar station at Peñas Blancas could have picked him up immediately. As he neared the Sonojal airstrip, the Russian radar station at Siuna probably followed his flight. Of course Fernando's body would have been discovered immediately. Ellen had thought they'd assume Fernando was the pilot. But now, through Marc's carelessness, the Captain had already surmised by Fernando's passport that Marc was the pilot and

Fernando the passenger. Now he realized why Fernando had been so tight-lipped about his mission. Marc knew nothing about it, so could reveal nothing. Would his interrogator believe it?

The truck driver down-shifted and braked as they rounded a curve. A tree had fallen across the road, and the truck ground to a stop. Quickly the Sandinista soldiers were alert, standing and pointing their Ak-47s at the dense woods. The machine gunner swiveled the barrel back and forth. The Captain was shouting commands from his seat inside the cab. They smelled an ambush.

Suddenly a rocket propelled grenade struck the right front of the truck. A second one followed immediately, hitting the left side. Wild firing began, with the Sandinistas spraying their 7.62mm bullets wildly in every direction. Miraculously, the truck engine was still running. The driver began backing the truck, which moved about fifty feet when Marc saw the driver slump. The machine gunner was hit in the same burst. The seven soldiers in back scrambled out of the truck. They were met with withering fire from a dozen or more assault rifles on both sides of the road. The truck had backed into well protected dug-in positions the ambushers had prepared. Marc awkwardly slid off the bench seat and flattened himself on the steel floor of the truck. The Captain's bodyguard, bleeding heavily, roughly pushed past the body of the cabin gunner. She unlatched the door, fell heavily to the ground, and fired her AK-47. As she began to lose consciousness her grip loosened. The 7.62mm bullets began hitting tree trunks, then higher branches, and a rain of shattered leaves fluttered to the ground. The Cuban, bleeding heavily from facial and shoulder wounds, slid from the door to the ground. He fired as he came to his knees.

A burst of automatic fire from the trees threw him against the side of the truck, and he collapsed on the ground.

Marc dared not raise his head to see what was going on. The firing had almost stopped except for one burst of gunfire that seemed to come from beneath him. One of the Sandinistas was still firing. Marc heard a dull explosion under the truck before he felt the thrust of the thick steel floor against his right cheekbone. The grenade had been thrown precisely. The firing underneath him had stopped.

Contras emerged from the dense cover from all sides, dodging and weaving as they ran towards the truck. Marc raised his head, just in time to see a stocky, red haired contra wearing a Miami Dolphins baseball cap walk up to the tailgate.

"Are you okay?" he asked with a mid-western accent.

"Yes, I think so," Marc answered. "Who're you?"

"Pete Givens," the Contra answered, as he climbed up into the truck. He set down an Uzi submachine gun, and pulled an eight inch knife from a scabbard attached to his shoulder harness. His blade sliced through the rope binding Marc's hands. Pete had piercing blue eyes, a striking contrast with his red hair. He was well muscled, obviously fit. Four grenades hung from his shoulder harness. A U.S. Army Ranger insignia was tattooed on Pete's left forearm.

His arms free, Marc rubbed his wrists and felt his cheekbone for blood, but found it dry. He extended his right hand to Pete.

"Marc DiAngelo. You with the Contras?"

"That's right. Our group is a Special Forces Commando Unit of the Jorge Salazar Task Force. We were supposed to meet you up on the mountain, but the Sandinistas found you first. Better late than never."

Marc nodded, surprised. A rescue plan had been directed from somewhere by someone who obviously had very good communications. He sat down on the back of the truck, and slid out to stand on the ground. Pete helped by holding his left arm. Marc flexed both arms, trying to relieve the soreness and stiffness.

"Pete, are you with the U.S. Army, CIA, or what?"

"I'm ex-Army. I was a ranger for eight years. I've been with the Contras for 15 months. We can talk later. Let's get the hell outta here. I think two of the Sandys got away. They're probably halfway to Comalapa by now."

Pete let out a shrill piercing whistle between his teeth, made a circling motion in the air with his right hand, and pointed towards the forest on the south side of the road.

"Todos las armas," he yelled. The Contras had already picked up some of the AK-47s and ammo clips, and removed grenades from the bodies of the Sandinista soldiers. One had recovered the light machine gun mounted on top of the truck cab, and waved it in the air triumphantly.

"Pete, there is a knapsack in the truck that has some important things in it. It should be in the cab where the Cuban captain was."

"Okay, go get it. There is a Cuban officer with every Sandinista battalion, and some with smaller special units. I don't mind wasting that guy at all. Most are from Cuban intelligence. Nasty guys."

After retrieving the knapsack, Marc followed Pete and the others through the forest and onto a cow path. He could see that the unit was going to continue downhill towards the distant lakeshore. This surprised him, as he expected them to head towards the refuge of the mountains to the east.

"Where're we headed?" Marc asked breathlessly as the contra column was walking at almost a half trot.

"We'll continue towards the lake, near Puerto Diaz. Those are my instructions." Marc had already seen one of the Contras with a field radio telephone on his back. It explained how the free-moving commando unit could be under orders from some distant headquarters. Following the Contras in front, Marc noted they were all wearing U.S.-style camouflage fatigues and Australian-type bush hats. He knew these were marks of an elite outfit. The briefings he had received at Point West had indicated that the usual Contra fatigues were dark green, and in some cases Sears brand dark blue work uniforms.

"Can you keep up?" Pete asked.

"Yeah, I'm okay," Marc answered, though his legs were tiring and his lungs burning as he followed the quickly moving column down the trails, sometimes veering, but always gradually downward to the west, toward the lakeshore. The camouflage uniforms of those leading the front of the column often blended into the surrounding trees. Two of the Contras were far ahead, taking measure of any possible ambush. Finally, the column pulled to a halt, and the two point men conferred with Pete.

Pete turned to Marc. "The Juigalpa-Managua road is half a kilometer away. We're going to cross it in groups of two and three," he said.

The commandos pulled up short of the paved road. For the past 15 minutes, Marc had heard the sound of occasional trucks and buses on the road below. It seemed the traffic was light.

The unit continued to walk in file until 2000 yards from the road. Pete sent six contras ahead. The rest spread out in defensive positions. Four of the contras returned in 15 minutes, and reported to Pete.

"Marc, we'll get half our unit across the road, then you and me, and then the rest."

"Okay, where are we heading?"

"We're going to go to a forested site a little north of Puerto Diaz. In fact, it's only about 10 miles from the airstrip where you had your crash landing."

"You seem to know the whole story," Marc said.

"I'll explain later, Marc. Let's get across the road and into cover."

Lookouts had been posted on each side of the road hidden in the trees. They both held up their hands for Marc and Pete to remain where they were. Within a minute they had coordinated the movement and Pete and Marc were waved across. Pete carried two AK-47s; one was the booty from the recent firefight. Marc clutched his knapsack and ran across with his head low.

Once the unit was across safely, they again walked single file, with two point men 500 yards ahead, and two trailing by the same distance. The commando unit resumed its quick pace.

Marc stumbled several times. Pete pretended not to notice. After a little more than two hours, the unit stopped on a heavily treed hillock.

"Okay, this is where we spend the night," Pete said. Already the commandos had slipped off their heavy backpacks. Hammocks were strung up to trees, and a small campfire lit. Two of the commandos brought out a large pot. Marc could not imagine how it would have fit into a backpack. Four of the commandos were dispersed to patrol a hundred yards from the main camp. A small plume of blue smoke erupted from a fire as one of the commandos boiled a pot of rice and beans. Pete threw Marc a canteen, and two packets of U.S. Army MRE.

"Every one of my guys has some additional MRE's," Pete said. "We don't always have time to cook, and many times we're so close to the Sandinistas we can't start a fire."

Pete walked over to the radioman, who attached the whip antenna to his equipment. Pete was making a call to his headquarters, Marc presumed. After Pete was done, he called two of his men. Marc noted Pete spoke fluent Spanish. Pete gave instructions; the two men nodded, picked up their AK-47s, and left.

"My guys are going almost all the way to Puerto Diaz, only a couple of miles. I have instructions to turn you over to one of our agents who will take you across the lake where it's safer. The Sandinistas will be looking for you – and us – on this side of the lake. You'll leave early in the morning. My unit will be long gone from here as soon as you leave. You've seen how fast we can move."

"I'm impressed. I had a tough time keeping up, even though your guys are carrying heavy backpacks and extra weapons."

"Yeah, and extra ammo now. The main reason we prefer the AK-47 is because we're mobile and re-supply is difficult. We can use captured Sandinista AK-47 ammo. That hammock over there is yours for the night."

"I don't want to take one of your commando's hammocks."

"Don't worry. There will be perimeter guards dispersed all night. They will rotate in the hammocks that are up."

"Pete, you said you would explain later how you knew who I was and where I was. So now's a good time."

"The Contras are well established in Boaco and Chontales. We have a large base of support in the population, and we know everything the Sandinistas do, and where they are. Through these local sources we learned that a Contra plane had crashed.

I don't know what your mission was, and I don't want to. We checked in with our headquarters by radio the day before yesterday. We were told that a Contra pilot was holed up in a cave at El Quizaltepe Mountain. We know that area pretty well. We thought we could get there later today, find you, and get you in the E and E pipeline. Unfortunately, the Sandinistas had an informant, at Comalapa probably, who knew you were at the mountain. A Sandinista patrol in the area was dispatched by radio to go find you. You may or may not know this. There are a number, I don't know how many, of mobile Contra listening posts on hilltops and mountain tops around the country. These listening posts have modern scanners that track Sandinista tactical frequencies. We were alerted early this morning that a Sandinista patrol had been sent up to the cave to capture you. That info was a result of an intercept. We couldn't get to you first, but we knew the road they would be traveling and we set up an ambush."

"That explains a lot," Marc said, shaking his head at descriptions of the behind the scenes operations he never would have imagined.

"Pete, these guys seem very professional, not like the Contras that have been described to me."

"They are professionals. Each one has been handpicked by me. None of them are from Somoza's National Guard, which had some bad apples. For the most part they were farm boys who became seasoned veterans. I took them to Florida for Ranger training. The 20 of us here have been together for almost a year. We're one of a dozen 10 to 100 man commando units in the north, east, and southeast of the country."

"Units just like yours?"

"Pretty much. A twenty man detachment is common for what we call commando or Special Forces teams. Each 20 man unit has a basic weapons package. We're given a choice of 16 AK-47s or FAL assault rifles. I prefer the AK-47 as I said before, so we can use captured Sandinista ammo. We are also issued a 60 millimeter mortar, an M-79 grenade launcher, a light machine gun, 50 grenades, and a sniper's rifle. My guys can fast for days with little food, carrying everything on their backs."

"You said you weren't U.S. Army or CIA. How do you happen to be in this war? Are you working privately?"

"I'm not sure I would call it work. I had Army Ranger training when I was 20 years old. Then, one year in Vietnam. I would have stayed for more but the peace accords were signed. We gave that away, in my book. Did everything wrong."

"Yeah, I know. I was flying C-47 gunships out of Da Nang. The Air Force started pounding Hanoi with B-52's in Linebacker I before Christmas '72, and then Linebacker II on and after Christmas. The North Vietnamese agreed to peace. After Linebacker II they had no more SAM's to defend their capitol. We had them by the throat, and then gave it away, as you said."

"I don't even like to talk about it," Pete said. "I stayed in the Army with the Rangers for three more years. I loved it, but decided to try civilian life, and worked for UPS. I just happened to read a friend's *Soldier of Fortune* magazine one day about the Contra fight. It appealed to me as a just fight. The Contras were the underdogs. I made a few calls, and ended up as a contract employee for the CIA giving Ranger training. These were handpicked Contra rebels I trained in the Florida Everglades. As far as any one is concerned, I'm still training them."

"Just can't let go of the kids, is that it?" Marc asked.

"Yeah, that's about it."

At this moment one of the commandos walked up and introduced himself.

"Mister Pilot, I am Harold Baker," he said, in an accent that sounded Jamaican. Harold was a black man, short, not more than five foot five, muscular with cat-like movement. Marc, who had been sitting on the ground, stood up and shook Harold's hand.

"Name's Marc, Harold. It's a pleasure. Where are you from?"

"I'm from Miskito country, a little village called Seven Bank, close to Puerto Cabezas on the Caribbean. People call me "Seven.""

"The Miskitos have been treated very badly by the Sandinistas. Many Miskitos have joined the counter-revolution," Pete said.

"Yes man, this is true. The Sandinistas decided to relocate the Miskitos. We live on the Río Coco, which separates Nicaragua and Honduras. The banks of the Rio Coco have been the ancestral home of the Miskitos for hundreds of years. The Sandinistas were afraid the Miskitos of the Rio Coco would give help to the Contras. So 4,000 of my people were moved from their villages to what the Sandinistas called "new communities," but there were no facilities. After they were moved, the Ejército Popular Sandinista burned their houses, killed their cows and destroyed their fields and grain storage. Many of the 4,000 were made to walk more than a hundred kilometers to these new camps. These were old men and women, mothers and fathers."

"I would think that brought many recruits to the Contras," Marc said.

"This is true. But there was even a worse tragedy. On the ninth of December in 1982 the Fuerza Aérea Sandinista began evacuation of children and some mothers from the Río Coco using MI-8 transport helicopters. On that day 800 Miskitos from the Río Coco were being evacuated from Ayapal to San José de Bocay. One helicopter just lifted off at Ayapal, then crashed. Seventy-five Miskito children and nine mothers died in the crash. The Sandinista propaganda machine blamed the Contras. Their story was that Contras had shot the helicopter down with a missile. They made the most of this *mentira*, this lie. The Sandinista newspaper, *Barricada*, had headlines blaming the Contras."

"You say it was not shot down?" Marc asked.

"No. Our intelligence within the Sandinista Air Force is good. We learned that the tail rotor failed, causing the helicopter to fall and explode. Our informants say this was the conclusion of Soviet technicians who investigated the crash. And it was learned that the helicopter had previous accidents and problems. The truth will be known some day. All we can do is deny the chopper was shot down by a Contra missile. Otherwise, if we go into more detail disproving the Sandinista lie, then we jeopardize our informants." Harold shrugged and fell quiet.

"Yeah, I see your point," Marc said.

Pete now added, "As a result of the forced evacuation, the Sandinistas cut their own throat. It was not only an inhuman thing, it was stupid. Now there are two militant Miskito organizations dedicated to fighting the Sandinistas. Before, they were just minding their own business, fishing the Rio Coco and doing a little farming."

"Not that I'm worried, Pete, but aren't we pretty much in the heart of Sandinista controlled country?" Marc asked.

"Well, like I said before, we enjoy a lot of support in this area. Normally we wouldn't set up camp overnight in an area where the lake blocks one direction of escape. First, I've been told to stay here till Comandante Flor arrives to take you in tow.

Second, here in the Sandinista Fifth Army Region, many of the regular army units have been withdrawn to Managua and Leon. They're the ones to provide extra security for Fidel Castro's visit which starts tomorrow. The Sandinista Junta is deathly afraid that the Contras, the CIA, or even the United States will provoke an attack. The goal might be to kill Castro or to embarrass the Sandinistas. The job here in Chontales and Boaco Departments has been left to a couple of what they call Batallón de Lucha Irregular or Irregular Warfare Battalions. We call them BLI's. These are supposed to be light mobile counter-insurgency units. Generally the battalions are made up of draftees who are poorly trained and then sent to the field. Even so, some have fought well. The regular Sandinista Army prefers to sit and guard Managua anyway. They're paranoid about a U.S. invasion. The BLI's are thrown against the Contra battalions, which are more experienced. Let me give you an example. The BLI Santa Lopez was operating in the Department of Nueva Segovia near the Honduran border. After a three month engagement, one of the BLI companies was down to a strength of 35 from 110 as a result of deaths, wounds, and desertions. You will never read this in the newspapers, of course."

"Who is this Comandante Flor that is taking me under his wing?" Marc asked.

"Vamos a ver, we will see," was Pete's non-committal answer.

"How long you going to do this?" Marc asked.

"Dunno. Till I get killed, wounded, forced out, or just get too tired. You've got to love these people. They've endured a lot of hardship. The campesino you meet on the farm or in the little villages is usually friendly and courteous despite these hardships. Your heart goes out to them, and you do what you can to help."

Marc had judged Pete to be a mercenary, a soldier of fortune, caught up in a dangerous adventure. Now he saw that for Pete it was much more.

"I admire your courage and conviction, Pete," Marc said.

Pete shrugged, did not reply, but cocked his head, listening. There were greetings exchanged in the distance, as someone passed the outlying perimeter guards.

Pete stood up, and Marc followed suit, brushing the forest floor debris from his clothes. Into the clearing walked the commando Pete had sent to meet Comandante Flor. Behind him was Comandante Flor.

"Hola Adriana," Pete said, kissing the blonde haired, blue eyed young woman on the cheek. She was in washed jeans and a T-shirt, about five foot six, her blond hair pulled back in a pony tail. She had a beautiful smile. Marc was speechless. Comandante Flor wore a shoulder holster with a 9 mm pistol under a loose vest.

"Marc, this is your surprise. This is Comandante Flor. I call her by her given name, Adriana." Pete then laughed at the expression on Marc's face. Even out in the jungle Marc managed to blush, and stammered his own introduction.

"I'm Marc DiAngelo. As you can see, I was a bit surprised to find that Comandante Flor is a woman."

"Don't you worry, Señor Marc, I will have you back to Costa Rica without even a scratch." Adriana spoke in a serious voice in contrast to her barely suppressed smile.

"Marc, I don't know Adriana very well. We've met a couple of times. But she is one of our best intelligence operatives. I have complete confidence in her," Pete said.

Marc hurried to respond. "Then so do I. I apologize, Adriana, if I seemed to feel otherwise. I was just surprised, that's all."

"No preocupe, do not worry, Marc," Adriana replied. "Tomorrow we will go to the Juigalpa-Puerto Diaz road. We will be picked up at a finca that is five kilometers north of Puerto Diaz. A car will take us to the dock at Puerto Diaz. That is enough for you to know now."

Marc understood he was only being told enough to keep him comfortable as a precaution in case of capture. He couldn't tell what he didn't know. Once again, he was grateful to Pete and company.

"Adriana, that's your hammock over there. I'm going to sleep," Pete said. It had been dark for over two hours.

"Tomorrow will be a long day, Marc. We should get some sleep," Adriana said, as she easily slipped into the hammock. Marc climbed more gingerly into his hammock, and stretched the best he could. Within minutes he was in a deep exhausted slumber.

CHAPTER 8—CROSSING COLCIBOLCA

Pete put his hand on Marc's shoulder and shook him gently. Marc rose up in the hammock, startled. Searing pain from deeply bruised ribs caused him to open his mouth, but pain as quick and sure as a sharp knife across his ribs left him unable to breathe for a moment, or even utter a groan.

"You okay Marc? We need to get Adriana and you on your way. You've got a rendezvous with your transportation to Puerto Diaz in two hours. I hope you're up to a fast hike."

"I'm okay, Pete." Marc swung his legs over the edge of the hammock. "Let me see if my legs will work. They feel like two fence posts."

"You've got a heck of a bruise on the right side of your face, Marc, and a real shiner on the right eye. Sorry we don't have a steak to put on it. Just MRE's this morning. Don't want smoke from a fire. Would you like a chili dinner or macaroni and cheese for breakfast?"

"Can't say I've had either for breakfast. Throw me the chili. I like to live dangerously."

"Well, you're doing that, amigo." Pete threw the MRE to Marc. Marc opened the package and found a chili dinner bar, apple sauce pop-top can, package of two Oreo cookies, and a package of two sticks of chewing gum.

Pete pointed off to his right. "Hombres bathroom that way." He pointed to the left. "Mujeres is over there" As if on cue, Adriana emerged from the trees.

"Buenos Dias, Marc. We should leave in 30 minutes. We will walk to a hacienda which is a kilometer and a half from here. So you must be prepared for more walking."

"Buenos Dias, Adriana, I'll be ready," Marc replied. He could see that Adrianna had the vigor of youth that permitted her to spend the night in a hammock in a tropical forest, and still manage to look fresh and alert. He felt much less so. He knew that stress had taken its toll on his energy level as much as the physical abuse his body had suffered.

"Breakfast, Adriana?" Marc asked.

"I had two tamales an hour ago, Marc," she said, adjusting the shoulder holster partially hidden by the embroidered khaki vest. "My tastes are not for the MRE, so I brought my own breakfast."

Marc finished his MRE quickly. It was apparent Pete and Adriana wanted to get the show on the road as soon as possible.

"Marc, six of my men will escort you and Comandante Flor to the hacienda. The Comandante knows the drill, how we deploy our patrols for ambush protection. Just follow her lead and you'll be okay. Good luck. Maybe we'll meet down the line."

"I hope so. I owe you guys. I will take Fernando's backpack with the KL-43, but I'm leaving you his passport, that you will probably want to destroy, and about $10,000 in U.S. dollars and Nicaraguan córdobas he was carrying. Anything else I can do, let me know," Marc said.

"Just keep dropping those supplies," Pete answered.

With that, Adriana, Marc, and the six Contras left the camp. Two of the Contras trotted ahead out of sight, two walked just ahead of Adriana and Marc. Two kept their distance far behind to prevent the encircling type of ambush favored by both the Sandinistas and Contras. They were not following an established trail that Marc could see. It seemed more of a trail blazing trek following a compass heading. They made their way around trees and bushes, stepped and climbed over fallen logs on a path that seemed to be southward rather than directly toward the lake. Adriana managed the terrain with grace, keeping a steady pace, while Marc stumbled now and then. He was quite aware that he had neither the athletic skill nor endurance to match Adriana and her fellow Contras.

The group filed silently through the woods. The pace was equivalent to the U.S. Army's "double time". Marc focused on the terrain in front of him. Adriana and the other two Contras in front of him constantly scanned ahead and to the sides.

Within 30 minutes they came to the edge of an open field. The two point men were seated on the ground, with tree trunks as back rests. Their AK-47s were at arm's reach crosswise on their legs. A large rambling ranch house was on the other side of the field. A porch surrounded all sides of the white adobe house. Marc could see a wash stand, or "pila" as it was called in Costa Rica, to the rear of the house. A frail old woman was hanging clothes on the barbed wire fence that enclosed the house. Marc had always marveled that barbed wire fence, also commonly used in rural Costa Rica as a handy clothes line, did not rip the clothes to shreds. This was particularly remarkable given the ferocious Guanacaste winds that blow in the early months of the year.

The old red tile roof of the house was mottled heavily with patches of green moss, black mold, and clumps of the cactus plant pitahaya. The purple blossoms of the cacti added bold contrasting color to the roof. The old woman stopped hanging the clothes and looked directly at the Contra group partially hidden in the trees. She turned; spoke to someone out of sight in the house. Then she returned to her task of reaching down into a plastic basket and hanging items of clothing on the barbed wire.

"We have the signal that the house is safe," Adriana said.

"What signal?" Marc asked.

"The clothes on the alambre de pua. I do not know the English words."

"Oh – the barbed wire," Marc said.

Adriana nodded that she understood. Then in rapid fire Spanish she gave instructions to her six Contra compatriots. Two went to the left along the tree line, two to the right. Adriana was not taking chances, Marc observed. Even though there had been the okay signal, she had directed her men into covering lines of fire positions.

"Now, Marc, vamanos," Adriana said, leaving the protection of the trees for the house. She had slipped her 9 mm pistol from the shoulder holster so deftly that Marc did not realize it until he saw it in her right hand. He thought for a moment he should pull out his .38 from his knapsack. Such a move now seemed awkward and late. It was luck that the Sandinistas had put both pistols in the knapsack which he recovered after the firefight. He could easily reach for the .25 caliber Browning automatic stuck under his belt at the small of his back if need be. But he knew that would be of little use if they were attacked from the trees at the far end of the field. Besides, he understood that his safety was in the hands of true professional soldiers.

Adriana said nothing. The two Contras that had remained with them stayed at the edge of the field, providing a third zone of covering fire. Meanwhile, the old lady continued hanging clothes as if it were just another day of household chores. A door on the back porch was open. The covered porch left it in deep shadows. As they got closer, Marc could see the figure of a large man filling the doorway.

"Hola, Doña María," Adriana said as she neared the fence.

"Hola, mi amor," Doña María answered, as if it was common for armed visitors to emerge from the woods and walk to her house. Adriana opened a simple gate of barbed wire strands nailed to a pole that was connected to a fence post with wire loops. Marc nodded to Doña María, who gave him a perfunctory glance but no acknowledgement. She bent back down to her laundry basket.

"Don Ricardo," Adriana addressed the heavy set gentleman in a white straw hat favored by the cattlemen of the provinces east of the lake. They exchanged kisses on the cheek, and Don Ricardo waved them both into the house. It was dark and cool inside, a testament to the thick adobe walls, tile roof, and small windows found in the old country homes. They sat in the wicker chairs Don Ricardo directed them to. He brought each a glass of water. Although the morning had been cool, the fast pace of the walk had left Marc parched. He gulped down the glass and gladly accepted a refill.

"Comandante, todo listo," Don Ricardo said. This Marc understood. Everything was ready. Don Ricardo continued and Marc could only understand bits and pieces of the conversation.

"Marc, it is all arranged. In five or ten minutes a pickup truck should arrive. If there are no Sandinista patrols or police between here and Puerto Diaz - - our driver will know that when he gets here - - we will go directly to the muelle or dock at Puerto Diaz."

Adriana and Don Ricardo chatted on for several minutes. Doña María entered the room quietly with "quesillos", warmed tortillas wrapped around a raw mozzarella/string cheese with onion and sour cream. The MRE had not satisfied Marc's early morning hunger. He gratefully accepted a second quesillo offered by Doña Maria. Adriana said something to Don Ricardo, and they both laughed. Marc, puzzled, looked at Adriana.

"You have a grande appetite, Marc."

"These quesillos, as you call them, are delicious. I'm probably making a pig of myself. Tell Doña Maria that this is the first time I have eaten quesillos, and I like them very much."

Adriana spoke to Doña Maria, who had pulled a straight-backed chair from the kitchen table into the living room area.

Doña Maria smiled, and asked, "Más, Don Marc?"

"No, gracias," Marc replied, and then looked at Adriana.

"That is the first time I have ever been called Don Marc."

"Marc, it is a sign of respect, and also of age," Adriana said, with a smile.

Marc was about to reply when the sound of a vehicle pulling up to the front of the house interrupted him.

"Eduardo is here. We shall leave, Marc," Both Adriana and Marc picked up their knapsacks and walked to the door.

"Buen viaje, Comandante Flor y Don Marc," said Don Ricardo, returning to a more formal tone. Adriana and he kissed cheeks, embraced briefly, and after a handshake with Marc he opened the door to the bright sunlight.

"Hola, tío," Adriana greeted Eduardo with the affectionate term "uncle" as she slid in on the bench seat of the old pickup.

"Mi Comandante, largo tiempo no verle," Eduardo replied, with an expressive frown that added emphasis to his disappointment that he had not seen Adriana for some time.

"Eso es verdad," Adriana replied, nodding her head sympathetically that it was too true. As Eduardo drove the pickup away from the farmhouse, an old Ford farm truck with two men in the cab pulled out of the trees on the far side of the house and followed at a distance. Adriana turned around for a better view, then looked back at Eduardo. "Nuestras guardas," he said, glancing at Adriana, and then directed his attention ahead. Adriana surmised Peter and Don Ricardo had arranged a discrete security escort to accompany them to Puerto Diaz.

The way to the Puerto Diaz dock was a dusty gravel road, pothole upon pothole. The old Nissan pickup clattered and rattled. There were no shocks, and the ball joints were so loose Marc expected the pickup's front end to hit the gravel at any moment. There were only a few poor farmhouses along the road, set well back with open doors, glassless windows, and the ubiquitous outhouse in back. Here there seemed little to suggest a war was in progress. They came into the small village of Puerto Diaz too fast for Marc's comfort, and approached the dock. With a last minute screech of brakes that could only be rivets of worn brake linings grinding against the brake drums, the pickup lurched to a stop.

Eduardo, his smile heightened by the edges of silver around each tooth, said triumphantly, "Estamos aqui!"

"Gracias a Dios, we are here" Adriana replied, glancing at Marc. She then took Eduardo aside. Marc saw her pass him some cordobas and peck him on the cheek.

"Adios, mi amor," he said.

"Hasta luego, Eduardo."

Adriana led Marc to the rickety dock, a double line of slender poles that supported a narrow walkway two boards wide. At the end of the dock two dark skinned men sat in a sturdy fiberglass panga. It had a prominent bow and more than two feet of freeboard for the large lake waves. A "T" top and control console were at the boat's midpoint. It must be 20 feet long, Marc thought, as he looked at the whitecaps on the lake whipped up by strong northeasterly trade winds. A 75 horsepower Johnson was mounted on the transom.

"Marc, these men can be trusted, but I'm not going to introduce you. The less everyone knows the better. We will cross the lake to Laguna La Calera, a small fishing village south of Granada."

"Okay, just show me my life jacket," Marc said. He was looking out at the wind-whipped white caps.

"We are going to have to do without, I am sure," Adriana said. "But you needn't worry. These two have fished the lake since they were boys. This is not the first time they have helped us."

Marc and Adriana sat in the seat directly in front of the control console. The 75 horsepower Johnson cranked over several times and finally fired in a cloud of blue smoke, much to Marc's relief. The panga pulled away from the dock as the late afternoon sun began its quick dive for the horizon.

"I think these guys have two throttle positions, idle and full power," Marc said, as the panga quickly accelerated and was skimming across the waves with the wind at their back.

Adriana looked at her watch.

"Marc, it will be almost dark when we get to Laguna La Calera."

As dusk approached, a large cluster of lights became visible to their right in the distance.

"Is that Granada over there?" Marc asked, nodding in that direction.

"Yes. Just to the south of Granada is Volcan Mombacho, with the ragged top. Also to the south of Granada are the isletas. There are 350 of them. Have you seen the islands from the air?"

"No. All the flying I've done over Nicaragua so far has been to the east side of the lake, and low."

"These islands are the reason Volcán Mombacho has no top. About 20,000 years ago it erupted, and the top blew off creating the many islands."

"You sure seem to know a lot about this part of Nicaragua."

"Our country is muy pequeño, very small, not like the Estados Unidos. It is easy to know."

What appeared to Marc to be solid lake shore from a distance turned out to be a mass of small islands. They clustered east, south and west of the southward protruding Peninsula de Asese. The Peninsula itself was but a few kilometers south of the shore city of Granada. Adriana and the boatmen spoke briefly. She turned to Marc.

"They say we will go between the south end of Peninsula Asese and some islands, then direct to Laguna La Calera. It is a well protected harbor. There are a few small homes of fishermen there, and no real road access. We will be safe there, and stay the night. Then we will find out tomorrow if it is safe to go to Puerto Santa Isabel, which is closer to Granada."

It was almost dark, and the panga had slowed to trolling speed. One of the boatmen knelt on the prow looking for rocks ahead. "Isleta Buena Vista," he called out, pointing to the left.

Marc looked in that direction to see an island of two acre size, with tall trees and surrounded by large rocks. The panga cleared the island and southern tip of the Peninsula. Then they headed due west towards Laguna La Calera. The boat glanced off a rock barely protruding from the water. Harsh words were exchanged between the helmsman and lookout. They kept moving forward slowly, with no apparent prop damage.

Once through the maze of the rocky isletas, the panga continued towards Laguna La Calera. As landfall neared, the panga made a hard left turn, entering into the north-facing entrance of Laguna La Calera. Marc saw that it was a small horseshoe-shaped bay. A few lights shone on shore at the southwest end of the Laguna. The panga slowed even more, and finally a flashlight illuminated ahead, then turned on and off several times, then remained on.

"Okay, parece bien," Adriana said. The boatmen nodded, and Marc understood that the universal "O.K. meant they were expected and all was well. The panga pulled up to a rickety wooden dock, not much more substantial than the one at Puerto Diaz. It was tied fore and aft, and the motor shut off. Adriana had already jumped lightly to the wooden planks, and walked to the end of the dock. An older man in his sixties waited there. Adriana and the old man were talking when Marc walked up. Adriana turned to Marc.

"Marc, this is Don Alfonso." Marc shook hands with the old gentleman, and they exchanged "Mucho gusto" greetings to each other.

"We are going with Don Alfonso to his house. We will stay there tonight, and leave tomorrow after we know that Puerto San Isabel is safe. Doña Luce, Don Alfonso's wife, will prepare some food. Our friends here will eat with us, and then sleep on the boat. They will return to Puerto Diaz at first light."

Don Alfonso and Doña Luce's home was a humble two room wooden cabin with a rusted zinc sheet roof. There were no glass windows, only wooden shutters. The kitchen was an outside roofed shelter to the rear of the house. The kitchen consisted of a rough table, a rounded wood-fired oven made of cement, and a fireplace made out of cement block and a grate of rebar lengths. Chickens roamed freely, and two pigs grunted and snorted a welcome.

Doña Luce had already started grilling chicken pieces over the outdoor wood-burning grill. Don Alfonso proudly showed the visitors the home. He then took simple wooden chairs from the house to the outside kitchen area, and invited everyone to sit.

"Marc, you can have a coke, water, or pinol. Don Alfonso apologized because the drinks aren't cold. The power in this village comes from a generator, which only runs a few hours in the day. Refrigeration is very limited."

"I would love to have a coke, even a warm one. Muchas gracias, Don Alfonso."

Marc and the two boatmen drank their warm cokes. All four visitors dined on charcoal broiled chicken, fried platano, and rice. The two boatmen finished, thanked their hosts, and left.

"Marc, you and I will sleep in the front room on the floor. They have foam pads and sheets. They wanted us to use their bedroom, which has two single beds. I told them no."

"Adriana, I could sleep on bare concrete tonight and not know the difference."

Adriana put the two four inch thick foam pads on the floor next to each other.

"There are two sheets we will have to share. Since you are so tired I won't have to worry," she said with a laugh.

With their hosts retired to the bedroom, Adriana stripped down to bra and panties without hesitation or any seeming self-consciousness. Marc thought "what the heck," stripped to his shorts, and slipped in between the sheets.

"Very comfy, he said."

"What did you say?" Adriana asked, rolling to face him, her hand landing on his arm.

"Very comfortable," Marc replied, very aware of her closeness. Breathing became harder.

"Claro que sí, muy confortable," she answered rolling her eyes.

Marc smiled. Adriana leaned over, kissed him on the cheek, and said "Buenas noches." She rolled back to her own foam bed, and closed her eyes.

"Buenas noches," Marc replied, thinking of his sleep mate for only a moment before falling into a deep sleep.

CHAPTER 9—GRANADA

"Buenos días, Marc."

Marc opened his eyes. Adriana had already dressed, and Marc could smell the wood burning in the kitchen fireplace outside.

"Buenos días."

"Doña Luce is boiling some coffee. That will help wake you up."

"That is just what I need."

Breakfast was more gallo pinto, as Marc had expected. Once again the monotony was relieved by a welcome serving of fried eggs and hot tortillas. Both Marc and Adriana ate generous helpings, much to Doña Luce's pleasure.

After breakfast, Adriana suggested they sit on the front steps of the cabin, facing the laguna. Doña Luce walked up quietly behind them as they talked.

"Comandante, pinol?" she asked, as she offered two rounded cups to Adriana, who took them and then handed one to Marc.

"Gracias, Doña Luce," Adriana said.

"What is it," Marc asked, looking at the drink he had just been handed.

"It is pinol, Marc, a traditional drink made from corn. Try it."

Marc sipped from the rounded bowl, nodded his approval, and sipped again.

"The corn is toasted in an iron kettle until it pops open and then it is ground in stone metates or simple grinders called mixtamaleros. Then it is soaked in water for several days. Doña Luce has added milk and sugar. That is the way I like it."

"The cup is made from a gourd, I see."

"The cup is made from the fruit of the jicaro tree. The fruits look like balls hanging from the branches. The campesinos make bowls, glasses, and cups from the dried balls. In Matagalpa, and all over Nicaragua, the meat inside the ball is fed to dairy cattle to increase their milk."

"Nothing goes to waste in this country," Marc said.

"We are a poor country, Marc. This is the way it must be."

As they sat on the steps, the morning trade wind blew over them from across the lake. The lake winds were calmest in the morning. Marc could see the dock below. A gentle slope led to the lake shore, beyond the brown sand beach with patches of small, smooth water-worn rocks. The two peaks of Concepción and Madera Volcanoes on Ometepe Island rose majestically out of the lake to their right. Zapatera Island, the spiritual island of the ancient Chorotegas, lay between them and Ometepe Island. Adriana was dressed in jeans and sleeveless knit top. Marc was also in jeans and golf shirt. To all appearances they were two friends or lovers enjoying a casual chat as they sat on the cabin's steps.

"Don Alfonso left earlier this morning to go to Puerto San Isabel. We should know shortly if it is safe to proceed," Adriana said.

"What happens when we get to Puerto San Isabel?"

"There will be a car waiting for us. All of this was arranged before we left Puerto Diaz."

"I'm amazed at how organized your group is."

"We have to be. It is very dangerous for us. The Dirección General de Seguridad, which is the Sandinista Security Office, has many informers, many spies. The Section F3 is in charge of anti-counterrevolutionary investigations. They are very ruthless to anyone even suspected of collaborating with the Contras. When one of us is caught, others who work with the unfortunate prisoner have 24 hours to disappear. That is the maximum time that any of us can hold out during an interrogation. Of course, it is much more than an interrogation. This is such a beautiful morning. Let us talk about more pleasant subjects. Can you see the smoke coming out of Volcán Concepción?"

"The one to the left?"

"Yes. Concepción is active. Its last eruption was 100 years ago. Madera is dormant. The Nahuatl Indians who first settled Ometepe considered the island sacred ground. Many of the people who live there still do. That must be true, because the Sandinistas seem to avoid it. I was told that the revolution has not changed the island. I hope to visit it someday."

"Well, maybe we can visit it together," Marc said.

"My, such a proposal, after only one night together," Adriana replied. Her face was serious for just a moment before she laughed. It seemed to Marc that Adriana was trying to make light of his remark.

"I think your Italian blood is showing," Adriana continued. "I think I should call you Marco. That is more Italian," she said. This time she allowed a bit of a playful teasing in her voice.

"Well, that leads to a question that I wanted to ask you. You are Nicaraguan, but you have light brown hair, blue eyes, and fair skin. You don't look like the typical Nicaraguan."

"In the area where I was born, Matagalpa, there are many people of German ancestry. Many Germans immigrated to the Department of Matagalpa in the 1800's and to other coffee growing areas. My grandfather was just a boy when he immigrated in the 1890's with his parents. Grandfather worked on a coffee plantation, and eventually bought his own finca. When he returned to Germany for a visit, he met my grandmother. They married, and returned to Matagalpa. My father grew up working on the family coffee farm. Like many others of German descent he went to the Jesuit school in Granada. He met my mother in Granada. Her family was from Jinotega, north of Matagalpa. She is half German. So there you are."

"How did you come to be with the Contras," Marc asked.

"This is a long story, but it seems we have the time. After high school, I went to the University of Centroamerica in Managua to study for entry to medical school. You would call it pre-med. After two years I was accepted at a German medical school in Hamburg. I spent two years there. Here is the story. A boy I had known when I was in colegio -- high school -- in Granada was also a medical student there. We became very good friends and became engaged. Enrique was from Ocotal in the Department of Nueva Segovia. That is near the Honduran border. In our second year of medical school, the Sandinistas confiscated Enrique's father's coffee finca. They put it in a cooperative. Enrique's father protested, and he was put in jail as a counter-revolutionary collaborator. Enrique immediately left school and returned to Nicaragua. The family protested his father's imprisonment. As punishment, the Sandinistas sent a gang of young men from the Juventud Sandinista movement. This gang burned down the family home and beat the family members. Enrique was killed trying to protect the home and his mother. After this happened I felt it was impossible to keep studying. So I returned to Nicaragua. I was soon in contact with others who were against the Sandinistas. I joined the counter-revolutionary movement or Contras as we are called."

"I'm sorry about Enrique. That is pretty tough."

"That is just my story. There are many others who have been driven to the Contra cause," Adriana said. I am sure that one day my father's coffee farm will be confiscated. Some of our workers whose families have worked there for more than a generation will go to the cooperatives. Some will go willingly, and some out of necessity. But some of our workers will go to the Contras. In many cases it is brother against brother, sister against sister."

"It's a damn shame," Marc said in a low voice, shaking his head.

Adriana looked up. "Marc, I think Don Alfonso's panga is entering the mouth of the laguna. Let us go down to the dock to meet him."

The old panga pulled alongside the wood pier. Don Alfonso and another man secured each end to the dock. Marc leaned over and gave a helping hand to Don Alfonso as he climbed up on the pier. Adriana and the old man conversed much too rapidly for Marc to comprehend.

Adriana relayed his information. "Marc, we will leave in a few minutes. Everything is arranged at Puerto San Isabel, and it is only about 30 minutes there."

Marc grabbed both his and Adriana's backpacks, bid adios to Doña Luce with a soft kiss on her cheek, and boarded the panga. He could sense that Adriana was no longer in the mood for small talk. The tenseness had returned. The panga motored past the entrance to the horseshoe-shaped laguna. Then they headed north, skirting the lakeshore on the left. The panga was heading parallel to the waves, now being whipped up by the easterly wind which had grown stiff. It wallowed as it passed over the tops of the waves into the troughs.

"We're only a kilometer from Puerto San Isabel, Marc," Adriana said. Marc felt for the reassuring lump of the .38 S&W in his backpack. He nodded.

Don Alfonso slowed the panga to a crawl as they neared Puerto San Isabel. Adriana was now even more tense, more on guard, as they drew closer to the concrete dock in the distance. She spoke to Don Alfonso, again much too fast for Marc's basic Spanish. Don Alfonso said nothing but simply nodded in agreement.

"I say to him if not all appears right, not to go to the dock." Marc also nodded his understanding, but said nothing. The tension was contagious.

The panga approached the small concrete dock which had old tires attached to its side for protection. There were two small fishing boats tied up. They bumped against the tires as each wave struck. No one was at the dock. Several houses were scattered on the hillside facing the dock. Marc could see a few women and children about. Pigs, chickens and bony horses roamed freely. The panga pulled alongside the dock. Adriana instructed Don Alfonso not to tie up the boat up and to keep the motor running. Holding his end of the boat to the dock with one hand, Marc reached into his backpack, slid the .38 out, and stuck it in his belt. Adriana climbed up on the dock and walked down to the end where a small car was parked. The car's original paint had long ago oxidized to a rusty red. A dirty rag was substituted for a gas cap. Adriana leaned in to talk briefly to the driver. She then ran back along the dock to the boat.

"Come, Marc. Our taxi waits." She blew a kiss to Don Alfonso and then made a sign of a silent hug meant just for him. Marc hoisted himself up on the dock. Don Alfonso and his panga sped away south to safety.

Marc sat with Adriana in the back of the old Datsun sedan. A yellow unlit taxi light perched on the driver's side of the roof. The driver, a portly middle-aged man, gave Marc a careful once over. No words were exchanged.

Adriana faced Marc. "If we are stopped by a Sandinista checkpoint, you are a Canadian writer who is writing about wonderful Sandinista reforms."

"That should take some imagination," Marc replied.

"Creo que sí, I think so," Adriana said, smiling briefly. "And, you are staying at the Alhambra Hotel in Granada, and you left your passport there for safekeeping. That is your story. But our driver knows the streets to take to avoid checkpoints and patrols."

"You said we would be staying at a safe house in Granada. Isn't that more dangerous than out in the country?"

"The problem with the campo is we don't know who our friends or enemies are. It is easier to know in the city. Granada is a very conservative town, mostly anti-Sandinista. We will meet Father Pablo at the Palacio Episcopal, on the Parque Central. It is the residence of the Archbishop of Granada. There are many rooms for the priests also."

The taxi drove north along a rough winding gravel road that followed the Lake Nicaragua shore line.

"We will pass very close to the entrance to Puerto Asese," Adriana said. "That is the main dock area for small boats. The Sandinista Army has a small guard post there. Before we get close, we will pass a small hotel on the lake shore. Armando will turn on his taxi light so it will appear that we are traveling from the hotel to the city."

The old Datsun veered off on a left fork in the road just after the entrance to Puerto Asese. Adriana heaved an audible sigh of relief, and Armando visibly relaxed. Their road continued away from the lake, heading straight northwest. The taxi entered the southern outskirts of Granada.

Armando made a right 45 degree turn onto a wide paved road. Much too fast, Marc thought.

"We are turning onto Calle Atravesada, the principal north-south road through Granada," Adriana said. She put her hand over Marc's, and squeezed it. Marc looked at her, smiled, and received a smile in return. He felt a flush of emotion. Was it just gratitude, he wondered?

"Armando! Directo! Directo!," Adriana shouted.

A block ahead, a Sandinista Russian-made Army truck was parked on the left. Soldiers were checking two cars they had stopped. In reaction, Armando made a violent right turn onto Calle Cuíscomo, overshooting and rocking the back end.

"Whew!" Marc exclaimed. Armando slammed on the brakes. One hundred feet ahead a Sandinista soldier was standing in the middle of the street. He motioned the car to stop. Two other soldiers, rifles slung over their shoulders, were standing on the sidewalk to share a patch of shade.

Adriana moved against Marc, put her arms around his neck, and kissed him full on the mouth. It was a particularly lingering kiss that caught Marc by surprise. Quickly sensing Adriana's intent, Marc lightly kissed her on the forehead, cheeks, and mouth.

The Sandinista soldier waved them on with a smirk and casually ambled back to his comrades in the shade.

Armando accelerated slowly. All three were quiet for a moment. Marc, grasping for something to say, blurted out "One more road block and we're going to have to get married."

Adriana did not answer for a moment. "Perhaps two," she said, but she was not smiling. It had been a close call.

The taxi continued east toward the Malecón, along the lakeside road, and after three blocks turned north again on Calle El Martirio. They continued north passing through the poorer neighborhoods of small cinder block homes with zinc sheet roofs. In a few blocks they entered the historic district. Rows of stately red tile-roofed colonial homes shared common walls. Each home had several gated doors fronting the street.

When they reached Calle Libertad, Armando turned the car west toward the Palacio Episcopal and the Parque Central. Armando honked as he stopped at the garage door of the Palacio. Two black steel doors opened. Armando pulled in, and the doors were closed behind them.

"Buenas tardes," a uniformed guard said as Adriana and Marc got out of the car.

"Buenas tardes," Adriana responded. "Padre Pablo, por favor."

"Un momento, Señorita."

The parking area was at the corner of a large garden enclosed by the twenty foot high walls of the Palacio. At the far end of the garden a two story building in colonial style dominated the courtyard. Its upper porch overlooked the garden, central fountain, and palm trees. The guard had disappeared inside. Marc and Adriana strolled over to the fountain. The priest walking toward them was over six feet tall, trim, and had a broad friendly face that anyone would call handsome. He had a full head of black hair and a commanding presence. He was dressed in black slacks and a black short sleeved shirt with cleric's collar. "This guy should be in Hollywood," Marc thought ruefully.

"I have been expecting you," Father Pablo said to Adriana. "You are Adriana Kupper. I know your family. And you are?" he questioned, looking at Marc. Father Pablo spoke near perfect English with only a trace of an accent. Marc thought he must have lived for some time in the States.

"I am Marc DiAngelo, Father. I hope I'm not a surprise."

"No, not at all. I knew Adriana would be arriving with someone important supporting the cause. Our communications are intentionally vague for our common protection. For now, we will go upstairs in the Palacio. The guard will bring along your things from the taxi."

"I hope that we won't have to be in Granada more than a few days. We will have to confirm further arrangements that have been made for Señor Marc's return to the south. For now, where shall we stay?" Adriana asked.

'My plan is to have the two of you stay here in the northern upstairs wing of the Palacio Episcopal. There is an area of several rooms there that are used by priests who visit from the diocese. We have none scheduled to come to Granada for a week. As I am the Administrative Assistant to the Archbishop, I can take care of these things. The cover story, if you like, is that the two of you are from a Catholic lay organization. Señor DiAngelo is from the States, and you Adriana, are the coordinator for this diocese. I will prepare some letters to substantiate this story. We will have to secure a fake passport for Marc with an entry stamp in Managua. That will take some time. Marc, the name DiAngelo would be Italian I think. So you must be Catholic as well?

"That's correct, Father, though I have not been very good at church attendance lately."

"Then you will be happy to know that the Cathedral is just to the south of us. Since it would not be wise for you to attend services, your absence from mass is to be prolonged."

Father Pablo showed them the way upstairs and to their rooms. It appeared there was no one else staying in the north wing. Marc was anxious to orient himself, but he knew better than to walk out on the porch. That would have to wait till dark.

"The two of you have had a very difficult travel day," Father Pablo said. "I am going to leave you now so that you can freshen up, as they say, and get some rest. You are quite safe here. One of our kitchen staff will bring you dinner. I will be back to see you an hour or so after dinner."

The rooms were on the east side of the north wing facing the garden below. Beyond, lay a succession of tile roofs and the cupolas of Convento San Francisco and Iglesia Guadalupe. Marc eyed the windswept waters of Lake Nicaragua a kilometer further.

"Well, Adriana, pick your room. The two rooms share a bathroom. Reminds me of my old Air Force days. That was a common arrangement in Bachelor Officers' Quarters and Visiting Officers' Quarters," Marc said.

"Oh, I don't mind sharing, as long as I get the first shower."

"Adriana, you've earned it. I'm just going to enjoy this room for a few moments. I thought it would be more Spartan, like a monk's cloister, with a straw pallet on the floor. But this is furnished very nicely. Tile floors, comfortable bed, desk, chairs, closet, and a great view toward the lake."

Later, Adriana rapped on the bathroom door leading to Marc's room, and then opened it.

"I left you some hot water."

Marc stared at her. A large white towel was wrapped around her slender body. Her wet hair framed a freshly scrubbed face. She looked more like 18 than 28.

"You are very fetching, I must say," Marc finally managed to say.

"Fetching? I do not know what that means. Is it good or bad?"

"It's an old fashioned word, but it is very good. I guess it means attractive in a desirable way," Marc replied.

"Muchas gracias, mi amor," Adriana said, fluttering her eyelashes, and disappeared back to her room through the bathroom with a laugh.

Later, as they sat on the porch overlooking the central park, a kitchen helper brought a tray with two plates of food and a pitcher of dark red tea and set it on the small porch table. To the west, the sun was setting and the evening lake breeze had picked up slightly. The city's pigeons fluttered among the roof tops looking for their evening's roost.

"Our dinner looks and smells wonderful," Marc said, as the warm aroma enveloped them.

"Yes, better than you have been eating for the past few days. This is a typical meal. Meat, beans, rice, fried platano, and cabbage salad."

"The tea is good, but very different," Marc said.

"It is Rosa de Jamaica tea, made from a dried flower. You know the hibiscus? The tea is very good for digestion, the kidneys. It even lowers cholesterol," Adriana replied.

They both ate with relish, enjoying the food and each other's company in silence. "Like I said, the tea was good, but a cold beer would be better. But, I'm not complaining."

At that moment Father Pablo walked onto the porch from the central corridor.

"Would you like a beer?" he asked Marc.

"No, No, Father. I was just kidding Adriana. I appreciate the hospitality and I know it's a dangerous for you to have us here. Tomorrow I would like to make a telephone call to the United States Embassy in Managua if that is possible. I have a telephone encryption device so my conversation cannot be understood by anyone who doesn't have a similar machine."

"I will arrange a phone for you in the morning. Are you two comfortable?"

Father Pablo asked.

"Yes, Father," they both chimed together, and then both laughed at the childish response.

"Leave your dishes on the table. The girl from the kitchen will come get them. Let us sit in the rocking chairs, Granada style, and enjoy the view from the porch," Father Pablo said.

The three sat in the rocking chairs, fixtures in every Granadino's house. As dusk settled in, they rocked back and forth as if they had not a care in the world. The branches of the palm trees in the garden swayed gracefully in the evening breeze. A three quarter moon had begun its rise.

"Muy tranquilo, que linda" Adriana said."

"Claro, muy tranquilo," Father Pablo answered.

Marc agreed. It was tranquil and beautiful here. He felt his first sense of security in many days, as he rocked slowly and savored the evening quiet.

"Father, I recall that the Pope's visit to Nicaragua went very badly," Marc said.

"This is true. There has been a split between the Sandinistas and the church which is now very wide. There are several reasons for this. In the beginning, when the revolution was formed against Somoza, the church was supportive of the Sandinistas. In fact, armed priests were killed in combat. One was Gaspar García killed near Rivas in 1978. He became a symbol for other priests and Catholics in opposition to dictator Somoza. Somoza's National Guard killed Padre Francisco Luis Mejia who was an activist priest.

"Many of the Sandinistas were sons of the rich, educated in catholic colleges. The Catholic Church hierarchy was, of course, in support of the poor people who the Sandinistas claimed to represent. In those early revolutionary days, Archbisop Obando y Bravo who now opposes the Sandinistas was an auxiliary bishop in Matagalpa. I was his assistant there, and that is the reason I know Adriana's family. Archbishop Obando y Bravo was loved and honored. He rode ox carts and horses to remote parishes to serve mass. He was named archbishop in 1970. Those were the days of liberation theology."

"Liberation theology?" Marc asked.

"I should explain that, of course," Father Pablo said. "The Sandinistas use what has been called liberation theology to drive a wedge between the traditional Catholic Church and the new government. Liberation theology promises social justice as defined in Marxist doctrine with the concept of Christian salvation. It has been called the Popular Church, and diminishes the power of the formal Catholic Church in its opposition to Sandinista political action wrapped up in theological garb."

"Allow me to continue. After the Sandinistas and their sympathizers overthrew the Somoza regime in 1979, there were four catholic priests in high Sandinista Junta positions. Ferdinand Cardenal was Minister of Education. His brother

Ernesto Cardenal was Minister of Culture. Edgard Parrales was Minister of Social Welfare, and Miguel D'Escoto was Foreign Minister. In the eyes of Archbishop Obando y Bravo, they had accepted political doctrine as predominant over religious doctrine. The Archbishop sent each one a letter asking him to resign his government post because of this conflict. They refused."

He paused to let that sink in, and then continued.

"Tomás Borge, who is Minister of Interior and therefore head of State Security, began attacking the Archbishop in speeches. The Archbishop was forbidden to televise his Sunday masses. He responded by telling all priests that they could not televise their masses until he was permitted to do so. The Sandinistas shut down the Catholic radio station. Sandinista gangs interrupted masses and staged sit-ins at churches whose priests were thought to be supportive of Archbishop Obando y Bravo. Many of those in the Sandinista government did not agree with these tactics. In fact, two FSLN Junta members who were staunch Catholics, Alfonso Robelo and Violeta Chamorro, resigned in 1980 when they saw the true Marxist nature of the Sandinista movement."

Adriana nodded her head thoughtfully in agreement. "Yes, that is when many people began to lose faith in the revolution," she murmured, almost to herself.

Father Pablo continued. "But here I have not talked about the Pope's visit in March of 1983 that you mentioned, Marc. When the Pope arrived at the Managua Airport, as was typical he kneeled and kissed the ground. There was a reception at the airport. Father Ernesto Cardenal, who you remember I said as the Sandinista Minister of Culture, kneeled down to kiss the Pope's ring. Pope John Paul would not allow it, withdrawing his hand. He told Father Cardenal that he needed to correct himself with the church. Later, the Pope's sermon in Managua was interrupted by shouting, chanting and the yelling of revolutionary slogans by a gang of Sandinista ruffians. Obviously planned in advance, the Sandinista group was given the space directly in front of the podium. While the sound system speakers on the Pope's microphones were turned down, those of the Sandinista gang were turned up. Then the Junta Comandantes on the platform with the Pope began to join in the chants. This disrespect was broadcast all over the world. It has caused the Sandinistas to lose support internationally."

"Father, you should tell of the Sandinista plot against Father Bismarck Carballo, which backfired on them," Adriana said.

"Oh yes. Bismarck Carballo was an assistant to Archbishop Obando y Bravo. He also had a strong following in his own parish. He was a vocal supporter of the Archbishop. In August of 1982 he visited a female acquaintance in Managua. Suddenly several State Security agents burst into the house, beat him, removed all his clothes, and chased him out in the street where Sandinista television crews were waiting. The Sandinistas said that he had been beaten by the deceived husband of the woman he was visiting. Of course all this was shown on the Sandinista-controlled television station. Ordinary people could see that this was a Sandinista plot, perhaps because of its clumsiness and stupidity."

"I can think of another incident the Sandinistas provoked that also brought them discredit," Adriana said.

"Which are you recalling?" Father Pablo asked.

"The Sandinistas accused the Bishop of Chontales, Pablo Antonio Vega, of subversive activities. Really that meant support of the Contras. Marc, Chontales is the area where you crashed your airplane. Bishop Pablo Antonio was taken by helicopter to the northern border town of El Espino. He was forced to ride to Honduras in the cab of a truck. This humiliating treatment of the Bishop only alienated the Catholic community more. Always, if a member of the clergy failed to denounce the Contras, which Archbishop Obando Y Bravo and Bishop Antonio would not do, then that priest was called subversive and dealt with by State Security."

Father Pablo turned to Marc.

"You must remember, Marc, 80 per cent of the people in Nicaragua are Catholic. They were forced to make a choice between the Church and the Sandinista government. Most chose the church. Church attendance in the country has grown every year since 1979 when the Sandinistas took power." He stopped rocking. "But it is late, and I am afraid I may have bored you with my rambling history lesson."

"Not at all, Father. It has been very interesting, this revolution within a revolution. It makes me feel much better about my part in the support of the Contras," Marc replied.

"Thank you. And buenas noches to you both," Father Pablo said, arising from the rocking chair.

"Buenas noches," Marc and Adriana replied in unison, as Father Pablo left.

"This has been a long day, Adriana. I will never be able to thank you enough for what you have done for me. If you'll excuse the language, especially here, you are one hell of a woman. Intelligent, courageous, and good looking."

Marc put his hands on Adriana's shoulders, pulled her towards him, and kissed her tenderly on the cheek. Adriana put her arms around Marc, hugged him for a few seconds, and returned a kiss on the cheek.

"Let us go to bed, Marc." With that, Adriana led Marc to his bedroom door, kissed him lightly again, and went into her room. Tired to the bone, Marc slipped into bed. But sleep would not come immediately. He thought of the past several days. The Air Force would call them "escape and evasion," the duty of any crew member downed in conflict to return to friendly territory. He thought of Ellen. Feelings not felt for years. And now, incredulously, here he was totally absorbed by another lovely woman. More than ever, Marc needed all his wits to get back to Point West. When and if he got back, he knew it would be because of the bravery of Adriana, Ellen, Pete, Father Pablo, and many others.

The roosters started crowing even before daylight. Marc woke and then drifted back to sleep several times.

CHAPTER 10—PALACIO EPISCOPAL

"Would you like coffee, Señor?" Adriana said, as she opened Marc's door.

"Absolutely, Señorita. What time is it anyway? Those roosters woke me up even before daylight."

"It is time to get up and enjoy the morning. And you cannot escape the roosters in Granada, no matter where you are. You just have to ignore them. There is a pot of coffee out on the porch. Father Pablo sent a note with the coffee. He will be here at 9:00 a.m. There is an office between the north and south wings where you can make your telephone call."

"That's great. After coffee I need to get familiar with the operation of the KL-43. But right now I need a caffeine fix. I'll be out on the porch in a minute."

After several minutes Marc joined Adriana on the porch. She poured a cup of coffee from a carafe and handed it to him.

"Muchas gracias. It looks like it's going to be a beautiful day."

"Yes, the Granada weather is almost always pleasant. Marc, other than the roosters, did you sleep well?"

"Very well, like a log, once I stopped thinking about you." Adriana laughed.

"And did you sleep well, and did you think of me?" Marc asked with a smile.

"Yes, I slept well, and tal vez, perhaps, I thought about you. But just a poquito." Adriana replied in a teasing voice.

After their breakfast on the porch, which was brought just as they finished their coffee, Marc went to his room, opened up the KL-43 case, and retrieved the slip of paper with the daily codes from his money belt. Adriana walked into the room, and he explained how the machine worked.

"It looks like a brief case," Adriana said.

"Yes. That's what the Sandinistas thought when they caught me at the cave. But the Cuban intelligence officer with them knew better. I keep thinking I should have destroyed it. But it's the only safe way that I can talk to our contacts in the Embassy."

Father Pablo poked his head in the door.

"Are you ready, Marc? I will open the office now, if you follow me."

Marc and Adriana followed Father Pablo to the office, which was spartanly furnished. There was a desk, bare except for a lamp and telephone; three chairs; and an empty bookcase along one wall. Marc sat the KL-43 case on the desk.

"How do I dial out, Father Pablo," he asked.

"I have written the Embassy telephone number on this piece of paper. Just dial that number directly. There are no area codes in Nicaragua like you have in the United States. You should have everything you need. When you are finished, just lock the door behind you. I will visit with you two later."

Marc opened the case. The KL-43 looked like a laptop computer.

"Adriana, there is an encryption chip in this machine. First I type in the message I want to send. It shows up on this little screen as I type. Then I review the message to make sure it's correct, push the "encode" button here, and everything will be scrambled. I will call the Embassy, ask for the right person, and when he gets on the phone I will advise him it is a KL-43 transmission. He will put his telephone receiver in the modem cradle of his machine. When I put my telephone in the modem cradle of my machine, there will be a beep, and then I will push the "transmit" button. A second beep will tell me that both machines are locked in together electronically. The agent at the Embassy will receive the encoded message. Then he'll hang up. After he hangs up his telephone, his machine will decode the message, and print it on the KL-43 printer. I have a code strip that gives the code for a two week period beginning the day of the airplane crash. When Fernando was killed I found the code strip in his billfold."

"It sounds very complicated," Adriana said.

"Fortunately, just by accident, I was shown how the machine works at our base at Point West. I was killing time in the Flight Operations office, and one of the duty officers explained it to me. There they have to use a satellite phone, but the procedure is exactly the same. Without the daily code, the machine is useless. I 'm entering today's code now."

Marc pressed the code button, keyed "Z639", and hit the enter key. An amber light came on next to the code button.

"Now I have to type a message. Adriana, would you hand me the paper pad and pen in the case?"

Adriana, who had been looking over Marc's shoulder, retrieved the pad and pen, handed it to Marc. He wrote out a draft message.

"I'm a two finger typist, as you will see," he said.

Marc typed the message which appeared on the small KL-43 screen.

"I am Marc DiAngelo based at Point West. The Maule aircraft I was piloting was destroyed at Sonojal due to a ditch cut across the runway. Fernando Lopez was killed. I have been escorted to a Granada safe house by Contra agents. Please advise any help you can give me to return to Point West or any safe haven outside Nicaragua. I will call at the same time tomorrow for your response. Marc DiAngelo."

Marc dialed in the Embassy telephone number. An operator answered, "United States Embassy, whom do you wish to speak to?"

Marc hoped he had guessed right.

"The Agent-in-Charge," he replied.

"And who is calling?"

"This is an operational emergency, please put me through," he said.

There were several clicks on the line and after three rings a phone was picked up.

"Yes," a gruff male voice said.

"This is a KL-43 call, are you equipped?" Marc said.

"Yes," the voice answered.

"I will call back tomorrow at the same time for a reply. Do you have a direct number?" Marc asked.

"No. Call through the main number," was the non-committal reply.

"All right, please put your telephone in the modem cradle and I will transmit in five seconds," Marc said.

"Okay," was the reply.

Marc put his telephone in the modem, a beep sounded, and he pushed the transmit button. The second beep sounded showing the two machines were locked electronically. After a few seconds the lights went out signifying the transmission was complete. Marc removed the phone, hung it up, and shut the KL-43 case.

"Now we have to wait and see, Adriana."

They left the room, locked the door, walked back to the porch, and sat down in the rocking chairs.

"Marc, what do you think the Embassy will tell you?"

"Right now I have no idea. I know the fellow I talked to is probably as worried about the KL-43 as he is about me. If anything should happen, if we're found out, it's very important to destroy the KL-43. The machines are used to secure transmissions between Point West, Ilopongo, Tegucigalpa, Miami, and Washington. I wouldn't be surprised if the agency people in Managua know exactly where I am now, that you're with me, and how we got here."

"You think so?"

"Like I say, I wouldn't be surprised," Marc answered.

"Then we should assume the likelihood that State Security also knows, don't you think?"

"Well, we should be prepared for anything. I'm worried that you have put yourself in so much danger on my account," Marc said.

"I believe in the counter-revolutionary cause, and with support of that cause brings danger. I have accepted that. The Marxist path of the Sandinistas is wrong for our country. Many of my countrymen feel the same, and that is the reason the Contra forces grow."

Just as Adriana finished speaking her convictions, a resounding BOOM shook the porch, and the windows rattled. Marc jumped out of the rocking chair and ran to the porch rail. Adriana remained calm, rocking slowly as she looked amusedly at Marc.

"Sounds like a big explosion," Marc said.

"No, this is a sound that is very common now, and you can almost set your clock by it. We hear it in Chontales and Boaco also. The United States sends SR-71 spy planes to check on the airport that was built at Punta Huete on the east shore of Lake Managua. It appears that the sonic booms are intentional, just to let the Sandinistas know that the United States is watching."

"I remember being briefed on the new airport, but there's apparently very little activity as I recall," Marc said.

"At one time we Contras were concerned that the Sandinista Air Force would be using Mig's at this air field against us. But now construction on the airfield has stopped, though it was nearly complete. The whole project was another huge Sandinista mistake."

"How was that?" Marc asked.

"The Russians promised Mig's to the Sandinistas, but there was not a suitable airport. So the Sandinista Junta decided to construct an airport at Punta Huete. Sixty Nicaraguan pilots were sent to Bulgaria to learn to fly the Mig. The construction of the airport consumed much of the nation's concrete and construction steel. And it cost so much that it caused high inflation in the country. There were thousands of tons of cement and hundreds of trucks carrying it from the plant at San Rafael del Sur. Then the United States protested to Russia the delivery of Mig's to Nicaragua. The Soviets backed down. I doubt that the United States would have allowed any Mig to operate in Nicaragua. Now the airport is used occasionally by the Fuerza Aérea Sandinista, but mainly as a staging field by the HIND-24 helicopters."

Marc and Adriana continued with small talk, chatting and rocking in the chairs until lunch time when they returned to the small table on the porch. Adriana was in good humor, obviously enjoying the respite from military duties and her conversation with Marc. The kitchen helper returned for their dishes and Adriana got up from her chair.

"Marc, I am going to leave by the side door next to the garage and go to the market."

"Okay, but don't take any chances."

"Do not worry. I blend in well," she said.

"Sure you do. A beautiful young lady that I'm sure all the guys stare at when you walk by."

"I think you exaggerate, Marc," Adriana said, in a mock stern voice, but blushing nevertheless.

"Adriana, if you can buy a deck of playing cards, we can play gin rummy to help kill the time."

"I will look, but you will have to teach me."

"Okay. Be careful," Marc said.

Adriana returned from the market and walked in the open door to Marc's room. She found him lying on his back in bed, fully clothed, eyes open.

"Did I wake you," she asked, as she set two plastic bags down on the desk.

"No, just day dreaming. What did you buy?" he asked as he stood up.

"Here are mangos, bananas, oranges and also yucca chips and dried papaya. Here are the playing cards. I could not find any new ones but I bought these from a street vendor who had them on his stand. And," she said as she held up a bottle in triumph, "I found this wine in a supermercado near here. We should have a glass of wine to celebrate our safe travel so far."

"You are wonderful," Marc said, hugging her.

"Claro que sí, of course," Adriana said, obviously pleased with herself.

Adriana's gin rummy lessons were interrupted by the sound of a small band. It sounded to Marc like a trumpet, tuba, and drums playing a dirge.

"What's that?" Marc asked.

"Oh, there is another celebration of one of the patron saints. We can go sneak a look on the front porch, if we stand back a bit."

Marc and Adriana stood in the shadows on the front porch. The sun had already receded in the west. It finally disappeared behind the old Granada Social Club that faced them on the other side of the Parque Central. On their right was a group of about 50 men, women, and children following the small band. The band played a short mournful tune that was repeated over and over. Between the small band and the entourage were four men carrying a four foot high figure of a saint mounted on an elaborate platform. The saint was dressed in red velvet with gold and silver trim. The group proceeded from the north end of the Parque towards the Cathedral, which was on the south side of the Palacio Episcopal.

"It is the beginning of a religious festival for a saint. I do not know which one he is. This is very common in Granada. By the end of the week the saint will be carried to various homes, and the band will play in front of the homes. Those people so honored make a donation to the saint through the church."

The group stopped in front of the Cathedral. The saint was carried into the church, and the entourage followed.

"Marc, do you see the house to your right, at the north end of the Parque, facing us? It's the house that the American filibuster William Walker lived in when he declared himself President of Nicaragua in 1855. The next building closer to us is the Casa de Leones, which is proposed to be a cultural center in a year or two with foreign help. Next is the colegio, or high school, that I attended.   The Spanish government consul is across the Parque in front of us. The Alhambra Hotel also faces us, next to the old Granada Social Club. On the south end of the Parque is the Alcaldía, or mayor's office. Some of the large two story homes are those of wealthy Granadinos. The Parque is a pleasant place to relax, with its palm and mango trees, fountain, bandstand, and benches. I wish we could do that together. But it will have to be another time, I am afraid."

"That would be something to look forward to," Marc said, putting his arm around Adriana's waist. She turned and smiled.

Marc taught Adriana gin rummy that evening, and found out she was an apt pupil. When the score was tallied it was nearly a draw. Adriana was slightly ahead.

"You're too tough for me," Marc said.

"I think that is called beginner's luck, is it not?" Adriana replied. Let's go out on the front porch now. It is dark and we won't be seen. The two stood at the rail, looking out at the now quiet scene of the Parque Central. The departing vendors pushed their hand carts piled high with stools, tables, and unsold goods or foods. Marc put his arm around Adriana, and she leaned into him. They stood there in silence for some time.

"I think it is time to go to bed, Adriana said.

"They walked to Adriana's door, and Marc kissed her soundly, which she returned with equal fervor.   After an awkward pause, Adriana said "Buenas noches."

"Buenas noches," Marc replied. As he walked to his door, he had the feeling that neither of them was sure what should come next.

From a deep sleep, Marc was awakened by a loud "Boom! Boom!" Two more followed in rapid succession. Though it was dark, he managed to get up, cross the room without stumbling, and walked through the bathroom. Fortunately both doors were open. He went to Adriana's bed, and woke her.

"Adriana. It sounds like there's some fighting going on. Maybe mortars. We had better get ready to get out of here," Marc said.

"Marc, sit down here," Adriana said, sliding over in her bed. Marc could see with the little bit of light from the Park that Adriana was shirtless. For the moment it had no bearing on his near panic. He sat.

"Remember I told you that the festival of the Saint would continue with more activity until Sunday? Those were just bombas going off. Fireworks you would call them. They will do this every morning starting at 4:00 a.m. through Sunday. They are just bombas, Marc. Nothing more." Adriana took Marc's hand, and pulled him towards her. The rest of the early morning hours passed. But Marc was no longer aware of the bombas.

Marc awoke, at first only dimly aware of knocks on the door. Adriana was curled up into his left side. It took a second to get his bearings. Then he realized the knocks were at his door, not Adriana's. He slid out of bed and crossed through the bathroom to open his door. Marc peered around the corner to see Lydia, the kitchen helper.

"Su desayuno está listo," she said, and Marc understood enough Spanish to know that breakfast was ready.

"Que hora es?" Marc said in his best high school Spanish.

"A las nueve. Padre Pablo quiere hablar con Ustedes," Lydia replied.

"Marc, if you did not understand, Father Pablo wants to talk to us." Adriana had slipped up behind Marc. Lydia gave her a sly knowing smile.

"Está bien. A que hora?" Adriana asked.

"Quince minutos, Señorita," Lydia said.

"Okay, gracias."

"De nada, Senorita," Lydia said. Once again the sly smile crossed her face for an instant.

Sharing shower and wash basin, Marc and Adriana rushed to get ready throwing any pretense of modesty aside. They both arrived at the breakfast table on the porch at the same time. Lydia had set out a vase of white hibiscus mixed with cuttings of purple bougainvillea. Adriana leaned over, kissed Marc on the cheek. He responded by taking her right hand and kissing the middle of the palm.

"If you hear the 'boom' tonight, you know where to come," Adriana said, with a devilish curl to her mouth.

"I'm sure I will hear it," Marc said with a laugh.

As they were finishing their breakfast, Father Pablo strode on the porch.

"Buenos Dias," he said.

"Buenos Dias," they both laughed as they responded in unison.

"Last night a visiting padre from Masaya was here for a special mass at the Cathedral. I cannot say that he is pro-Sandinista, but his comments were disturbing. He first assured me that to him "rumors are rumors." Then he said he had heard that an American pilot was being hidden in Granada. He asked me if I had heard the same thing. I could truthfully tell him no. Nevertheless, I have become suspicious of his motives. There are many Sandinista supporters in Masaya, including those in positions of responsibility in the church.

"Father, perhaps it would be better if we moved," Marc said.

"No, no, not at this point. The staff here at the Archbishop's residence knows you only as catholic lay association officials. But we must be very careful. Now, if you want to use the telephone again, I will open the office."

"Thank you, Father," Marc said. "Adriana and I will stay alert and be ready to leave at a moment's notice."

"Yes, that we will do," Adriana echoed.

Marc and Adriana went to the office. Marc placed the KL-43 case on the desk, opened it, and activated the machine to standby. He called the Embassy, asked for the Agent-in-Charge, and this time he was immediately connected.

"Yes", the same gruff voice answered.

"I am ready for your answer," Marc said.

"Transmitting now," the voice said.

The KL-43 indicated a message was received. Marc picked up the phone from the cradle to say received and thanks, but the line was dead.

Marc pushed the decoder button, and the message flashed on the screen.

For DiAngelo. Proceed to La Paloma airstrip on Ometepe Island using your current assets. You will be picked up by a Maule arriving at exactly 4:30 p.m. on Thursday. The airstrip will be secured by a commando unit from the Jorge Salazar Task Force at least 30 minutes before Maule arrival. If unable, respond within two hours. Destroy KL-43 before departure for Ometepe. Intel says you are being hunted as a spy in Chontales, Boaco, and Granada Departments. Do not attempt land travel in Rivas area and south due to numerous Sandinista Army checkpoints. If airlift fails, recommend make your way to San Carlos and cross there.

"What do you think, Adriana? We will have to leave tomorrow for Ometepe. How long would a boat ride be to Ometepe? Will you return with your commando unit to the eastern shore? I don't want to leave you like that," Marc said, with a worried look.

"Marc, we can be at Ometepe in three hours by fast boat if the waves are not too high. That depends on the wind. Yes, I will return to the eastern shore with my unit. Even if there were room for me in your airplane, I could not go. There is much unfinished work to do, and I would not desert my comrades."

"I feel I am deserting you," Marc said.

"Mi amor, there is a Nicaraguan saying: Amor y dar son lo que dan valor a la vida. Love and giving are what makes life worth living. Your escape to Costa Rica, your freedom, is my gift to you. I give it without reservation. Your gift to me will come later, when you return to Nicaragua to find me."

Marc did not look happy, and remained silent. He closed the KL-43, and they left the office.

"Marc, I will be going to the market again after we eat lunch."

"I see. I think I can guess why."

"I won't be very long. I want to spend the afternoon with you. We enjoy each other, don't you think?" Adriana said.

"Absolutely," Marc replied, now feeling a bit giddy and lightheaded to hear her open her feelings to him, feelings that were very much his own. Damn, it must be love, he thought ruefully, and for a moment thought guiltily of Ellen.

After lunch, true to her word, Adriana was only gone for 45 minutes. They sat on the porch, in their rocking chairs.

"Want to play gin rummy?" Marc asked.

"No, not now. I am enjoying just sitting here with you in this peaceful place. It is so different from the mountains and little villages of my last two years.

A loud "whump, whump, whump" sound broke into their silence. Looking to the north, Marc saw a large helicopter flying down the beach from the north.

"That is a Hind, a Russian helicopter," Adriana said. When the Russians sent the helicopters to the Sandinistas, it was very bad for us. They are armed with four barrel Gatling machine guns, rockets, 500 and 1,000 pound bombs. Also, they have laser targeting and infrared sensors that detect movement on the ground. They have heavy armor plate. We are not able to shoot them down with our automatic rifles. Now, we have Chinese-made SA-7 shoulder-fired ground-to-air missiles and the American Red-Eye missiles. We have been successful in downing some. When we do shoot down a HIND with our missiles, either it is not reported in the Sandinista newspapers or they write that the helicopter crashed due to a mechanical malfunction."

"I've heard a little bit about the HIND," Marc said, and continued. "We were told in flight briefings that we definitely should avoid them, and head the other way if we see one. The HIND maximum speed is about the same as the C-47, 170 miles per hour, so we can't out run it. The best we can do is stay out of cannon and rocket range. The C-47 has a higher service ceiling than the HIND. But to begin a climb to get above the HIND's max ceiling means we have a slower climb speed. So that's not the answer. That is the first HIND I've seen. I've only seen pictures at our operations office."

The HIND continued its southward trek along the lake shore towards Puerto Asese. They were both quiet for a moment.

"Adriana, when the war is over and I hope soon, what will you do?" Marc asked.

"I want to complete my medical studies, either in Germany or somewhere in Latin America, perhaps even in the United

States. Then I would work in some of the mountain areas where we have been fighting. There is a great need for doctors there. What will you do when there is no more flying for the Contras?"

Marc rocked slowly back and forth, trying to formulate an answer. He was embarrassed that he really had no plan.

"Maybe I will come find you," he answered.

"That would be nice, but you might have a novia by that time."

"I doubt it. I've been thinking of maybe running a small air taxi or charter business in Costa Rica. I wouldn't make a lot of money, but it would keep me flying. Besides, I have my Air Force retirement to keep me in frijoles."

"Marc, this may sound presumptuous. I have told you before that my parents, Luis and Dolores María Kupper, live in Matagalpa. Anyone in Matagalpa can tell how to find their house. And they can tell you where I am." Adriana looked directly in Marc's eyes as she said this, with a hint of tears forming in the corners of her eyes.

Marc was touched to see Adriana's softening emotions. They matched his own.

"You can count on me visiting your parents, mi amor," Marc said softly, stroking Adriana's cheek.

A few tears ran down Adriana's face, but she was smiling. "I like your Spanish," she said. "Let's play some gin rummy. Perhaps you will be able to beat me this time."

"Adriana," Marc said as he dealt the cards, "It seems that Father Pablo is worried about spies. Do you think there is that much danger?"

"Spies have been part of our lives for many years. One of the most famous incidents happened just before the revolution. Nora Astorga was a secret agent for the Sandinistas. One of Somoza's top generals was General Pérez Vega, who was in charge of the National Guard's counter-intelligence. He became infatuated with Nora, who was a tall, attractive divorcee. She arranged for him to come to her home, and when they arrived they went directly to her bedroom. In great anticipation the General undressed. Two men with knives were hiding in a closet. They jumped out and stabbed the General to death. His genitals were cut off and stuffed in his mouth. Some say he was tortured before he was killed. Nora left with the attackers, who had covered the General's body with a Sandinista flag. Not that one cries for General Vega, for he was an evil man. But it shows what the FSLN is capable of. Under Somoza, there were about 400 State Security agents. The FSLN's Dirección General de Seguridad del Estado has 2,000 security agents. State Security has its own spies and even has its own jail cells at El Chipotle prison. The FSLN's theory is that if you are not in agreement with them, then you are against them."

Adriana continued. "Let me give you an example of how State Security sets traps for persons they suspect as subversives. Jorge Salazar was a businessman who originally supported the revolution. But then he became critical of the FSLN and was meeting with other businessmen who felt the same way. These meetings were reported to Lenin Cerna, the head of State Security. A trap was set for Salazar. State Security agents posed as Sandinista Army members disaffected with the regime. The agents developed a plot in which Salazar would be assassinated. Nestor Moncada, a friend of Salazar's, was involved in the plot. He just happened to also work for State Security, but, of course, Salazar did not know this. Moncada told Salazar he had important information and wanted a meeting where they could talk. They met on the fringes of Managua. When Salazar arrived at the meeting place, Moncada was there, but also the Deputy Chief of State Security, Juan José Ubeda. Ubeda shot

Salazar. Several M-16 automatic rifles were placed in Salazar's car to make it look like he was a counter-revolutionary. This happened in 1980, with the full approval of the ruling Junta."

"That is a very chilling picture," Marc said.

"There are many more stories I could tell you, but I do not want to pass our time with these unpleasant subjects," Adriana said.

"I agree. Time for our glass of wine."

The two sat on the porch in darkness, chatting and sipping their wine.

"What is that?" Marc asked. Animals were running, hissing, and snarling on the rooftop in front of them.

You are seeing the famous Granada cats. They run across the roofs of the city, mostly at night. Sometimes have fights among themselves. It keeps the rats off the roof. That is the good part. They also move the tiles as they run on the roof, causing water leaks that have to be fixed."

With the wine bottle emptied, Marc stood up and walked to the porch rail.

"I think I hear a bomba," he said, cupping his hand to his ear.

"I also heard the bomba," Adriana said, joining him at the rail. Marc put his arm around her waist, and she leaned her head against his shoulder.

"Your place or mine," Marc asked.

"I think I will come visit you," she answered.

Later Adriana came to Marc's bed, sat down, and he pulled her in beside him.

"Marc, I am going to miss you," she said.

"And I will miss you, my love. But all this should soon be over, and I will be back. I will head straight for Matagalpa."

"That is a promise," she responded, kissing him on the shoulder, the neck, and then the mouth.

It was still dark when Mac awoke with a grim foreboding. This was to be the final day of his escape. If things went right, he would be back at Point West tonight. He knew there was much risk and uncertainty in the rescue operation. In Vietnam it would have been called an extraction operation. And he worried about Adriana. Not that she would want his worries. After all, she was one of the counter-revolutionaries. Marc dozed off again, in a fitful and nightmarish sleep.

Marc awoke to daylight. Adriana was in the bathroom, humming a tune.

"Adriana, when you're done, I will take a shower," Marc said through the partially open bathroom door.

"Join me, querido," she said.

"With pleasure," Marc answered.

They soaped each other down, with a few caressing strokes here and there that provoked laughter as they played.

After showering and dressing, Marc opened the KL-43 case, and began disassembling parts, twisting, bending, and mutilating with his knife as best he could. Finally he put the open case on the floor, and began to crush it with his feet.

Adriana looked in the room with amusement.

"There is no more communication with the Embassy now. I believe you belong to me," she said, with a mock air of authority.

"More than you know," Marc answered, still stomping on the KL-43. He took out the code strip from his billfold, walked to the bathroom, and tore it into small pieces over the commode and flushed. A knock on the door announced Lydia and breakfast had arrived. They walked to the porch for their last breakfast together.

"Marc," Adriana said, putting her coffee cup down.

"Yes?" he answered.

"Our boat should be at Ometepe at 3:00 p.m. We can wait there until after the task force has made La Paloma airport secure. It will take the boat three hours to get us to Ometepe from Granada. We should leave here at 11:00 a.m. and go straight to the docks that are a bit north of Puerto Asese. Our panga is all arranged," she said.

"Thanks to your visit to the market yesterday, right?"

"Perhaps," Adriana said with a smile.

She poured both another cup of coffee, but had not yet set the carafe down when Father Pablo hurried out on the porch.

"My friends, it appears your stay here is compromised. I received a call that the Security Police are on their way. We must leave immediately. Get your things together. I will return in a moment."

CHAPTER 11—THE TUNNELS

Marc looked out the window at the Parque Central in time to see two olive drab four-wheel drive pickup trucks pull up to the front of the Palacio Episcopal. Each had four security police armed with AK-47s. As the men stepped out of the trucks they were approached by a tall white-haired cleric. A vigorous but brief discussion began.

Father Pablo returned to their rooms in a run. He threw a black cleric's shirt and pants to Marc, and went to Adriana's room and handed her a nun's simple street habit.

"Dress quickly," he urged.

In a matter of minutes Adriana and Marc were dressed. They put their street clothes in their backpacks, and followed Father Pablo down the stairs.

"Father, I've destroyed the KL-43, but it's still in the closet of my room."

"I will have Lydia dispose of it," Father Pablo said.

"Lydia?" Marc blurted out in surprise. Then it sunk in. The Contras and their supporters were much better organized than he had imagined.

"We will go through the garden to the garage and out the side door on Calle Libertad," Father Pablo said.

Marc was sure he must look like a scarecrow. His pants were much too large and the shirt with a clerical collar left an inch of clearance around his neck. On the other hand, Adriana's white calf-length street habit fit very nicely. It showed off her figure unlike any nun's habit he had seen.

They exited the side door onto Calle Libertad, and walked hurriedly away from the Parque Central. A security force four-wheel drive truck sped past them. The three soldiers in back only glanced at them. Father Pablo turned left at the end of the short block, onto narrow Calle Cervantes. To welcome the morning, the owners of those old adobe colonial homes had opened the high wooden doors to the fresh lake breezes that flowed in through the ornate wrought iron security doors. But the three looked neither right nor left as they walked hurriedly past. The sound of a siren pierced the morning air as another security force truck drove towards the north end of the Parque on Calle El Arsenal.

The long-legged Father Pablo slowed his walk to a normal pace and allowed Adriana and Marc to catch up. When they reached the corner at Calle El Arsenal, Father Pablo grasped Marc's arm below the shoulder, and spoke to him softly as if they were on a pastoral stroll.

"Now we will cross the street, go up the stairs to Convento San Francisco, and enter the door just to the left of the church."

The Convento San Francisco was more imposing at close hand than when seen from the upper porch of the Palacio Episcopal. More than a dozen steps up led to the large plaza that fronted the convent and its church. The entire complex stood above the homes in the blocks that surrounded the convent. A four story high façade faced with columns formed the entrance to the church. A double bell tower dominated the façade on the right side. A wall encircled the entire city block that housed the convent-church complex except for the plaza in front of the church and the convent portal.

Marc and Adriana followed Father Pablo to a heavy wooden door that was about 12 feet high and just to the left of the church entrance. Father Pablo pounded on the door with his fist. In a matter of seconds it opened.

"Adelante," said a gray haired old man, a caretaker, Marc assumed.

They walked into the convent's large courtyard of high palm trees and grass lawn. Leading them on, the caretaker stopped at a side door on the church. He unlocked the high 20 foot wrought iron security door, unlocked the giant brass padlock that secured a massive sliding bolt on the thick oak door and pushed the door open and they followed him into the church. The old man said nothing, but simply turned around, left the church, and closed the huge wooden door behind him. They heard the "clank" as the sliding bolt was moved in place. Marc looked at Adriana and shrugged.

Father Pablo took over the lead. Adriana and Marc followed him to the center aisle of the church and down to the altar. They climbed the two steps to the altar, proceeding behind the altar and to the right. Father Pablo opened a door that led to a room that appeared to be the church office. The room had two desks, a wooden storage cabinet, and several high backed chairs. It seemed little used if at all, Marc observed. The office's barred windows looked to the south across an expanse of red-tiled roofs and framed a view of Volcán Mombacho.

Father Pablo stopped and turned.

"The security police will have set up road blocks all around the Parque Central. They will start a house to house search, if they follow their usual procedure. There is an old tunnel from Convento San Francisco that goes towards the Lake to Iglesia Guadalupe.   Its existence is known by a few of the older Granadinos. I would say very few. The tunnel was used as an escape route. Pirates would come up the Rio San Juan from the Caribbean, sail across Lake Nicaragua, and pillage Granada. It has been many years since the tunnel has been explored. Gerardo, the caretaker who let us in here has been in the tunnel in years past. He believes it to be safe. We will see."

Marc and Adriana looked at each other, and March shrugged his shoulders.

"Lead on, Father. I like your plan," Marc said.

"And after we arrive at Iglesia Guadalupe?" Adriana asked.

"I think it best to take a carriage or taxi to the docks. I would expect all of the security police and soldiers to be called for the search around the Parque Central," Father Pablo said.

"If we keep our new clothes to wear to the dock, it would be better, I think," Adriana said.

"I agree. Dispose of them in the Lake with a rock to weigh them down," Father Pablo said. He turned and opened what appeared to be a closet door that was no more than five feet high. Stooping, he entered and they followed. The windowless room was dark and musty. An old armoire rested against the wall opposite the door. A table and several large wooden chests on legs outlined the other sides of the room. Father Pablo pulled a small flashlight from his pocket, and gave it to Adriana.

"Marc, please help me move this armoire away from the wall."

Marc and Father Pablo slid the armoire toward the right side of the room. The flashlight revealed a rusted steel plate three feet by four feet recessed a half inch into the concrete floor.

"Marc, use your fingers in the holes at that end of the steel cover. We will slide it toward the center of the room," Father Pablo said.

Once the steel cover was moved, Adriana shone the flashlight into a black hole it had covered. She focused the beam on a stone staircase that led below.

"Close the door, Adriana, and put the wooden bar across it," Father Pablo said. He then walked over to the wooden bar, pulled down the end of a rope that was hanging on a peg. He tied it to the midpoint of the bar.

"The caretaker, Gerardo, knows how to find the other end of this rope in the loft above. Once we are on our way, he will pull the inside wooden bar away from the iron supports, enter the room, cover the tunnel entrance, and move the armoire back in place. Then the room will arouse no suspicion. We have rehearsed this bit of drama in the last two days as part of an emergency escape plan. I would say that my premonition was correct. We must not delay further. Be careful, these are very steep steps."

"Father, have you been in the tunnel before?" Adriana asked.

"I have seen the entrance, but I have never been down in the tunnel. Gerardo has told me what to expect," Father Pablo said.

Marc had an uneasy feeling. His escape plan would have been to run for it outside. He saw Adriana had not hesitated. Should he be a wimp, he thought to himself, as he peered down into the tunnel. The sound of sirens as Adriana closed the door convinced him.

"Adriana, please give me the flashlight, I will go down first," Father Pablo said. Marc and Adriana stood above and watched the beam of the flashlight descend and bounce off the rock walls below.

"Now, Adriana, come down the steps. Watch your head."

As he followed Adriana, Marc felt his way down the steps. The rock sides of the stairwell were damp. The stone walls swallowed the light from the flashlight. The tunnel was no more than a meter wide and arched two meters high at the middle. Father Pablo had to stoop as he shuffled to avoid hitting his head.

"The citizens and clergy of Granada were much shorter a hundred and fifty years ago," Father Pablo said, his voice echoing and disappearing into the unknown.

"How far is it to Iglesia Guadalupe, Father?" Marc asked.

"It is about four blocks toward the lake. We should gradually be going downhill."

It was more a shuffle than a walk with Father Pablo in the lead, then Adriana, and Marc. Adriana and Marc received little help from the flashlight. They used their hands as guides, sliding them along the sides of the tunnel. Every so often they would hear an exclamation from Father Pablo as he tired of bending over and rose just enough to scrape his head on the rock above. Marc also scraped his scalp a few times. Adriana, at five foot four, was spared this particular problem.

"Oh, Oh, I did not anticipate this," Father Pablo said, stopping his shuffle. Adriana bumped into Father Pablo, and Marc bumped into Adriana. Marc stifled a laugh.

"What is it?" Adriana asked.

"Just like a Marx brothers' movie," he whispered.

"I don't understand," Adriana said.

"I know. I'm sorry. I'll explain it to you later. What is the problem, Father Pablo?"

"It seems that the tunnel branches here. It has been said that there are several tunnels that connect various churches. I have heard that there is a tunnel from the Cathedral to Iglesia Xalteva to the west. No one really knows, but I have also heard a tunnel connects Convento San Francisco to the Cathedral. Since it branches here to the right in the direction of the Cathedral we will assume that it is the tunnel to the Cathedral, and we will continue straight ahead."

Marc felt drops of perspiration on his head, face, and neck. The clamminess and lack of air movement were stifling.

"This is like a sauna," he said. Adriana, next to him, felt about his face, and lightly touched her fingers to his lips. Marc marveled at her coolness.

"Father, I think you are right," Adriana said.

"Yes, I agree also," Marc added.

The threesome started off again in their shuffle. Adriana asked the question that had been on Marc's mind.

"Father," Adriana said, her voice echoing down distant walls, "Are you sure that we have a way to exit at the end of the tunnel?"

"Gerardo has assured me that there is an exit in the small confessional room which is in a vestibule of a small chapel on the west side of the church. It is disguised as a concrete cover for a registro. That, Marc, is a cover over an underground collection box of pipes of sewer or rain water drainage. Two days ago Gerardo went to Guadelupe after we formulated this emergency escape plan. Gerardo removed the cover and went down into the tunnel to confirm the tunnel entrance was still usable."

"Gerardo is a very brave man, Father. Please thank him for us," Adriana said.

"I will do that. I think we should be very close to Guadelupe," Father Pablo replied.

In another fifty feet Father Pablo stopped. He focused the flashlight beam on the wall. There was writing engraved on the stone. When he put the light on the other side of the tunnel, there was the same. Father Pablo walked forward slowly, shining the light on both sides of the tunnel. There were more inscriptions as they walked along.

"The catacombs," Father Pablo said, without further explanation.

"They must be very old," Adriana said.

"Yes, here is the grave of the Governor of Granada, who was buried in 1755," he said. There were several short stone walled corridors that branched off the main tunnel, forming part of the catacombs.

Within 25 feet they came to narrow steps that led to a ceiling. The moment of truth, Marc thought to himself.

Father Pablo handed the flashlight to Adriana and pushed on the cement square above. It did not budge. Marc went up the steps alongside Adriana and helped Father Pablo push. Gaining leverage was difficult, as both men had to lean slightly forward as they pushed. The cement cover still did not move.

"Father, instead of pushing in the middle, let's both push on one end."

As they pushed on the closest end of the concrete cover, there was upward movement, first an inch, then two inches, and the weight began to decrease. A scraping sound accompanied the lessening of resistance on the cover.

"There is something on top of the cover, Father," Marc said. As they continued to push, there was a "thud" as the object that was on the cover fell. Then the cover came up easily, and Father Pablo and Marc were momentarily blinded by the daylight. First Father Pablo and then Marc climbed up through the hole in the floor. Both were breathing heavily, and rivulets of sweat were streaming down their faces. Adriana climbed up through the opening, paused, and made the sign of the cross.

"That was more frightening than a Sandinista ambush," she said.

"The Lord is with us," Father Pablo said with a wan smile.

"Marc, help me replace the cover," Father Pablo said, "But first we should pick up this cofre that has fallen over. Someone moved this since Gerardo was here." Marc helped Father Pablo pick up the large wooden chest, which had separated from its separate four-legged base as it fell to the floor. Then they replaced the concrete cover which was tiled to match the floor over the tunnel entrance, and moved the cofre back over it.

"Wait here," Father Pablo said. "I will make sure the church is safe."

He returned in five minutes. "Everything is normal. I will walk back to the Palacio Episcopal as if I had been here to Guadalupe on an errand. Remain in your clerical clothes until you get to the docks, as we have said. I see that Gerardo has arranged for a horse carriage to meet you here. The carriage will take the road along the malecón. Marc, you say nothing if stopped. Sister Adriana will do the talking. But I would expect no checkpoints along the lake shore now."

Father Pablo and Marc shook hands. Adriana kissed the Father on the right cheek.

"Father, be careful," Adriana said.

"I can't thank you enough, Father," Marc added.

"Hurry, the two of you," Father Pablo said. "I will pray for your safety."

"And I for yours," Adriana said in an uncharacteristically broken voice.

Father Pablo walked to the massive front doors of the church that faced the lake. A horse carriage waited at the curb at the bottom of a dozen steps that led to the sidewalk. It was the same type of horse carriage "taxi" that Marc had seen in Granada when he watched from the upper porch of the Palacio Episcopal.

"That is your carriage," Father Pablo said, and March and Adriana walked down the broad steps of the church to the curb.

The driver only nodded as Marc and Adriana climbed aboard. The carriage pulled out onto the Calle Caimito and headed down the short distance to the lake and the malecón.

"No inglés," Adriana whispered. The competing clatter of the horses' hooves and the rumble of the iron wheels covered her voice.

The carriage turned south on the malecón road and followed the lake shore towards the lesser docks above Puerto Asese. The driver turned and spoke quickly to Adriana. All Marc understood was the word "adelante".

"Marc, there is a roadblock ahead. We dare not turn around. We will continue. Marc had his backpack at his feet. He reached down, pulled out the .38 revolver, and stuck it in his belt behind his back. Adriana put her backpack on the seat next to her, unzipped the outer pocket, and pulled out a double barreled .32 derringer, and slipped it into the nun's habit. Neither said a word.

A soldier waved the carriage to a stop. The soldier was young, perhaps no more than 17 years old. "Buenos días," he said to the driver, Adriana, and Marc.

"A donde Ustedes van?" he asked, clearly wanting to know where they were going, but asked in a not unfriendly way.

"Vamos a Puerto Asese a encontrar los padres de Ometepe," Adriana answered with a smile, telling the young soldier they were going to Puerto Asese to meet clerics arriving from Ometepe Island.

"Está bien, buen viaje," the young soldier replied, flashing a wide smile and wishing them a good trip.

As the carriage continued down the road, Adriana said "It is good that the hydrofoil from Ometepe is scheduled to arrive at mid day."

"Hydrofoil?" Marc said.

"Yes. There are four large hydrofoil boats that were given to the Sandinistas by the Russians. They have a schedule between Granada, Ometepe, San Carlos, and San Jorge. They are based in Puerto Asese, so it is logical we would go there to meet visiting priests from Ometepe."

"I'm glad that young soldier was not a problem. He's just a kid," Marc said.

"Yes, there are many young boys from the campo who have been forced into the army. Most are sent almost immediately into the hills to fight with little or no training. There are many grieving mothers. That boy is lucky to be in Granada."

At the south end of the malecón the road veered to the right leading to Puerto Asese and the little bay formed by Peninsula Asese and the mainland. Instead, the carriage followed a straight narrow dirt road that led to a small dock area on the east side of the Peninsula that was a short distance from the open lake. The carriage pulled up to a parking area in front of a small lakeshore restaurant.

Marc and Adriana stepped down from the carriage, and Adriana asked the driver how much was owed.

"Nada," the driver replied.

"Gracias por su ayuda," she said, thanking the driver for his help.

As the carriage departed, Adriana and Marc walked into the small open air restaurant. Through the seating area with roof overhead, they could see several pangas tied up at docks which were immediately on the other side of the restaurant. Three middle-aged men sat at a table playing cards. Marc and Adriana were surprised to see two soldiers drinking beer at the far end of the seating area. Their AK-47s were leaned against a wall. One of the card players got up, walked over to them, and introduced himself as Ernesto Aguilar. Ernesto was of medium height, powerfully built, with a round face and full mustache.

"Mucho gusto," Adriana said. "Soy Hermana Adriana, y el es Padre Marco," Adriana explained, introducing herself as Sister Adriana and Marc as Father Marco. Ernesto gave a small crooked smile that said "I know your secret" and replied, "Mucho gusto."

"Estamas listo para salir," Adriana said. "Marc, I told Ernesto we're ready to leave," Adriana whispered in Marc's ear. Now the two soldiers halted their discussion and were looking at the threesome with interest.

"Vamanos," Ernesto said a bit nervously.

The three walked through the restaurant to the dock side, and Ernesto helped them step off the cement dock into a 25 foot panga. He began untying the lines. Marc untied the stern line, and was surprised to look up and see the two soldiers standing alongside.

"Sus documentos," demanded the taller one who had a wildly unkempt wide mustache. His long hair hung out from beneath the small green fatigue cap perched on top of his head.

"No tenemos aqui," Adriana replied. The boatman looked wary now, alert to impending trouble as Adriana informed the soldiers they did not have their identification documents with them.

"Sus documentos," the soldier said again. His speech was slightly slurred by one too many beers. He was not going to drop the matter. When they entered the restaurant Marc had noticed that neither was armed. He had seen their AK-47s casually placed against the wall next to their table.

"Tendremos nuestros documentos por Ustedes más tarde," Adriana replied. She was trying to mollify the increasingly agitated soldier by telling him they would show him their documents later.

The soldier shifted his attention to Marc.

"Su documento, Padre," he said.

Marc did not reply, but was gauging his options. If the outboard started up immediately would the soldiers be able to get to their AK-47s and fire before the panga was out of range? He doubted it.

Adriana loosened the straps holding down the cover of her backpack, then unzipped the main compartment and fiddled inside for a moment.

"Vengan aqui, tengo algunos documentos," she said with a smile, motioning both soldiers onto the boat to see the documents she was about to produce. As they climbed aboard and clambered over the seats to Adriana, she pulled the.32 derringer out of the backpack and pointed at them.

Sientan!" she ordered. Both sat down as directed, with a mixture of fear and surprise on their faces. Marc had replaced his .38 in his backpack earlier, and had it out in a matter of seconds. Now the soldiers looked even more confused.

"Silencio! Adriana hissed. The soldiers were truly speechless at this point. This warning to be quiet was unnecessary.

"Ernesto, vamanos," Adriana said, and Ernesto went to the center console and started the 100 horsepower Yamaha outboard. He backed the panga away from the dock, put it in forward gear, and headed for the isletas channels. Marc looked back at the restaurant. The two card players continued their game as if nothing had happened. He noticed the two AK-47s were no longer leaning against the wall.

"Marc, watch our two hostages closely. If we have to shoot them, we will," Adriana said.

Marc looked at wonder at Adriana. She was a young lady of many contradictions; tender, warm, feminine, and tough as nails if the situation dictated it.

Ernesto steered the panga through the isletas, heading south towards Ometepe Island at a moderate speed that would not attract attention. The two soldiers were sullen, the effects of alcohol rapidly dissipating as they realized their predicament.

"Tranquilo amigos. No tienen miedo. Ustedes pueden salir al Isla Zapatera," Adriana said, calming the two soldiers in a quiet voice, assuring them that they need not be afraid and that they would be turned loose at the Zapatera Island.

"Esta bien," the taller one said, with little enthusiasm.

"Marc, we will pass Zapatera Island on the way to Ometepe. We are going to have to delay at Zapatera. Otherwise, we will be much too early at Ometepe, which would be dangerous for us. So it is better to stop at Zapatera and wait."

"Sounds like a good idea, Adriana. What about these two guys?"

"I told them not to worry, that we would release them at Zapatera. We will keep them under guard until we leave Zapatera. Not many people live on the island, less than 500 I think. There is only one small village on the east end. We will leave our two friends on shore far from any houses. It will be several hours or more before they can notify authorities. By then you will be back in Costa Rica and I will be with the Task Force in Chontales."

Marc nodded, while directing his attention to the two hostages.

Adriana continued. "Zapatera is only 40 kilometers from Granada, so it should take us about an hour and a half. As soon as we are out of the isletas channels you will be able to see it."

The panga wove its way through the channels, passing the small islands, some no more than a few rocks, others two or three acres in size. Only a few seemed to be inhabited, wooden shacks with tin roofs, and the inevitable laundry line between trees with clothes flapping in the stiff lake wind. Now and then they would pass fishermen in dugout canoes and planked rowboats. Waves were exchanged. Finally they cleared the last isleta and were in the open lake. A strong east wind was blowing. White caps had formed, and the panga wallowed as it traversed the troughs of the waves.

"There Marc, adelante. Zapatera. Do you remember, we saw it when we were at the Laguna?"

"Yes, but it is looking much bigger now. Looks rugged."

"It was a burial ground of the ancient Indians. There are many petroglyphs and stone idols there. The forest grows right up to the top of the volcano, which is dormant. There are many birds, deer, jaguar, ocelots and other wild animals. In 1983 the Island was made a national park. I have to give recognition to the Sandinistas for doing that."

As the panga neared Zapatera, Adriana directed Ernesto to the western part of the island. "Poca gente alla," she told him, to emphasize that the west part was more remote with fewer inhabitants. Ernesto slowed, and he began to look for an isolated beach that was not too rocky. He steered the boat to a small beach with steep promontories on each side. The beach was a mixture of sand and rock, and from there the terrain rose rapidly into dense forest.

"Perfecto, Ernesto," Adriana said, as Ernesto slowed the boat as it neared the beach. The boat landed with a bump. Both Adriana and Marc held their guns on the two soldiers as Ernesto hopped out in calf deep water and pulled the front of the panga up on the sand.

"Marc, we will have to wait here two hours. We should tie the two men up."

"Good idea, Adriana. It is better that Ernesto do it while we keep a little distance."

Adriana asked Ernesto to tie the hands of each of the soldiers with rope that was in the boat. Then they were told to get out and sit on the sand. Ernesto filled a plastic coke bottle, and gave each one a drink. They seemed grateful.

Adriana and Marc sat on a large log that had drifted up on the beach, keeping themselves between the men and the forest.

"I imagine those guys are trying to think of what they are going to tell their commanders when they get back to Granada," Marc said. He nodded towards the two glum soldiers.

"The Sandinistas can be very unforgiving. These two may think long and hard about returning. They might be considered deserters rather than hostages. They might even become Contras," Adriana said.

"Well, I wouldn't want to be in their shoes. But come to think of it, I'm not sure they would want to be in our shoes."

"You have given me a thought. We should take their boots when we leave. That should make their travel to civilization much slower," Adriana said.

"Maybe Ernesto needs a couple of pairs. Marc was feeling better and his sense of humor returning.

"Adriana, we should be at the La Paloma airstrip no later than 4:30, right? By then it should be secured by your task force commandos from Chontales."

"Yes," Adriana said. "We should leave the island at 2:30 to make sure we are at Ometepe on time. The airfield is half a kilometer from the lake shore. We can be there from the boat in 15 minutes."

"Will Ernesto wait with the boat so that we have an alternate escape if something goes wrong?"

"Ernesto will go to the landing field with us, and then return to Chontales with the commando unit. He cannot return to Granada if we let these two soldiers go free. You and I are not the type that would execute them here. So that is the only option. But if there is a problem, the three of us will return to the boat, and perhaps head for San Carlos."

At that moment Ernesto walked down from the forest edges and handed Mark two large ripe mangoes.

"Gracias, Ernesto."

Marc rummaged in his backpack and found the hunting knife.

"Marc, please give me the knife and I will show you how to prepare the mangos." Adriana skillfully peeled the first mango, then sliced off an oblong piece, gave it to Marc, and sliced one for her.

"Marc, inside my backpack are tortillas wrapped in paper from this morning's breakfast. Tortillas and mangoes will be our lunch.

Then she called Ernesto and gave him several tortillas.

"Los soldados pueden comer mas tarde. Por ellos, agua solamente."

"We don't have enough food for the two soldiers, only water. But they will find food even before they arrive at the little village of La Merced on the other side of the island."

Well, I think they are full of beer anyway," Marc said. "If I could forget what is ahead of us, I could really enjoy sitting here on the log, eating our lunch, with the sun shining, a nice breeze, toucans and parrots up in the trees," Marc said.

"Yes, it is very tranquilo here. Even our Sandinista friends seem to be content for the moment. We should leave in 15 minutes, Marc."

Ernesto had gone to the boat and was transferring gasoline from a spare can into the main tank. With this activity, the two soldiers became alert, still not sure of their fate.

"Time passes too quickly. We must go," Adriana said.

"Yes, it's time," Marc said, as he glanced at his watch and got up.

They approached the two soldiers sitting in the sand.

"We will keep our distance as before, Marc," Adriana said. Both she and Marc aimed their pistols at the two soldiers.

Adriana told Ernesto to remove the soldiers' shoes and put them in the boat. A look of fear crossed the faces of the two Sandinistas. As a matter of necessity both the Sandinistas and Contras removed the shoes and boots from the dead, regardless of whether friend or foe. Adriana then directed Ernesto to untie the ropes. The two Sandinista soldiers stood up uncertainly as Marc and Adriana continued to train their weapons on the pair.

"Vayan, muchachos. Al este está La Merced," Adriana advised. Both barefooted soldiers hastily began a climb up to the point where the beach met the forest, looked over their shoulders once, and quickly disappeared in the foliage.

"Now is our time to leave," Adriana said. "We should change our clothes now. We will sink the church's clothes in the lake with rocks as Father Pablo instructed."

"Okay, I'll help Ernesto push the boat off the beach. You can put my backpack and shoes in the boat," Marc replied.

CHAPTER 12—OMETEPE ISLAND

Ernesto started the outboard after Adriana was seated while Marc pushed the bow clear of the beach and climbed in over the side. Ernesto headed the boat around the west end of the Island, and soon they were in clear water. Both Marc and Adriana relaxed on the seat in front of the console. They were not holding hands, but pressed their shoulders together tightly as they studied the twin peaks of Ometepe's volcanos Concepción and Maderas.

A roaring noise behind them broke their reverie. Closing fast upon them a hydrofoil passenger boat pounded the waves.

"It must be going 30 knots or better, and it has to be at least 80 feet long," Marc said. About a dozen passengers were standing along the bow rails. Marc noticed at least two armed soldiers.

"We will just be friendly and wave," Adriana said. In a matter of minutes the hydrofoil was abeam, 200 yards to their right. Adriana and Marc waved, and the passengers waved back. Soon the hydrofoil was far beyond.

"The Russians gave the Sandinistas four hydrofoils. Unfortunately, they are meant for smooth water, and often cannot operate on the lake because the water is too rough," Adriana said.

"It must be going to Ometepe," Marc said.

"Yes, it is probably going to Moyogalpa, and then to San Jorge on the shore next to Rivas. Ernesto will stay well clear of the port of Moyogalpa. The La Paloma airstrip is on the west side of Ometepe, a little further south than Moyogalpa, and not far from San Jorge on the mainland. My concern is that there is an airport near San Jorge used by the Sandinista Air Force. There is a squadron of HIND helicopters there."

"Hopefully we will have come and gone before the Sandinistas know what happened."

"Yes, I think that is the way it will be."

The panga was soon abeam Moyogalpa a kilometer to the west. As they passed, Ernesto angled the boat towards the island shore. Marc looked at his watch.

"Three forty-five, Adriana. The commando unit should be near."

"Yes, they would have landed on the eastern shore of the Island between the two volcanoes, and traveled by truck over farm roads to La Paloma."

Marc could not see any evidence of an airfield from the boat. The terrain rose rapidly to about 30 feet above the lake, but then was relatively flat to the base of Volcán Concepción.

The boat continued angling toward shore. Ernesto looked at his watch, and nodded to Adriana. He gunned the outboard, and the panga dashed the last 50 feet and ran up on the sandy shore. Both Adriana and Marc had braced for a sudden stop. Instead, the boat glided up on the sand and came to a slow stop on the steep beach. Marc jumped out of the boat, his pistol in his belt. Ernesto quickly unwrapped a rolled up canvas tarp, revealing two assault rifles. One was an M-16, which he handed to Adriana. The other was a heavier Belgium-made FAL for himself. Adriana slung the rifle strap over her shoulder, obviously familiar with the weapon. She was already wearing her backpack. Marc slid his on.

"Sigame," Ernesto said, and Adriana and Marc followed him in single file.

"Marc, Ernesto's home is Ometepe."

"Good. That makes me feel better."

The three climbed the steep bank beyond the beach, and found themselves immediately entering a field of tall platano plants. Ernesto headed directly inland down the rows of platano, which were heavy with the banana-like fruit. Adriana had moved over three rows. She followed slightly behind Ernesto, both of them with rifles at the ready. Marc was intrigued by Adriana's military skills.

The sound of gunfire erupted.

"Those are AK-47s and FAL's," Adriana shouted, sliding the M-16 action.

When they approached the end of the platano field, Ernesto held up his hand to stop. It was evident to Marc that Ernesto was much more than an itinerant boatman from Granada. Straight ahead was the east end of the gravel runway. On both sides there were more fields of platano. At the west end of the runway was Volcán Conception two kilometers away.

"Sandinistas. This may be an ambush," Adriana said to Marc.

There were more long bursts of staccato firing.

"AK-47s," Ernesto said. Then short bursts of another type of rifle. Those are our FAL's and AK-47s," Adriana said. "The Sandinistas fire their AK-47s on full automatic. We use three second bursts to conserve ammunition."

Ernesto pointed to the left side of the runway. Halfway along they could see two cattle trucks, one blocking a dirt road that entered onto the landing strip.

Marc could see half a dozen Contras in their U.S. style camouflage uniforms, behind the truck blocking the road. More had spread out in the platano field and were firing down the road.

Ernesto waved Adriana to follow him.

"Marc, you remain here," she said, and followed Ernesto. She stayed inside the cover offered by the platanos, her M-16 at the ready.

Marc pulled his .38 from his belt, and ran after them. Both Ernesto and Adriana were darting from plant to plant, and he followed suit.

Adriana stopped, turned and saw him. She pointed to the ground. "Stay here," she said in a no-nonsense voice. Her face showed she meant it.

The firing had slowed to an occasional burst of gunfire. Finally there was silence. The Contra commandos, who had crouched behind the truck, began to advance cautiously down the sides of the road. They stayed well hidden among the platanos, and fired short bursts now and then. Return fire had almost ceased. It appeared the Sandinistas were in retreat down the dirt road away from the airstrip.

Adriana joined two other Contras beside the truck and was talking to them when Marc walked up.

"Hola, Marc, we meet again." It was Pete Givens who Marc had last seen at the camp near Puerto Diaz.

"Hola amigo," Marc retorted, and shook hands with Pete and the other Contra, José Miguel, who he remembered from his stay at the camp.

"Marc, Pete thinks it was just bad luck that a Sandinista patrol stumbled on them here. There were 8 or 10 Sandinistas in that East German IFA truck that drove up to the airstrip. Our boys heard the truck and ambushed them. They think one or two got away. The rest are dead. Those that escaped will return to Moyogalpa for reinforcements. There may be none. Your plane should be here in 15 minutes," Adriana said.

The Contra commandos set up an ambush along the road that dead-ended into the airstrip. They positioned themselves on either side of the disabled IFA truck that sat in the middle of the road. The cattle truck was left blocking the road at the entrance to the airstrip. Someone backed the second truck into the platano field.

Adriana, Ernesto, Marc and Pete remained by the truck. Adriana took three swigs from a canteen which Pete handed her first. She passed it next to Marc. Ernesto and Pete leaned casually against the truck and they appeared not to have a care in the world. Pete's fatigue cap was pushed back on his head, and Ernesto was taking deep drags on a cigarette.

"Five minutes to go," Marc said, looking at his watch. Adriana looked at him, and held his gaze for a few seconds. Pete, Adriana, and Marc walked onto the airstrip. They all scanned the sky.

"He will be low, probably not more than 200 feet. With these winds he will land to the east, towards Concepción Volcano," Marc said.

Suddenly there was a "Whump, Whump, Whump." The three turned to see a HIND no more than 50 feet off the ground coming straight at them. The five rotor blades made a deafening sound. Marc could plainly see the two pilots, sitting in bubble-shaped cockpits in tandem, the back pilot sitting higher than the one forward. Two large engine inlets were above the pilots' bubbles. Each of the HIND's two short stubby wings at the fuselage mid-section carried pylons with two anti-tank rocket launchers, two 23 mm guns, and a rocket pod. The co-pilot in front sat behind a four barrel Gatling gun mounted in the nose of the HIND.

Ugly and lethal, was Marc's first thought. The HIND flew over them from the north to south without firing, and then turned back. Pete, Marc, and Adriana were already running towards the platano field when the Gatling gun fired. They all turned and fired at the helicopter. The rounds from the Contra's FAL's and AK-47s bounced off the armor plate of the HIND and failed to damage the titanium rotor head.

The HIND turned south again, reversed its course, and fired its 57 mm rockets. One scored a direct hit on the cattle truck blocking the entrance to the airstrip. Two Contras firing from behind the truck were blown in the air.

One Contra fired a rocket propelled grenade which barely missed the HIND as it turned for another pass.

Marc thought briefly of the Maule. It was time for it to arrive. For the moment immediate survival was much more on his mind.

The Contras continued to fire their assault rifles at the HIND. Then the HIND landed on the eastern end of the runway. Eight Sandinista soldiers got out and ran into the platano field.

Pete dispersed his commandos to a protective arc in the platano field just east of the entrance to the airstrip. The HIND lifted off, swung south, gained altitude to about 200 feet, and came back north again towards the middle of the airstrip firing its Gatling gun. Marc saw three more commandos fall in the platano field. After a nod from Pete, Luis Miguel lifted a Red-Eye anti-aircraft missile launcher from the back of the truck. He raised the 29 pound missile launcher to his shoulder, and activated the Red-Eye's sensors with a switch. A series of beeps indicated the system was activated. Positioned correctly, the missile's sensors picked up the heat of the MI-25's turbine engines. Then the beep became a continuous sound. The HIND turned right once more. The slow turning speed caused an excessive roll. At that perfect moment, Luis launched the rocket. It gained speed first under the propulsion of its booster motor. Three seconds later the sustainer motor fired and the missile streaked to the port engine of the MI-25. A few seconds after the impact, the HIND rolled on its left side, then banked even more steeply, and dropped in a tight spiral. When it hit the ground, the blast shook the ground where Marc was standing. The heat of the fireball reached him a few seconds later.

Pete signaled his remaining commandos and they began moving east towards the Sandinistas.

The Maule appeared almost as if by magic flying low over the strip from the shore. It pulled up in a right climbing turn to 300 feet, flew a low downwind, and disappeared out of sight over the lake as it turned back to the strip to land. Marc was surprised. He had assumed with the firefight and the helicopter burning that the Maule would not land.

Marc and Adriana sprinted to the middle of the runway, ignoring the bursts of rifle fire as the Contras approached the Sandinistas' positions on the northeast side of the runway.

"Querido," Adriana said, as she reached out for Marc's hand. She looked up at him, her eyes pleading for his full attention. "Do not forget you have promised to come to Matagalpa." Marc put his arm around Adriana's waist, struck for the moment at the beauty and heroism of his lover, friend, and protector. "My love, I promise I will return to Matagalpa when the war is over so we can be together."

Adriana smiled and squeezed his arm tightly. "I love you. Please hurry back to me!"

Marc had no chance to reply. At that moment the Maule suddenly reappeared, on short final with full flaps, just over the tops of the trees that bordered the platano field. It dropped solidly in a three-point landing at the very edge of the landing strip. The pilot braked the craft heavily. It rolled to a stop a short distance from Marc and Adriana.

As Marc and Adriana ran for the Maule, two Sandinistas broke from the platano field and began firing at them. Adriana raised her M-16, firing back in three second bursts. One Sandinista went down. The Maule taxied up to where they were standing. The pilot motioned Marc to get in. Marc turned to Adriana, but she was no longer standing next to him.

Adriana lay face down on the ground, her M-16 still in her hand, and a large splotch of blood on the back of her blouse. Horrified, Marc ran to her and turned her over. Then he could see that at least two AK-47 rounds had hit her in the chest. Marc looked at her perfectly composed face. Adriana was serene in death despite the horror of her last 15 minutes.

"Marc," the pilot yelled. "Now!"

He pointed to the remaining Sandinista soldier now running toward the Maule, firing wildly. Marc's feet were leaden. He could hardly feel himself moving. He opened the door on the right side of the plane, got in, and automatically fastened his seat belt.

The pilot jammed the throttle forward, and the Maule accelerated quickly. Its tail came off the ground and it was airborne in 1,000 feet. The pilot started a turn so soon it seemed the right wing tip would hit the ground. It was a dangerous maneuver at low takeoff airspeed, but not as dangerous as the AK-47s at the end of the runway. Marc looked back to see Adriana's body sprawled in the dirt near the middle of the runway.

Not until Marc turned back to speak to the pilot did he realize it was Joe. Joe had obviously escaped the HIND helicopters that were chasing him as he headed south to the Costa Rican border. How many days ago, wondered Marc as he remembered the crash.

"Thanks, Joe," was all he could muster.

"Sorry about that young lady. She saved our butts," Joe said. Marc nodded, but couldn't speak. He should not have left her, he thought. There was nothing left for him to do. Still, he should not have left her.

"I'm going to keep it down close to the ground," Joe said. The Maule was at max power now, the manifold pressure indicator clearly in the red danger zone on the gauge. They were headed for the right side of Maderas Volcano which was on the south side of Ometepe Island, flying just above the tree tops.

"Scarlet, this is Swift One, departing target, squawking code five," Joe called over the radio.

"Swift One, this is Scarlet. Ident."

"Swift One Ident."

"Swift One, Scarlet here. No contact."

"Swift One, understand."

"Marc, I think when we're around the other side of Maderas Scarlet will pick us up on their radar, even though we are down in the trees," Joe said.

Marc had been turning around in his seat constantly. He was checking behind to make sure they were not being followed by either a HIND or the Sandinista Air Force's so-called fighter, the Cessna twin engine Skymaster. The Skymaster was armed with 20 mm cannon. Marc had seen the Skymasters used in

Vietnam in close air support operations, spotting targets for fighter aircraft. The Maule was an even match in speed with the Skymaster so only the HIND helicopter was the real threat.

Joe banked the Maule to the right as it came around the base of Maderas Volcano. He headed directly for the lake shoreline and Costa Rican soil just beyond.

"Swift One, this is Scarlet, Ident."

Joe hit the Identify button on the IFF panel, and Scarlet called immediately.

"Swift One, we have contact. You are 35 miles from the border. We show no bogies following you. We had a second slow moving target, probably a HIND, approach the target area. It disappeared at the target area while in a straight line of flight. We suspect it was a missile hit."

"Swift One understand," Joe answered, and turned to Marc. "Looks like the Sandys launched another HIND from Rivas, and it got hit also."

"Good. That will give Pete and his commandos a chance to get out of the area and back to the east side of the lake. I hope they're able to take Adriana with them," Marc said.

"Sounds like Pete must be a gringo Contra. And I'm guessing Adriana must be the young lady who took out the first Sandinista that was firing at us," Joe said.

"You've got it right on both counts. I'll tell you all about it when we get back," Marc said.

"Marc, it looks like you might have been hit in the hand or arms. You've got splotches of blood on your hands and your left arm and pants." Marc had been totally occupied in looking for a pursuer. He checked his arm, hands, and upper body. He found nothing. It was most likely Adriana's blood he had touched when he had lifted her after she was shot.

"It's not mine," Marc said, without the need to elaborate.

"Okay," came the muted response from Joe.

The Maule was close to the waves, out over the lake, and nearing the shoreline.

"Swift one, Scarlet here. 15 miles."

"In about seven minutes we'll be over the border, Marc. Then it's a short hop to Point West."

"Roger that. I'm beat. Think I've had enough of this."

"I don't blame you. I'm getting too old for this myself."

"Thanks again for picking me up. It was a risky mission."

"More than I would have imagined. Wasn't the way it was briefed, I will say, but you would do the same for me."

"That's affirmative."

CHAPTER 13—AGENCY BUSINESS

"Marc, you awake?" Jerry Jones asked, as he rapped his knuckles on Marc's door, and opened it partway.

"Go away," Marc grunted sleepily.

"It's almost 9:00 o'clock, and the van is ready to leave for San Jose. Jimmy up at Point West Ops said he had orders that you are to be on it. No ifs, ands or buts. Besides that, you look like you need to get out of here," Jerry said.

"Yeah, I know. It's an enforced R and R, plus I have a scheduled debriefing at the Embassy tomorrow with the Company guys. Then a week at the Cariari Hotel, with some pool time and even a chance to resurrect my golf game. Sounds good."

"I'm going down with you. Have to renew my passport. See you in fifteen," Jerry said.

Jerry, Marc, and the driver were the only occupants of the Toyota van as it sped south on the Interamerican Highway, the driver expertly dodging the numerous potholes. Marc, unable to shake the weariness that permeated his body, felt a deep depression that heightened his fatigue. He dozed fitfully on the four hour trip, haunted by a recurring nightmarish dream. It always ended with the image of Adriana lying face down on the Ometepe Airstrip. The crimson patch of blood on the back of her white blouse doubled in size every second. He would jerk awake, stare dully out the van window for a few minutes, and once more doze off.

"Marc, we're at the Cariari," Jerry said, shaking Marc gently on the shoulder. "I'm staying here too."

The driver handed the two duffle bags to the bellman, and told Marc he would be back at 10:00 a.m. the next morning to take him to the Embassy.

"Let's get checked in, and then have a late lunch," Jerry said.

"Thanks anyway, Jerry. I'm going to do room service and catch up on my sleep. See you in the morning. You going to the Embassy with me?"

"That's affirm. Hasta mañana," Jerry said.

The next morning Marc, in clean pressed khaki's and a white short sleeve sport shirt, met Jerry for breakfast. They were seated at a poolside table, surrounded by the lush greenery of potted palms, broad-leafed elephant ears, bougainvillea, and hibiscus.

"What a change here in the Central Valley, everything always green, and cooler than Guanacaste," Jerry said.

"Yeah. Four thousand foot elevation and a lot more rain here. Said to be one of the world's most perfect climates. An average 72 degrees year-round. Sort of a third-world Hawaii."

"You notice I haven't asked you about your time up in Nicaragua. Quite frankly, Ops told me not to. Let's get the hell out of here. The van should be here by now."

As soon as Marc and Jerry stepped out to the curbside entrance of the Cariari, the Toyota van pulled up. Their driver headed east on the autopista, turning right at Sabana Park, and towards the upscale Rohrmoser area where the Embassy was located.

"Wasn't too many years ago that Sabana Park was San José's airport, and DC-3's were flying in and out, right here on the edge of town," Jerry said.

"Yeah, the old control tower is down the street about a half block from where we turned," Marc replied. "I'm anxious to get this debriefing over. Not my idea of fun."

"Know what you mean," Jerry said.

The van turned onto a narrow side street, and pulled to a stop at the side gate to the Embassy. A guard carefully examined the driver's badge and, nodding to Marc and Jerry, waved them through to the parking area behind the Embassy.

"Well, I'm off to the passport section. I'll check at the Commercial Section office to see if you are debriefed and ready to go back to the Cariari. If not, I'll catch a cab and go on back. I want to get some pool time in," Jerry said.

"I'm sure pool time means looking at the bikinis from a chaise lounge with a cold Imperial in your hand," Marc said.

"Just what I had in mind," Jerry said, with a chuckle.

Marc went upstairs to the Commercial Section, where the agency offices were located. The Station Chief held the title of Chief of the Economic Development Branch, though it was widely known throughout the diplomatic community that this was a thinly disguised cover. A narrow faced gringa, in her early fifties with shoulder length red hair, sat at a desk inside the door. The photo ID tag clipped to a light blue blazer pocket identified her as Margaret Jones. Marc had met Margaret before when he received his in-country briefing and signed a contract that outlined the conditions of his employment. His copy, he had been told, would be held for him in his file in that office. It was the only proof he had of his employment with the

Point West operation. The Agency would never be identified officially as his employer should he be shot down over Nicaragua.

"Hello Marc, nice to see you again. Mr. Blandon will be with you in a minute. Have a seat."

"Thanks, Margaret. How have you been?"

"Fine. But I'm ready for a week or two back in the real world."

At that moment the door behind Margaret opened and a short, stocky man with close cropped salt and pepper hair emerged. Wearing a white long-sleeved shirt, his tie loosened, the CIA Station Chief greeted Marc with a smile, a handshake, and a friendly clap on the back. Marc had only met Francisco briefly when he arrived in-country, and had talked to him for a short time when Francisco visited Point West. Francisco was known to be a decisive, demanding leader, but not an unreasonable one.

"Hello Marc. Come on in, and have a seat on the couch. Coffee?"

"That sounds good. Make it black, please."

"Marc, how are you feeling? I've read the ops and intel reports on your E&E in Nicaragua. That was a harrowing time. You did well."

"Thanks. Just a little tired. I think a week's rest will bring me up to par. The Doc gave me a clean bill of health. Said with a little rest I could be flying again."

Francisco walked over to the table next to his desk. He filled two Styrofoam cups from a vacuum pot, and handed one to Marc. Francisco, though not more than five years older than Marc, had a fatherly approach that played well with the Point West operations and support contingent. A few had mistaken his genteel, deferential Latin air for softness. They later regretted it. Francisco was hard as nails, and tightly controlled a fiery temper. But he was known to be fair. He defended his troops when higher ups decided to cover their own mistakes by putting the blame on the guys on the front lines.

"Marc, I have discussed your status with my superiors in Washington. To be totally frank, my recommendation was that you no longer fly any combat support missions. You have a great deal of information now on Contra assets. People, locations, and tactics," Francisco said, emphasizing each point as he counted them out one finger at a time. Francisco continued.

"You got out of Nicaragua thanks to your own courage and initiative, and also with the help of covert assets that must not be compromised. We can't risk your being shot down and captured a second time."

Marc sat there, waiting for the other shoe to drop. What Francisco said was true. In so many words, he was a liability.

"Marc, we are giving you a new assignment. You will be the new Assistant Operations Officer at Point West, replacing Bud Knight. We are sending him to open up a new support base in the Caribbean. Your flying will be restricted to check-outs of new pilots, offshore supply flights between Ilopango and Point West, and flights down here to San José. How does that sound?"

"Sounds fair enough. I assume the compensation package remains the same?"

"The same. I have to tell you the days of Point West are numbered. The Costa Rican government does not like the attention the press is giving to Point West and the support of the Contra's. They say it is an affront to their sovereignty."

"I find that rather ironic. The Nicaraguan revolutionaries operated for years from San José in the 1970's. They even operated a clandestine radio station right in the middle of San

José.   The government allowed arms to be ferried into Nicaragua from Costa Rica, and it was widely known," Marc said.

"All true. At that time, of course, it was a revolution against Somoza, originally a worthwhile endeavor, and supported across the world. Now many of those who were involved in the revolution are back in San José, opposed to the people's revolution which was hijacked by the Marxist faction. All I'm saying is don't count on this work continuing forever. It's time to do some future planning. If I can help in any way, let me know. Meanwhile, get some rest. You're not expected back at Point West till next Thursday."

Marc took this as a cue that the interview was over.

"Francisco, thanks for the advice and the offer to help. I may just take you up on that." He got up, shook Francisco's hand, and went out to the outer office.

"Marc, here's a note for you," Margaret said. Marc opened the folded sheet of paper, which was a note from Jerry saying he had decided not to wait and would take a cab back to the Cariari Hotel.

Marc left by the back stairway to the parking lot, and found the van and driver waiting.

"Manuel, I want to go to the Aeropuerto Tobias Bolaños in Pavas.

"Si, señor. It is very close," Manuel said.

Within 15 minutes they were at the small general aviation airport that boasted several hangars, a tower, and one asphalt runway. It was, in fact, the only other airport with services in Costa Rica other than Juan Santa María International Airport on the west side of San José. Liberia, the only other sizable airport, had no tower, seldom had fuel, and no hangars. They passed through the airport entrance, and Manuel asked "A donde?"

"Adelante. The Cessna building on the right," Marc answered.

The van pulled up in front of the wide double door to the hangar office and Marc went inside. It was a typical general aviation operations business that offered fuel, aircraft tie downs, maintenance, flight instruction, and often charter and air taxi service. Inside the office there were several lounge chairs, a coffee table with flying magazines scattered on it, and coffee pot. A display counter with a glass face was home for charts, headsets, ball caps, and other paraphernalia for sale. The odor of stale, overheated coffee permeated the air.

"Don Ricardo está aqui?" he asked the young man behind the service counter.

"Sure, down the corridor, first office on the right," he answered, with only a slight trace of an accent.

Marc found the office, and rapped on the partially open door. He could see Ricardo hunched over an oversize wooden desk, piled high with correspondence, manuals, and magazines. A large ashtray made from an engine cylinder was off to one side. Behind Don Ricardo was a plaque on the wall that proclaimed Cessna had awarded a "Best Customer Service" award to the Cessna Central American Regional Office, and its manager, Ricardo Salinas Araya.

"Ricardo, Marc DiAngelo. We met at the Liberia Airport a couple of months ago."

"I remember very well, Marc. You were flying a Maule, and had flown in from that non-existent airfield up on Santa Elena peninsula," Ricardo said with a smile.

"Yes, it was a Maule, a great airplane. I'm in San José for a week, and was nearby at the Embassy this morning. I thought I'd take you up on your invitation to stop by and say hello."

Ricardo was of medium height, sported a wide thick mustache, had slightly bulging eyes, and reminded Marc of a Latin Groucho Marx. Ricardo leaned back in his swivel chair and waved Marc to a seat in front of his desk. Marc guessed that Ricardo probably knew more about general aviation in this part of the world than anyone. That was precisely the reason for his visit.

"Ricardo, my current contract will probably end in a year or less. I have been thinking that a small charter operation out of the Pavas Airport might make sense, if it is feasible, and if I can get the Directorate of Civil Aviation approval. I would need a good used Cessna 206 or similar aircraft, like a Piper Cherokee Six.

Ricardo visibly winced at the word Piper, his competitor, and brought his chair to an upright position.

"As they say, Marc, the handwriting is on the wall. The President is going to have you guys shut down pretty soon. The scuttlebutt is that all the various ranches on the Santa Elena Peninsula will be expropriated, and the entire Peninsula made into a national park. That's how President Arias is going to solve what he feels is a national embarrassment. That's how your operation is going to be shut down, they say. Now to your question, there is very little here in Costa Rica in the way of charter, air taxi, and med evac. I do a little charter work here, and some instruction. There's always room for one more. I know of a good 1965 Cessna 206 for sale at Guatemala City's La Aurora International Airport. It is parked at my Cessna dealership hangar there. It has a recent overhaul, original paint and interior. And it is in good shape. You're looking at about $35,000."

"That's in my ballpark. I've got the week off, as I said. Any chance you'll be going up that way?"

"Well, I always have business there, in fact all over Central America. Sure, I could make a trip up there. Tomorrow I have a meeting with the Directorate of Civil Aviation's Technical Advisory Board. Day after tomorrow?"

"Two things, Ricardo. First, I need to clear leaving the country with my company. Second, if they give approval, it will be on the condition of no over-flight of Nicaragua. So an off shore route is necessary."

"Not a problem. I don't like flying over Nicaragua anyway. I normally fly about 20 miles west of the Nicaraguan Pacific coastline till I get abeam the middle of the Bay of Fonseca, then head to Guatemala City."

"I'll give you a call this afternoon, after I get the flight cleared," Marc said.

Two days later Marc returned to the Pavas Airport. His apprehension that he would not be permitted to fly out of Costa Rica was unfounded. Margaret had called him to relay Francisco's approval. At the Pavas Airport the morning of departure, he found Ricardo in the Airport Operations Office filling out an ICAO flight plan.

"All set, amigo?" Ricardo asked, looking up from the paperwork.

"You bet. I'm already getting a little bored just sitting around."

"The weather is CAVU as they say - clear and visibility unlimited. At Guatemala City the normal early morning fog is burning off. Visibility is forecast to be 15 miles by landing time there. We're ready to file the flight plan. I've already pre-flighted the 210, and cleared customs for both of us. You are listed as a pilot on the flight plan, so you won't need a departure stamp on your passport from Migración."

The Cessna 210 departed Pavas on Runway 9 for the two hour flight to Guatemala City. Once on the ground, they taxied to the Cessna hangar, cleared immigration at the nearby office, and returned to the hangar

"There she is," Ricardo said, pointing to the Cessna 206 that they had parked next to.

"It looks good, Ricardo. I'd like to go up with you on a test flight."

"We can do that. Let's go into the hangar office."

They walked across the ramp and through open hangar doors into a small office on the south side.

"Emilio, this is Marc. He is here to look at the 206."

"Mucho gusto, Señor Marc," Emilio said.

"A pleasure," Marc responded.

"Emilio, Marc is going to take a test hop in a Cessna 206," Ricardo said. "It's really a pre-purchase check of the aircraft," Marc added. "If I like its condition and the price, then consider it sold."

"Marc, shall we make the test flight right now?" Ricardo asked.

"Yes. Tell me more about the plane. I also want to look over the maintenance log books."

"It was manufactured in 1965. It has been in Guatemala two years. A Guatemalan businessman in the city has a large cotton farm 30 miles east of here. He bought the plane in Phoenix and has been using it to go back and forth from the city to the cotton farm. It's about an "8" in and out. It has 1,750 hours on the engine and airframe. He's asking $31,500. If you like it, you can write a stateside check to my company. We have a Miami bank account that we use for international transactions."

"I like the fact that it was an Arizona airplane. There is much less chance of corrosion and deterioration due to weather. Let's go ahead and do the test flight."

By the time Marc, in the left seat, had taken off and flown the Cessna for10 minutes, he knew he was going to buy it. It handled beautifully, the engine was smooth, and the condition of the interior and exterior was better than average for its age. He estimated it was $5,000 less than it would be in the States. They landed after 45 minutes of flight, disembarked, and Marc and Ricardo shook hands on the deal.

"I'll have it fueled and ready to go, Marc. Also, I'll take care of the change in registration from Guatemala to Costa Rica."

"Sounds great," Marc said, beaming at the thought of his new acquisition. With six seats and a large load bearing capacity, the 206 would be perfect for tourist charter and air taxi operations. After refueling and a weather check, Marc departed the Guatemala City La Aurora Airport for the Pavas Airport at San José. He was elated. The 206 seemed even more responsive and the engine quieter and smoother. His thoughts turned to the future, a very satisfying outlook of having his own little one airplane airline, every pilot's dream. His Air Force pension would allow him to follow the dream without the pressure that a small business might otherwise generate. Off to the left he saw the twin peaks of Ometepe Island, Concepcion and Maderas, and suddenly felt a twinge of nostalgia and sadness. His thoughts turned to Adriana, so young, so beautiful, with a zest for life that had enveloped him in their short time together. Beyond Ometepe he could see the hills of Chontales, and he wondered if Ellen was still there. He shook himself back to the business of flying, and called Coco Control, which directed Costa Rican airspace, with an initial position report.

CHAPTER 14–RESCUE AT THE RIO SAN JUAN

Rodrigo Morales, the "handler" for the Contra re-supply flights, pulled up in front of the flight crew safe house in San Salvador at 4:00 a.m. in his Chevy Suburban. The lights in the house were ablaze, telling him that pilots Bill and Gerry, and the cargo kicker Vince were up and getting ready.

The door was unlocked, and Rodrigo announced his presence with a loud "Hurry up, guys." He sat down on the sofa in the living room. Rodrigo, a compact muscled Latin with a full mustache man and a receding hairline with specks of gray, was naturally impatient. Sitting and waiting for any period of time was uncomfortable. The fidgeting and shifting about on the sofa started almost immediately. Carmen, the cook, brought him a cup of strong Salvadoran coffee. "Deysayuno?" She asked. Rodrigo declined. He hoped the three man crew, who would meet their Nicaraguan communications specialist at the airport, would hurry through the American-style breakfast Carmen was preparing.

Rodrigo was uneasy. Daylight drops were dangerous. Today's mission was to be a re-supply drop just 20 miles north of San Carlos on the southern end of Lake Nicaragua. Roving teams of Sandinista anti-aircraft patrols with heat-seeking anti-aircraft missiles made these missions particularly dangerous. The daylight drops required the re-supply aircraft to fly low to visually spot the Contra drop zone. Increasing their vulnerability, it was often necessary to cross and re-cross the same terrain to find the drop zone. The Sandinista patrols had the advantage of seeing the aircraft in the daylight and being able to immediately identify it as the enemy.

Rodrigo had argued with the higher-ups in Tegucigalpa. Danger was neither foreign nor distasteful to Rodrigo. He had stormed ashore in 1961 at the Bay of Pigs, leading a company of his fellow Cuban exiles of Brigade 2506. Pinned down on the beach, they waited in vain for the promised air support that never came. After serving time in jail in Cuba, he made his way to the States. He was offered a commission in the United States Army, as were many of his fellow Brigade 2506 officers. He served four years, and then went to work for the CIA. The aircrews he handled in San Salvador, flying out of Ilopango in contracted Southern Air Transport aircraft were well aware that Rodrigo was a legend in his own right. An avowed and hardened anti-communist, he had participated in the capture and interrogation of Che Guevara in Bolivia.

No, Rodrigo thought, sipping his coffee as the crew ate their breakfast in the dining room; this mission is not to my liking.

Rodrigo drove the crew to the Ilopango Airport and right out onto the flight line to the waiting C-123. The loading crew had finished strapping down the pallets and stood near the lowered aft ramp. Bill headed for the flight deck, Jerry began the co-pilot's exterior walk-around, and Vince strode up the loading ramp and began checking all tie-down straps and parachute attachments. Rodrigo went up on the flight deck and sat down in the co-pilot's seat.

"Bill, just to double check, your flight plan takes you off the coasts of El Salvador and Nicaragua till you get abeam Costa Rica's Santa Elena Peninsula and Point West. Right now you're loaded with 9,500 pounds of assault rifles, grenade launchers, ammunition, and boots. At point West you'll pick up 500 pounds of medical supplies. You're to be over the drop zone at 12:30 p.m. The maps with route coordinates and your discrete radio frequencies are in the mission folder. Good luck."

In the back of the C-123, Vince slipped on his parachute, the only crew member that used one; in fact, the only crew member that had one. He had paid for it himself.

Near the village of El Tule, 20 miles from San Carlos, the 10 man Sandinista anti-aircraft patrol assigned to the Sandinista 5th Military Region was resting. Some were cooking bananas and rice, others were dozing. The sound of an aircraft drew them to their feet. Binoculars came out, and within seconds they were able to identify the low flying C-123 as an enemy aircraft. A 19 year old conscript raised a Soviet-made heat-seeking SAM-7 to his shoulder and fired.

"Operations, DiAngelo," Marc answered on the radio telephone in the Operations shack at Point West. The date on the office calendar was October 6, 1986, a date that would be remembered as the beginning of the end for Point West.

"Marc, this is Francisco at the Embassy. It has just been confirmed that the missing C-123 was shot down yesterday at 12:45 p.m. in southeastern Nicaragua. One of the crew members has been captured. They were out of Ilopango but I believe re-supplied at Point West. Is that correct?"

"Yes, Francisco. They staged out of here. Another damned daylight mission. I knew we were going to get bitten in the ass eventually."

"Yeah, I know. They were re-supplying one of the Task Force units that have been in a continual firefight for a month with the EPS Fifth Irregular Battalion. There were two previous night re-supply attempts but they couldn't identify the drop zone. The guys were out of ammunition and living on monkey meat. It was a risk, and turned out to be costly. Not only in terms of men and machines, but also bad publicity. Just the kind our Costa Rica President Oscar Arias will capitalize on. It gives him more ammo to expropriate the land you're sitting on up there."

"I understand, Francisco. Was there something you wanted us to do up here?"

"Just you, Marc. Specifically you. I heard your Cessna is sitting on the ramp at the Liberia Airport right now."

"Fernando, I'd not want to try to keep a secret from you. You have eyes and ears everywhere. Yes, I flew it up here last week. I usually keep it in the hangar at the Pavas Airport."

"Marc, here's the deal. We have heard from a source that one, two, or all three of the other crew members may have survived the crash and are attempting to get to the Costa Rican border. The "123" was shot down by a Sam-7 near the village of El Tule, which is 20 miles from the border town of San Carlos. The known surviving crewmember was the kicker, who had a chute on and bailed out the rear cargo door. The two pilots and the radioman may have survived the crash. I have sent an infiltration team to Los Chiles, across the Río San Juan from San Carlos. I would like you to fly your Cessna over to Los Chiles. We will know in a day or two if there are surviving crew members on the run south to the river. If the team finds any of the crew members, they will bring them across the river to Los Chiles. You are to fly them direct to San José for debriefing. We need to know what records and what cargo were destroyed in the crash. By the way, this is a request. It is your airplane. We don't dare use one of the Maules. That would arouse certain suspicion."

"I can do it, Fernando. But I don't want to jeopardize my Costa Rican aircraft registration. If you will keep me from any problems in that area, I'll do it."

"You won't have any problem. I guarantee it. We do a lot for the Directorate of Civil Aviation. We will just consider it your time off and a chance to fly around the country as a tourist. That's your story."

"All right, I understand. When do you want me there?"

"Today if the weather is okay."

"Our PIREPS - pilot reports that is - show some broken cumulus clouds east over the cordillera. I don't have any reports further east of the mountain range."

"I'll call Los Chiles and, if it looks bad weather-wise, I'll call you back. Otherwise, consider it okay"

"Got it. I'll be on my way in a couple of hours. I've got back-up here. I'll stop by the crew house in Liberia on the way to the airport and pickup clothes for a couple of nights. I'll call my flight plan in from there."

"Call me on a land line when you get to Los Chiles. Your contact there is Alvarado Medina. Ex-Marine. He will be at the Hospedaje Carolina."

Marc drove to Liberia, filed his flight plan over the phone, packed a small knapsack and stuck his .25 automatic in as an afterthought. He drove to the Liberia Airport, 15 minutes away. The Cessna 206 was tied down in the grass to portable screw-type anchors he carried in the plane. He worked those out of the turf, made a hurried preflight, started the engine, taxied, and took off. Stiff trade winds were blowing straight down the runway. Marc trimmed the nose to a high angle of attack, maintaining a best climb speed of 90 knots in order to cross the mountain range east of Liberia. He crossed the range in the gap between the Miravalles Volcano and the Rincón de La Vieja Volcano, dodging cumulus clouds. The border town of Upala came into view within minutes. He scanned the horizon for Los Chiles, which was only 20 miles further East in a direct line.

Landing at Los Chiles, Marc parked in front of the Civil Guard station, a small wooden shack flying the red, white, and blue striped Costa Rican flag. He spoke to the two guards there, who appeared to be half asleep and only mildly interested in a gringo arriving in his own airplane at this out-of-the-way outpost. They said they would watch over the Cessna 206. Marc knew how to convey the promise of a propina or tip when he returned without being so crude as to be explicit. It was an art one learned in Latin countries. There were no taxis at Los Chiles, so Marc swung his knapsack over his shoulder and began a hike into town, which was less than a quarter of a kilometer. He found the Hospedaje Carolina in the center of town, on the east side of the little town park. The hospedaje was a Spartan affair, a one story wooden building with three tables with chairs out in front on the sidewalk. Marc walked inside to a large, dark room that served as a bar and restaurant. The only occupant was a skinny brown dog asleep under a table. Mark followed a corridor along the right side of the room which opened to an office area bordered by a small interior garden. A heavy set young man sat at a desk reading a newspaper. Behind him was a varnished board mounted on the wall with a dozen or so keys hanging on nails. A gray and white cat slept on the old wooden desk curled up next to a dust covered hand-crank calculator.

"Hola," Marc said.

"Hola," the young man answered. He did not look up from the newspaper.

"Necesito una habitación. Está Señor Alvarado Medina aqui?" Marc wasn't sure asking for a room and Alvarado Medina would tear the young man away from his paper.

"Firma y numero de su cédula o pasaporte," the young man said, slowly putting the paper down. He handed a ledger book to Marc. Marc signed his name and entered his passport number, and handed the ledger back to the young man, brushing the side of the cat's head with a corner of the ledger. It opened its eyes, hissed at Marc, and went back to sleep. Just as lazy as his owner, Marc decided. The clerk wrote #7 next to Marc's name in the ledger, and handed Marc the room key without comment.

"Señor Medina?" Marc asked again.

"Numero ocho," the young man answered. He immediately opened the newspaper and leaned back in his chair. Marc walked to Room 8, down the corridor past the office, and knocked.

"Adelante, Señor DiAngelo."

Marc opened the door, and found a shirtless man sitting at a table with a portable VHF transmitter/receiver on it. He was all muscle, in his late forties or early fifties, and clean shaven, including his head. Tattoos adorned both upper arms and forearms. On his left arm was the U.S. Marines' emblem with "Semper Fi" written below. Despite his name, Medina appeared to be light skinned but heavily tanned. Medina set the paperback down that he was reading.

"DiAngelo, have a seat," he said, motioning Marc to the bed, the only other piece of furniture in the room.

"Thanks, Medina," Marc said, deciding they were going to be on a last name basis like the detectives on popular TV programs.

"Heard about your travels in Nicaragua. Pretty hairy."

"Yeah, for sure. I had a lot of help getting out. I assume you're working out of San José?"

"Only for the time being, it's temporary duty. I've been an advisor to the Salvadoran government on the FMLN insurgency there. The leftists receive their weapons and ammunition from Nicaragua and from Panama, Venezuela, and Cuba, using Nicaragua as a transit route. I was in San José working on the arms smuggling network, which includes Costa Rica, when Francisco asked me to bring the infiltration team up here and honcho the search for the C-123 crew. I'm in contact with the team by radio."

"What do you hear from your guys?" Marc asked.

"Last night they traveled up the Río Medio Queso on the east side of town to the Río San Juan. The Río Frio to the west of town might be faster, as it is a wider river, but it is well guarded by the Sandinistas where it enters Lake Nicaragua and the Río San Juan at San Carlos. The Río Medio Queso enters the Río San Juan about halfway between San Carlos and El Castillo , and is a shorter route to the mouth of the Río Sábalos. El Castillo is the old Spanish fort that was built to keep the pirate ships from entering Lake Nicaragua from the Caribbean. Then the team traveled down river to the Río Sábalos, and went up that river about a kilometer and a half. That's pretty close to the crash site."

"Any contact since then?"

"I've had several radio calls, the last one about an hour ago. They expect a lot of Sandinista activity around the crash area. They've had one radio contact. It appears to be one of the USAF

Survival Radios that uses the emergency frequency 121.5, but it was garbled. They think it could be one of the crew." As if on cue, a call came over the radio.

"Red Dog, Red Dog, this is Pancho, over." The call was weak and slightly garbled.

Medina grabbed the mike. "Roger, Pancho, this is Red Dog, go ahead."

"Red Dog, we estimate two kilometers from the target."

"Pancho, avoid the immediate target area. It will be heavily guarded. Make your search south, continue to monitor frequency 121.5. Have you received any more calls on 121.5?"

"That's affirmative. We have received two calls within the last 20 minutes, still not good reception. They were unreadable."

"Keep me informed. Red Dog out."

"Pancho out."

"What is the extraction plan for the team?" Marc asked Medina.

"They'll return the same route. Down the Río Sábalos to the Río San Juan, west to the Río Medio Queso, then up the river to Los Chiles. Should be no more than an hour and a half, except it will be dark by the time they get to Río Sábalos, and then they'll have to navigate by flashlight.

A heavy knock on the door brought Medina to his feet and he strode to the door. When Medina opened the door, the hotel clerk was about to pound it once more with his ham-like fist.

"Señor, teléfono," the clerk said.

"Be back in a minute, DiAngelo. Monitor the radio." Marc suppressed the urge to reply "Aye Aye Sir," and moved over to Medina's chair. He picked up Medina's book and turned it over to the front cover. Marc raised his eyebrows in surprise. It was titled *The Selected Tales and Sketches of Nathaniel Hawthorne*. At this moment the radio crackled again.

"Red Dog, Red Dog, Pancho here, over." Marc picked up the mike and keyed the side transmit button.

"Go ahead, Pancho."

"We're getting a strong signal on 121.5, and some garbled transmission. Our direction finder shows it northwest of us. We are in heavy cover, proceeding in that direction."

At this moment, Medina rushed into the room.

"What was that?" he asked.

"The insertion team has a strong 121.5 signal and a garbled transmission which the DF shows is to their northwest. They're heading that way."

"Good God," Medina said, grabbing the mike.

"Pancho, Pancho, this is Red Dog! Abort! Abort your mission! It has been confirmed that the two pilots and the radioman are dead and the kicker taken prisoner. The 121.5 signal is a trap. I repeat, abort. Acknowledge, Pancho."

"Pancho understands abort. We're on our way back."

"That was Francisco on the phone. The loadmaster, a kicker as you guys call them, has been captured and is already singing like a bird. He apparently made no attempt to escape south to the river or to destroy any of the documents at the crash site. The Sandinistas just struck a PR bonanza. The two CIA pilots and the Nicaraguan radioman were killed in the crash. That's based on communications intercepts. It looks to me like the Sandinistas have one of the survival kit radios and are trying to draw any rescuers, either airborne or on the ground, into a trap. We'll have to keep glued to this radio till our guys get back. I'm thirsty. I'll buy cokes if you go get them."

"It's a deal," Marc said, and walked to the bar at the front of the hospedaje.

When he returned, he handed one to Medina and sat down on the bed.

"I see you're reading Hawthorne. It's not what I would expect an ex-Marine to be reading."

"I was an English Lit. major in college. It's right up my alley."

"Well, there you go. One should never make quick judgments," Marc said.

"What do you read, DiAngelo?"

"Just about every book Clive Cussler has written."

"He's a good writer. Easy and entertaining."

"I'm going to put my knapsack in my room and lie down. I'll be back in a few minutes."

"Not a problem. I'll be monitoring for periodic reports as the team makes its way back here."

Marc unpacked the knapsack. There was no closet, just a couple of rusted hangars on a nail. Like Medina's room, the window was screened but there was no glass in the widows. Shutters that swung to the inside of the room were for protection against the rain. A small floor fan sat in one corner. Marc turned it on and lay down on the cot-like bed, fully clothed. He was awakened from a deep sleep by Medina's call from the doorway.

"DiAngelo, we got a problem. You better come now." Medina turned and hurried back to his room.

"What's up?" Marc asked as walked into Medina's room.

"Our guys either stumbled on a Sandy patrol or the patrol was looking for them. It was our six to their fifteen they estimate, but our guys got the first shot. They figure they killed or wounded at least half. One of ours got hit in the arm. They're double-timing it back to the boat."

Medina got up from the chair and began pacing the floor. "Shit! Shit!" he said shaking his head. "I didn't feel right about this mission. It was thrown together too fast with almost no intell. About as dumb as the resupply flight during daylight hours. We'll just have to sit and wait. Were you in Vietnam, DiAngelo?"

"Yep. I was with Special Ops flying C-47 gunships. How about you?"

"I was in Laos, with a MACV team. We were training the Montagnard hill people on guerilla tactics."

"How long were you there?"

"I did two tours consecutively. Would have done three if the whole shooting match hadn't fallen apart. Where were you stationed? What kind of action?"

"I was at Da Nang. The most action, in terms of intensity, was during the siege of Khe Sanh. We were flying day and night. Those Marines on the ground were just holding on by their fingernails. The North Vietnamese finally took so many losses they gave up."

"Yeah, that was a tough one. I've seen the gunships in action. I wouldn't want to be on the receiving end of those Gatling guns." Medina was interrupted by the radio.

"Red Dog, Pancho here. We're aboard, will hit the big river in about 15 minutes."

"Red Dog copies. I'll meet you at the entrance to our river," Medina said, intentionally omitting the use of the geographical name.

"Pancho copies. Our man that was hit in the arm was also hit in the stomach. He's not doing well."

"Okay Pancho. Let's get him back here."

Medina set the mike down and looked at Marc. "DiAngelo, let's go. We have a spare river boat at the dock. I had rented two so that there would be a back-up in case of engine problems. We'll go down to the Río San Juan to meet them. I'll take along a hand-held VHF radio. Here," he said, taking a small bottle of mosquito repellent out of an olive green gym bag and throwing it to Marc. "The mosquitoes are going to be fierce." Then Medina unwrapped an M-16 from its canvas cover, brought out a bag of ammunition clips from the gym bag, and checked the weapon's mechanism.

Marc walked back to his room, slathered mosquito repellent on his arms, face, neck and ankles, and put on a long sleeve khaki shirt. He slipped the .25 automatic into his pants pocket, and put on a floppy fatigue hat. He grabbed a flashlight from his bag and left, locking the door. He hoped Medina was as savvy as he said he was. Marc followed Medina to a newer black Toyota pickup truck parked on the side of the hospedaje. The small dock on the Río Medio Queso was only a kilometer on the other side of the nearby town airstrip, and they were there in minutes. Medina pulled up to the side of a small dock, guarded by an elderly watchman. Two blue Toyota trucks were parked nearby. Medina exchanged words with the watchman at the dock, who was armed with an old single shot 12 gauge visible-hammer shotgun.

The boat was the type commonly used on the rivers. It was about 20 feet long; narrow in beam, with enough seats for 10 passengers. Medina fired up the outboard and Marc positioned himself at the bow with his flashlight. The Río Medio Queso was only 30 feet wide, but was a shorter route to the Río San Juan that the Río Frio on the west side of Los Chiles. The river boat motored slowly away from the dock, and Marc swung his flashlight back and forth to highlight the banks of the river. Occasionally there would be the sound of a large splash as a caiman left the river bank for the safety of the turbid water.

An urgent call came over the VHF radio. "Red Dog, Red Dog. Pancho taking fire at the entry to Río San Juan. We're holding back about 500 meters."

"Okay Pancho, hold on. The cavalry is on its way," Medina answered over the radio. Marc grimaced as he considered the cavalry's firepower, the M-16 and his mini-automatic.

"About time one of you flyboys got a chance to see how the other half lives," Medina yelled to Marc, almost gleefully. He gunned the engine abruptly, nearly causing Marc to fall backward into the boat. Marc kept the flashlight on the water ahead, and Medina increased the throttle even more.

"When we planned the mission, it was seven and a half kilometers or five miles to the Río San Juan. That will take 15 minutes," Medina yelled. "Then it's another 20 kilometers or 12 miles down the Río San Juan to the mouth of the Río Sábalos. That's another thirty minutes. So the boys need to hold on for another 45 minutes."

Marc was still puzzled as to how they were going to make a difference. Medina may have read his mind.

"DiAngelo, the element of surprise is ours. There's less than a quarter moon now. The Sandinistas on shore at the river junction will have no idea another boat will be coming down the river. We'll draw their fire, and the infiltration team can get out of there."

"Great," Marc said. "I always wanted to be a diversionary target."

Medina laughed, obviously relishing the opportunity for combat.

"Well, that's what you're going to be."

In a few minutes they entered the broad Río San Juan, its current stronger than the Río Medio Queso. Medina steered the boat into the middle of the river and they headed downstream to where the Río Sabalos flows from the north into the Río San Juan.

"Since we're going with the current, we'll beat that thirty minutes a bit. Come back and take the steering wheel. I want to get the M-16 ready. In fact, since I've got the firepower, you might as well be Captain. I'll be the gunner in the bow. Now you can push that damned throttle all the way forward."

The boat was not built to plane, but the front of the boat came well out of the water even with Medina perched forward. They cruised down river, the Honda four-cycle outboard running smoothly and quietly. Ten minutes later, Medina motioned for Marc to pull the throttle back to idle. Marc thought Medina had spied a log or some other debris in the river ahead. But then he heard it; the sound of intermittent gun fire not too far down river. Medina motioned for Marc to advance the throttle, and the boat regained its speed. They continued on for another ten minutes, and once again Medina motioned for Marc to pull the power back. He unclipped the transceiver from his belt and called the infiltration team.

"Pancho, Red Dog over."

"Go ahead, Red Dog."

"We're about 5 minutes away. What's your situation?"

We've moved back another 500 meters upriver. The bad guys are on the east side of the river mouth. They know they've got us bottled up. We've already had two RPG's fired at us."

"Pancho, be ready to make a run for it in about five minutes."

"Okay Red Dog. We're ready."

"DiAngelo, give it about half throttle. We're pretty close now. There's enough light that we'll be able to see them on the far bank. If we hug the southern river bank the Sandys will have trouble seeing us on this side of the river. When they see my muzzle flash, they'll return fire to that location. So when I fire, be ready to move the boat forward a hundred feet or so."

"Aye Aye," Marc answered.

Within a few more minutes the boat came around a gentle bend. On the east bank of the Río Sábalos where it empties into the Río San Juan they could see muzzle flashes. The rapid fire of an M-16 answered the Sandinista fire.

"DiAngelo, slow it down a bit, slide closer to the right and get as close to the bank as you safely can." Now Marc and Medina were abeam the point from where the Sandinistas were firing.

"Power off," Medina whispered to Marc. "I don't want to go much further downstream or my fire will angle back into our other boat when they make their dash down to the San Juan."

The boat was drifting slowly. Medina picked up the microphone and told the team he was ready to fire, and to be ready to make their escape. He raised the M-16, and fired on full automatic, emptying the clip.

"Move!" he said to Marc. Marc gave the engine enough throttle to move it quickly another 100 feet downstream. For a moment there was no response, and then a hail of AK-47 fire erupted from the opposite bank hitting the water and shoreline where they had been. Medina inserted another clip. He fired a full round of tracers. Impressive, Marc thought, and knew it pinpointed their boat's location to the Sandinista gunners. Marc immediately moved the throttle forward and the boat moved further downstream.

"Turn it around now, a 180," Medina ordered. Marc did as directed. Medina fired another clip in two and three second bursts.

"Back up, DiAngelo. I think we've got their attention. It looks like every sorry one of them is firing at us now. Our guys came down the river; I could see their muzzle flashes too. Got 'em confused. Like I said, surprise is our biggest advantage."

"Red Dog, Red Dog, this is Pancho. We're in the clear, we're heading up river. We took some hits, we have one more wounded."

"Red Dog copies. We'll be right behind you. Let's go," Medina said. As they passed abeam the Sandinistas, Mark took out his .25 automatic and emptied it in the general area of the Sandinista position on the far side of the river.

Medina turned around. "What in God's name are you doing?"

"Medina, I spent a long time being chased by the Sandinistas without even firing a shot. I think I got one."

"Yah, sure, DiAngelo. Put that toy away and let's get the hell out of here."

The infiltrators' boat had accelerated rapidly, propelled by two Honda 125's, but with a heavier load, its top speed was about the same as the boat following it. There was no conversation now, only the urgency to get back to the dock on the Río Medio Queso. When they arrived at the dock and tied up behind the lead boat, four members of the infiltration team, dressed in dark jungle camouflage suits and hats, faces and hands darkened black with face paint, were lifting the more seriously wounded man out of the boat. One hundred feet from the dock were the two parked dark blue Toyota crew cab trucks. The other two team members were loading equipment and weapons into them. Medina walked over to the group carrying the wounded man, spoke briefly, and returned.

"DiAngelo, we've got to get our wounded men out immediately to San José. Our medical guy has the wounds patched up as much as possible. Los Chiles won't have the medical facilities to deal with their injuries. It's up to you to get them to San José tonight. One is bad off. The other has a clean wound in the thigh."

"Medina, there are no runway lights at the Los Chiles Airport. I'm going to need some kind of artificial lights."

"Okay, I'll take care of that. We have spare gas cans in the trucks that we drove up from San José. We can scrounge some scrap wood or brush, and light up several fires alongside the runway. Let's get going."

"All I need is fires along one side of the runway, the last one marking the end of the runway. I assume you will send your medic with me. We can put both wounded in my plane, the most serious in the third row of seats, the one with the thigh wound in the right front seat next to me, and the medic in the middle row. That'll take care of my weight and balance. Don't forget to pick up my things in the room at the hospedaje and bring them down with you."

At the airport the Cessna 206 was loaded as Marc directed, and fires were lit alongside the north side of the runway. Marc started the engine, taxied to the end of the runway using his taxi lights to guide the way. He accelerated the engine to 2000 RPM with the brakes on, checking the engine oil pressure and cylinder head temperature until both were near the "green" arc on their respective dials, then advanced the throttles to maximum manifold pressure and rolled down the runway. Once airborne, he found it necessary to fly using total reference to his flight instruments. Though the sky was clear of clouds and full of millions of stars and a bit of moonlight, there were almost no ground lights to provide a reference to the horizon.

He arrived at the Pavas Airport after 10:00 p.m. The tower closed at 9:00 p.m., and Marc used the alternate procedure available to pilots to activate the runway lights by clicking the transmitter button three times on the tower frequency of 118.1.

On final approach to runway 9, Marc could see an ambulance waiting near his hangar, its red light flashing. Marc landed, taxied to the door of his hangar, and the ambulance and another car pulled up next to the Cessna as he shut the engine down. Francisco walked up and opened the airplane door.

"I got the call from Medina. How's the guy with the stomach wound?"

"I don't know, Francisco, but he didn't look good when we loaded him on the airplane. Better ask the team's medic. The one with the thigh wound appears to be in good shape, took the flight well."

With difficulty the two ambulance EMTs and the team medic unloaded the seriously wounded team member from the rear seat of the 206. He appeared unconscious. After speaking to the ambulance crew, Francisco returned to Marc, who was opening the hangar doors.

"Marc, the one in back didn't survive."

"Damn," was all Marc could say.

"Marc, what you did for me was, as they say, above and beyond. I owe you. Things have changed rapidly since the C-123 was shot down. I guess you could say we're dealing with almost hourly political developments. Those in our Congress opposed to helping the Democratic Resistance Forces are using this incident. Plus, there's new information that funding of the Contras was done illegally through the sale of weapon systems to Iran. Congress may cut all support to the Contras. My advice to you is to be prepared to have your contract terminated. Looks like your Aguila or Eagle Aviation is going to be a full time job for you from now on. I'll use what contacts I have to get you some charter business."

"I appreciate that, Fernando. I knew the day was coming and, in fact, I'm ready for a change."

"U.S. Embassy switchboard. How may I direct your call?"

"Señor Morales in San Salvador for Mr. Blandon. We need a secure line please."

"One moment please."

"Francisco Blandon here."

"Hello my friend. This is your old buddy Rodrigo."

"It's been a while Rodrigo. What's up?"

"I wanted to bring you up-to-date on our Swan Island venture. How much do you know?"

"I've heard a few things, Rodrigo. Actually, I know the Island. It's 120 miles off the coast of Honduras, and no more than about four square miles. I was involved in setting up Radio Swan there before our fiasco at the Bay of Pigs. I'm sure you remember. Our propaganda broadcasts to Cuba were laced with coded messages. But to tell you the truth, I'm out of the loop on the new Swan Island program."

"Well, we both know Point West will be out of business soon. My operation here at Ilopango will be closed right after that. Congressional approval last month of the additional $100 million gives us another couple of years to finish the job. With the Iran-Contra scandal breaking loose, I believe it probably is the last appropriation we will see."

"I agree"

"We will use the 3,500 foot runway at Swan Island. The plan is to shift all Ilopango, Point West, and some Honduran air re-supply to Swan Island. Almost all aircraft will move to Swan Island. We've already hired a dozen Rhodesian contract pilots. More than 100 Nicaraguans will live on the Island. They will unload CIA freighters, package the drops, and load the airplanes. We are training some Contras on the Island. Some are receiving specialized training in the handling and firing of the Red-Eye anti-aircraft missile. We have a Red-Eye simulator there, and the training is going well."

"I'm glad to hear that. Every time one of those 29 pound suckers is fired, it's another $20,000."

"Yeah, I know. With the new funding we have at the moment we are getting new uniforms, weapons, and even computerized field radios. The plans are for the Contras to move out of their Honduran base camps and break up into small fighting units. We should have 10,000 to 20,000 fighting throughout Nicaragua in a year.

"I like the plan. Somehow I don't think you called me just to bring me up-to-date."

"You're right. We need an experienced Air Operations Chief at Swan Island. Your Marc DiAngelo seems to be well thought of. Would you recommend him for the job?"

"He just got back from our aborted rescue attempt at the Río San Juan. You couldn't do any better than DiAngelo. He and I had a few discussions since the closure of Point West became evident. He has set up a single airplane charter operation out of San José. Both you and I know the Swan Island operation probably won't last more than a couple of years. Marc's earned his keep. I'm even sending him off with a bonus. We should let him go ahead with his plans here."

Well, I guess you're right. He's paid his dues. Good talking to you."

"Likewise."

CHAPTER 15–RETURN TO NICARAGUA

It was the beginning of a warm March day in 1990 for the normally temperate San José. The telephone rang twice before Marc could get to his desk. He put his cup of coffee down on the corner of his desk, picked up the phone and announced "Aguila Aviation."

"Marc, this is Ricardo. Did you get the 100 hour inspection on the Cessna 206 completed yesterday?"

"Sure did, Ricardo. By early afternoon, in fact. The only squawk was worn brake pads and those were replaced. The Emergency Locator Transmitter battery had to be changed, but that's standard with the two year life limitation. All of the cylinder compression checks were in the 70's. So no unpleasant surprises."

"You know, with Violeta Chamorro winning the presidential election in Nicaragua, there are quite a few Nicaraguans living in Costa Rica who want to go to Managua and sample the political climate change. Many of the Nicaraguan expatriates who live here were businessmen, and, with the Sandinista's Daniel Ortega losing the presidential election, they're keen on returning to re-establish the democratic market economy there.

I have flights scheduled to Managua the next three days, and have another party of three who want to go tomorrow. Can you help me out?"

"You bet. I've got nothing scheduled for a week. It's sort of slow right now. What time will they be here?"

"Hold on a minute, Marc," Ricardo said. Within 30 seconds he was back on the phone. "I told them to be at your office at 7:30 a.m. for an 8:00 a.m. takeoff. Okay with you?"

"That'll work for me, Ricardo. Thanks for the business."

"Anytime amigo. Bye."

Marc hung up the phone and leaned back in his chair. The prospect of returning to Nicaragua was not unpleasant. He was surprised that a strong feeling of anticipation arose in his chest.

The next morning three Nicaraguan men arrived at the office and introduced themselves. All were political exiles, they and their families now living in Costa Rica. Haroldo Mendez was a business owner whose cotton gin operation in Chinandega was one of the first businesses to be expropriated in 1980. Orlando Martinez had a coffee finca near Jinotega that was expropriated and placed into a coffee cooperative. Carlos Montoya was more the political refugee than victim of the change to a communist controlled economy. Carlos had been a comandante hero in the mountains of Nueva Segovia during the revolution against Somoza. He had resisted the Marxist-Leninist shift adopted by the Sandinista ruling junta, and organized a protest group. One day he had been told by a cousin who was in State Internal Security that his name was on a list of dissenters that were to be dealt with. Carlos and his family had driven to the Costa Rica border that same day.

Haroldo had been a private pilot in Nicaragua, and asked to sit in the right seat. The other two seemed a bit nervous. In his short passenger briefing, Marc pointed out the barf bags in the seat pockets facing them.

In 45 minutes they were over Liberia. Coco Control passed him to Sandino Control as he neared the Costa Rican border town of La Cruz. After that frequency change, he called and received a response in perfect English without a trace of an accent.

"Cessna 8163 Tango, we have you in radar contact. Squawk 5333 and ident."

Marc pushed the "ident" button on the transponder.

"Cessna 8163 Tango, you are 53 miles south of Sandino International Airport. You are cleared direct at pilot's discretion. Expect a right base to Runway nine."

"Cessna 8163 Tango, roger," Marc replied.

"Haroldo, this is just like the old days, isn't it?"

"Yes. It seems so. It is hard to erase the memory of Nicaragua as a police state. I am glad to be going home, but there is a little fear. You know that Violeta had to agree to let Humberto Ortega, Daniel's brother, remain head of the Ministry of Defense. The Sandinistas remain in control of the police and the judiciary as well. This will change, but not all at once, and Violeta knows it.

Marc turned to tell Orlando and Carlos, who did not have head phones that they would be landing soon. With Lake Nicaragua on the right side as a huge landmark, he was quite sure they already knew. Masaya Volcano, smoking as always, was dead on the nose. The airport lay 15 miles beyond that.

Sandino Control turned Marc over to Sandino Tower. There was no other traffic reported. They landed and parked next to the hangar of the old Managua Aero Club, now deserted. A military jeep, followed by a mid-sixties blue Ford station wagon, came out to greet them as Marc shut down the engine. Their passports were examined, and Marc's 206 received scant attention after he showed a copy of the Aguila Aviation corporation papers.

The three Nicaraguans were met inside the terminal by family members who had stayed in Nicaragua. Marc found his passport and aircraft documents once again scrutinized, and then he was released to the street side of the terminal, where he hired a cab. Ricardo's office had made reservations for him at the Inter-Continental, the best hotel in Managua. It took thirty minutes to get to the hotel. The driver, who had introduced himself as Antonio, exited the airport crossing the two eastbound lanes of the four lane Autopista Pedro Joaquin Chamorro. He turned west toward the city. Antonio spoke fair English, and was in a talkative mood. He told Marc that the Inter-Continental Hotel was located in Barrio Martha Quezada, a center for hotels, hospedajes, and restaurants.

Their route was not direct. They left the autopista and wove through a maze of wide streets, narrow streets, made several quick turns through densely populated neighborhoods, dashed back out onto a boulevard, then darted around a circle and off in what seemed to be the opposite direction. Still, the general direction seemed to be west. Marc had always prided himself on his sense of direction, but knew he would never be able to find the airport if left to his own devices. Finally the car pulled onto Avenida Bolivar, and Antonio assured Marc the hotel was not far. They passed the Palacio Nacional and Antonio continued with his patter on the local sights.

"It was here in 1978 that a Sandinista commando group seized the Palacio Nacional and held 2,000 legislators and others in the building hostage, to be released when political demands were met. Somoza capitulated to the kidnappers' demands and this is thought to be the most significant event leading to the armed revolution of 1979 and the ouster of Somoza."

They continued south on Avenida Bolivar and the Hotel Inter-Continental soon came into sight. It was immense and its architecture overwhelming to the senses. It resembled a huge Mayan pyramid painted white. Marc confirmed his reservation at the desk. A bellman led him to the elevator and escorted him to his room, which overlooked Momotombo Volcano. Marc had heard about the hotel, which was the center for international travelers of all types and frequented by local businessmen and politicians. He could understand why. Though the interior of his room was a bit on the shabby side, Marc thought the hotel rated four stars based on its elegant wood paneled lobby, marble floors and lounge furniture handcrafted of exotic woods.

The room air conditioning was turned down to the low 70's, much too cold for someone like Marc, whose body had acclimated to the tropics. He asked the bellboy to adjust it before he left. He unpacked his soft-sided suitcase and then sat down in a chair and looked out the window at Volcán Momotombo for a few minutes. He was excited to be back in Nicaragua. He was also hungry as he had eaten an early breakfast. He rode the elevator down to the first floor informal café. The décor was rattan with cushions in tropical print. It would have been just as appropriate in Hawaii or the Caribbean. Marc favored this décor and found it relaxing. His order was taken immediately, quite different, he noted gratefully, from the casual restaurant service he had found typical in San José. The coffee he had ordered arrived just as promptly. When it was suitably mixed with warm milk and sugar, he sipped it and looked about. As he scanned the other tables he saw the profile of a face he knew. But he could not recall the man. He studied the face, and watched the man as he conversed with two other male diners. Then it struck him. It was Pete Givens, the leader of the contra commando group that had rescued him from the Sandinistas in Chontales and secured the airstrip on Ometepe Island. He watched for another two minutes to make sure that it was Pete. Then he stood up and walked over to the table.

"Pete Givens, I believe," he said.

Pete looked up, with a momentary blank look, then jumped up from his chair as he recognized Marc.

"Well I'll be damned," he said, shaking Marc's hand and then hugged him.

"You got out, Marc, but just barely. And we lost Adriana in the firefight. We have some catching up to do. Let me introduce you to my friends, Jack Durand and Blake Leeds."

The introductions were made, and Pete invited Marc to join them. They were nearly finished with their lunch so Marc declined. Besides, he wanted to talk over old times with Pete in a more private setting. There was much to recount.

"Let's get together this evening, Pete, if you're available. Early drinks in the bar? I see that twofers start at 5:30."

"Great! It's so good to see you Marc. I'll meet you in the bar."

Marc went to the concierge's desk after lunch and arranged a rental car for the next day. She was able to provide him with a Xerox copy of a road map, which he took up to his room to study. A short afternoon map refreshed him, and he cleaned up for his meeting with Pete at the hotel bar. Marc walked into the bar at exactly 5:30. His military training had never failed him. He had never adapted to Latin time, which generally meant thirty minutes or an hour late was perfectly acceptable and normal. He ordered a Campari and soda, and was served two "Happy Hour" drinks, along with a small bowl of peanuts. Pete walked in wearing a light yellow guayabera shirt and sat down.

"Okay Marc, it's your turn first. What in the heck are you doing here?"

"Pete, I've got my own one airplane airline in San José. It's a Cessna 206, six seats including mine, and a capacity for 200 pounds of luggage. It's perfect for the national airports scattered around the country with 3,000 foot long runways. I've been doing that ever since the operation at Point West closed down. I'm flying tourists around the country, doing some business charters, and every now and then an air evac to bring patients into San José from the outlying airports. I was asked to bring some of the exiles up here that are interested in returning to Nicaragua. It looks like that may be a good source of business for a while. What are you doing?"

"You wouldn't believe it, Marc. I'm working with an investment group out of Miami that wants to acquire Pacific Coast beach property. They have seen what is happening in Costa Rica, and they want to buy cheap. I'm the guy who works with local attorneys here to study the land documents and make sure it is free and clear. Much of the rural land was expropriated by the Sandinistas, some paid for at prices the Sandinistas set, others never paid for, and title was given to local Sandinista party followers. So title search is very important. I go out with attorneys and talk to the people involved, to see if the filed documents are the same as what they tell us. You can't be too careful."

"Property investment is a long look down the road, it seems to me. This country is going to have to heal itself from 10 years of war, and that will take some time."

"That's true. But the big money will go to those who are on the ground floor."

"Yeah, as the saying goes, the more risk, the more reward."

"Well, Mexico beach resorts are getting very popular and North Americans are buying property there. Belize is in play now, and investors are looking at Panama in areas like Bocas del Toro on the Caribbean."

"I haven't invested in any property in Costa Rica except a small hangar at the Pavas Airport. I'll probably be sorry."

"How long you here for, Marc?"

"My passengers want a full week here. I plan to drive to Matagalpa tomorrow and meet Adriana's parents. I have been thinking I would do that some day and now I have the opportunity. It'll help me put the tragedy to rest, and I feel I owe it to her parents. Adriana died in the effort to get me out safely. I'll never forget that when she first met me in your camp she told me she would get me out safely. And she did. She was beautiful, caring, and brave. A most exceptional young lady. She has always been on my mind, and I guess I feel guilty that I was indirectly the cause of her death." Marc's voice choked. He picked up his glass of Campari and soda and sipped it slowly, as he attempted to regain his composure.

"I understand completely, Marc. Those were difficult times. I lost several good men, and when I say good, I mean good hearted and morally courageous. Adriana was certainly that. I sometimes think over some of my decisions that may have cost lives unnecessarily. But one can't really go back. We all did what we thought best and usually under tremendous pressure. The war was costly on both sides. Much like our own civil war, I suppose." Pete leaned back in the rattan chair and shook his head, as if that would banish the unpleasant memories.

"How do you see the outlook for the country, Pete?"

"In the long term, I am very hopeful. Certainly my company has a positive outlook, and they are shrewd businessmen. Who would have believed that the FSLN's Daniel Ortega would lose the February elections, and so badly? There is a lot of economic restructuring that needs to be done. But I believe it is just a matter of time," Pete said.

At this moment a man walked up to their table and clapped Pete on the back. He was of medium height, slender, with a trim mustache, a blue-eyed Nicaraguan in a white shirt and tie, shirt sleeves rolled up above his wrists.

"Pete, how are you," he said, extending his right hand. Pete stood up, shook hands and from the wide smile on his face Marc guessed he knew the man well.

"Jorge, when did you get in Managua?" Pete asked.

"This afternoon. I'm working with an international law firm here in Managua on expropriation issues."

"Jorge, pardon my manners. This is Marc DiAngelo, from Costa Rica. He has a charter air service in San José and flew some Nicaraguan clients here this morning. Marc, this is my old friend Jorge Vado"

"Mucho gusto," Jorge said, and Marc responded "Igualmente."

"Marc, Jorge was based in Honduras with the contra headquarters. He saw some fighting early in the conflict, but ended up as one of the primary Contra representatives seeking private donations when Congress cut off the funds. He traveled all over the United States in the late eighties on a lecture circuit and in meetings with private donors and conservative groups. Without that private money coming in, we could not have continued and the FSLN would never have been forced to agree to elections in 1990. Jorge, Marc was flying support missions for the Contras from the Point West airfield in Costa Rica. I have told you before about the firefight we had with the Sandinista soldiers in Chontales when we were sent to rescue Marc."

"Yes, I remember. Marc, those supplies that were dropped kept our forces in business. I want to personally thank you," Jorge said.

"It gave me a great sense of satisfaction to be able to help the good guys," Marc said with a slight shrug of the shoulders. It was an "aw shucks" mannerism he often adopted when offered someone's gratitude.

"How long will you stay in Nicaragua, Marc?" Jorge asked.

"I'll be in-country a week. I'm heading for Matagalpa tomorrow in a rental car," Marc replied.

"Jorge, do you still own the auto hotel between Tipitapa and Matagalpa," Pete asked.

"Yes, my cousin is managing it for me. I was able to keep the property during the war years because it was in my mother's name. She had several friends who were Sandinista officials in the Matagalpa Department."

"I'm going to Matagalpa, so I should make a reservation at your auto hotel," Marc said.

Both Pete and Jorge laughed.

"Marc, there are only two reasons to go to an auto hotel. You either have your girl friend with you or another man's wife. They are a place for liaisons. The rooms rent by the hour. It should give you an idea when you see the names of the auto hotels. Intima, Amor, Fantasía. Jorge can tell you auto hotel stories for hours," Pete said.

"The idea," Jorge said, "is to provide privacy, fast check in and checkout, discretion, and service. One drives in, usually to a prearranged unit by reservation. A canvas cover over the carport entrance hides the car. An attendant comes to the window of the room and receives payment and takes any order for food or drink. No names are given. Inside, the beds may be round, or even in the shape of a heart, and there are mirrors on the walls and ceiling. This is nothing new. Auto hotels have been in Nicaragua since the 1940's. I won't tell you all the stories, there are too many. For example, one time a girl and her boyfriend were leaving the Auto Hotel just as her father and his mistress were entering. The father expressed disgust at his daughter for being there. She was even madder at him for being there with a woman who was not her mother. In another case, a man's wife discovered his car at the auto hotel. When she could not find out which unit he was in, she broke all the windows in his car. Our client was told she was outside and waiting, and he would not leave his room until she tired and departed. Another time a wife discovered her husband's pickup at our hotel and waited for him to come out. My staff had warned him, and he left by another door on the back side of the room. Then he sent a friend to come get the pickup. The friend went in the back door and out the front door and told the waiting wife he had borrowed the pickup. My employees have seen everything, but they were shocked when one of the local priests showed up with a woman. They were embarrassed, but it did not seem to bother him. I asked if the priest always comes with the same woman. They said no, he was bringing many of his sheep there. There are many other stories. Like the couple who checked in and out in five minutes, or the couple that rented the room for three hours and left five used condoms."

"Maybe I'll just find a nice hotel in Matagalpa," Marc said.

"I can make you a recommendation," Jorge said.

"That would be nice. I appreciate it. Jorge, are you going to join us for dinner?"

Jorge accepted the dinner invitation without hesitation. The hotel had three dining rooms, and Pete suggested that Marc choose one of the three. Marc chose the Il Venetio which Pete had said had wonderful Italian cuisine. It turned out to be a wise choice.   A six course dinner started with melon balls wrapped in prosciutto, followed by Italian wedding soup, caprese salad, then by homemade ravioli stuffed with cheeses and ground pork, a large platter of rosemary chicken, and a moist Italian cream cake for dessert.   Volumes of Chianti accompanied the courses.   Both Pete and Jorge were lively conversationalists, and the evening passed quickly.

"Marc, do you think you can find your way to Matagalpa?" Pete asked.

"Sure, but only if I can find my way out of Managua first."

"The best bet is don't try any shortcuts.   Go north on Avenida Bolivar towards the old city, about one kilometer.   Turn on the road just past the Palacio Nacional and head east toward the airport.   From there it's pretty straight forward.   You go direct to Tipitapa, then north to Matagalpa.   The road branches at Sébaco, the left to Estelí, the right to Matagalpa.   I'm curious. Do you know how to find Adriana's parents' house?"

"I really haven't thought that out very well.   I know her last name was Kupper and her family has a large coffee finca on the outskirts of Matagalpa.   So I plan on asking for directions when I get to Matagalpa."

"Marc, I will have directions for you at the concierge's desk in the morning before you leave.   Though I have met Adriana's parents once some time ago, I don't know them well.   I know Matagalpinas who know them and I will get you proper directions."

"That would be great, Pete."

"Why don't you swing by Granada on your return?   I'll be there this week, staying at the Hotel Alhambra.   My company is interested in acquiring one of the large isletas to develop as a destination resort.   There are some friends there that I would like you to meet.   You know one of them"

Marc was puzzled. Who would he know in Granada? But then he remembered a recent article in San José's *La Nacion* that mentioned there were three Nicaraguan priests being considered for selection as the new Archbishop of Granada. Father Pablo was one of them. Though Pete appeared to be intentionally non-committal, it was likely Father Pablo, and seeing him again would be a treat.

"I'll try to do that, Pete. Remember, I stayed at the Archbishop's Palacio in Granada four years ago. I could see the Hotel Alhambra on the other side of the park, but I had to always keep hidden. I think I have a good idea of how Ann Frank felt while the Nazi's were hunting her family. I'm going to call it a night, gentlemen. Thanks for your company," Marc said, as he stood and shook hands with Pete and Jorge.

"Just a minute, Marc. Let me write down the name of a good hotel in Matagalpa and the directions. It is a small hotel, which is all you will find in Matagalpa. But it is clean and comfortable," Jorge said.

Jorge wrote on the back of his business card and handed it to Marc. It read "Hotel San Gregorio, one block north and one-half block east of Parque Ruben Dario." He had also written "Restaurante La Posada, across the street from the hotel — recommended." Marc took the card and again bid the men goodnight.

CHAPTER 16—THE JOURNEY ENDS

Marc awoke with a slight Chianti hangover. He rummaged for a couple of aspirin, slipped on khaki slacks and a white cotton sport shirt and packed his small suitcase. After breakfast he went to the hotel desk for checkout. Pete had indeed left him instructions on how to make contact with the Adriana's parents, the Kupper's. He was to ask the hotel to call them upon his arrival. They had been told he was coming and would send someone for him. Marc was relieved that Pete had broken the ice. Obviously Pete had anticipated that it would be very awkward for Marc to explain his visit to the Kupper's. Marc stopped at the concierge's desk and signed a one page rental contract for a 1988 Nissan Sentra, was handed the keys, and found his car in the reserved section in front of the hotel. He followed Pete's instructions for getting out of the city. It seemed surprisingly easy in comparison with the drive into the city the day before. Marc was grateful that he didn't have to fight the heavy late morning traffic. He was soon on the autopista that passed the International Airport and on his way to Tipitapa. The road bordered the south side of Lake Managua. At Tipitapa he saw the junction with the road to Masaya. He tried to memorize landmarks near the junction so that he would know where to turn on his return trip to Masaya and on to Granada.

The highway swung north at Tipitapa toward Sébaco, the small town where the road split to the northwest to Estelí and north to Matagalpa. Within a few kilometers after leaving Tipitapa, he came upon the road junction to Juigalpa in Chontales Department. He had noticed on the map the day before that Comalapa, near Juigalpa, was not very far from the road he would be traveling. He doubted that Ellen would still be at the village. It had been four years now, he mused, as he drove down the nearly vacant road. Ellen had said that the church limited its missionaries to two year stays. Besides, Ellen had said the Sandinistas intended to expel all the foreign missionaries as they were potential Contra supporters. Some, he was sure, had been in fact sympathetic to the Sandinista cause. But it was probably a case of throwing the baby out with the bathwater. He slowed down for the intersection, and read the road sign, which said Juigalpa was 99 kilometers. That's only 65 miles, he thought, and Comalapa was not even that far. Well, he would see how long his visit would be. Perhaps.

When Marc arrived at the small pueblo of Sébaco, he was relieved to see that the branch in the road to Estelí and Matagalpa was well marked. He had just passed the intersection when he came to a large fruit and vegetable market that lined both sides of the road for a quarter of a kilometer. The profusion of fruits and vegetables surprised him, after having just emerged from a very drought stricken area of brown dusty fields. But in this oasis huge carrots and giant heads of lettuce were stacked high in rows in front of the stalls. Strings of garlic hung from the tin roofs of the stalls. Woven cane baskets overflowed with onions, beets, bell peppers, yucca roots, potatoes and tomatoes. Stall shelves and bins displayed limes, mangos, bananas, platano, apples, pineapples, oranges and tangerines. Marc found the abundance staggering. He pulled off the road and bought six tangerines for the equivalent price of six cents.

The road out of Sébaco began the ascent toward the blue-green mountains ahead. The temperature became cooler and the air seemed fresher as the Sentra climbed the highway's curves. He could see coffee fields on the distant hillsides and along the road. Marc passed coffee processing plants with huge expanses of concrete. They resembled giant parking lots where the coffee beans were spread out to dry. Only a few buses and trucks and an occasional horse cart shared the road with Marc as he followed the road to Matagalpa. The city lay in the center of a long valley. He passed the outskirts of Matagalpa which gave Marc a view of the center of the city below and to the right. As he drove north, he could see the bell towers of the Cathedral of San Pedro. The map placed the Cathedral on Parque Morazan, which was to the north of Parque Darío, his key landmark to find the Hotel San Gregorio. It was easier than he expected. He saw the Parque Darío a block away, turned left and drove right up to the front door of the hotel. A young man dressed in dark blue pants and shirt with light blue shoulder tabs ran to his car and carried Marc's suitcase into the hotel.

The hotel was built in the form of a rectangle, a single story that surrounded a garden. A small oval-shaped swimming pool filled the center of the garden. The rooms were lined along deep corridors that faced the garden. The young man who had introduced himself as Juan led Marc directly to a room. He swung open the massive oak door and stood politely aside for Marc to enter. Though it was mid day and warm in Matagalpa, the coolness of the room hit Marc like a refreshing shower. Two matrimonial beds, as the double beds were called, rested against one wall. Marc looked approvingly at the other furnishings: a desk, large armoire, a small table and side chairs. They were all priceless antiques he was sure. Marc tipped Juan, unpacked his suitcase, and walked to the hotel desk to register. Juan had known his name and had taken him straight to his room. He had been expected, that was certain. It seemed that Jorge's introduction must carry some weight in Matagalpa. Marc passed a large open dining area of tables and chairs. All were fastidiously set with white tablecloths, crystal goblets, and china place settings. The only diners were an old white haired couple, elegantly dressed. Two attentive waiters stood a few feet away.

At the desk Marc was handed a card, which he filled out, and was asked for his passport. "Don Marc, this is for you," the clerk said. He handed Marc a hand-made envelope. It was addressed to Sr. Marc DiAngelo. The hand-writing was in elegant old world flourishes.

My dearest Marc,

My husband Don Luis and I look forward to your visit. Our foreman, Don José Lacayo, will pick you up at the hotel at 1:00 p.m. We will have lunch when you arrive.

Dolores María Vorwald de Kupper

It was nearly 1:00 p.m. Marc hurried back to his room to get the light windbreaker jacket he had brought along. The Inter-Continental Hotel's concierge had warned him he would need a light jacket or sweater if he was going to a finca in the

Matagalpa area. When he returned to the front entrance of the little hotel, he saw an old Landcruiser waiting out front. A man in his sixties with a weather beaten face and wearing a white straw rancher's hat was waiting at the desk.

"Don José?" Marc asked, as he walked up to the old gentleman.

"Sí, Don Marc," he said, as he offered a handshake. "Listo para salir?" he asked.

"Sí, Señor," Marc replied, acknowledging he was ready to leave. It appeared Don José spoke no English, and Marc was not enthused about spending an hour or so struggling in a conversation in Spanish. Perhaps the hotel clerk sensed that as he interjected. "Don Marc, it is only 30 minutes to the Kupper finca."

"Gracias," Marc replied. Don José motioned to Marc with a nod of his head and Marc followed him.

They drove up out of the city to the road going north to Jinotega and followed that road for about five miles. Then Don José made a left turn onto a gravel road and the old Landcruiser began a slow climb in second gear. They passed through orderly rows of coffee plants on both sides of the road.

"La finca Kupper," Don José said, sweeping his hand from left to right. Marc nodded. He knew a little about coffee farming from his travels in Costa Rica. The Kupper finca was producing shade grown coffee, as there was a smattering of trees scattered through the coffee fields. This, he had learned, increased the life span of the coffee plants and reduced the need for chemical fertilizers. Trees lined the narrow gravel road. Various colors of impatiens grew wild in the shady spots. Within 15 minutes Don José slowed the old Landcruiser and entered a driveway that led to a sprawling one-story brick and stone house. The car pulled up to a porch entrance and stopped. At that moment a lady who appeared to be in her seventies came out on the porch. She was followed by a tall, erect, white haired man. This has to be Adriana's mother, Marc thought. The resemblance was remarkable. Her hair was darker blond than Adriana's with very little grey showing. She was dressed in a peach colored outfit, with blouse overlaying the skirt. Her face was nearly devoid of wrinkles. She carried herself with elegant dignity. Don Luis was tanned and tall, without an ounce of fat. He wore ironed jeans, western style belt, and a striped short sleeve business shirt without tie. A real Marlboro man, if there was ever one, Marc reflected. But his attention turned towards Doña Dolores María. She had the same blue eyes as her daughter, the same graceful body movements and confident poise of her daughter.

Doña Dolores María waited for Marc on the porch, and gave him a motherly kiss on the cheek and an embrace. This was to be a special visit. Don Luis' handshake was firm and strong. Both of the parents spoke good English, he discovered, but with more of a German than Spanish accent. Doña Dolores María ushered them through the spacious house, which was airy and sparsely furnished by North American standards. The back porch ran the full length of the house, covered by a tile roof supported by heavy wood beams and posts. The view from the porch was the valley below. In the distance Marc could see a range of purple hills, each higher than the previous, rising from the other side of the valley floor. A grass lawn sloped down gently from the house to a line of huge old oak trees. Lines of coffee plants were beyond, descending toward the valley floor.

Doña Dolores María motioned for Marc to sit in one of the cushioned rustic coffee wood chairs. She and Don Luis also sat down, and a maid immediately walked in with a tray of glasses of lemonade.

Marc raised his glass and offered "Salud". The two septuagenarians raised their glasses in response and answered "Salud". They said nothing for the moment, allowing Marc to take in the scene before him. There was an extra chair to his left, and suddenly he pictured Adriana sitting there, her blonde hair in a pony tail, her blue eyes shining and a warm "Salud" lighting up her face as she smiled at him.

"Marc, it was so nice that you came to see us," Doña Dolores María said. "Señor Peter Givens explained to us the reason for your visit. We have been told of the circumstances of our Adriana's death. We know that she was very brave on Ometepe Island." Don Luis had said nothing, and Marc was worried that Don Luis might hold him accountable for Adriana's death. Now he began to doubt that. Tears had welled up in Don Luis' eyes as his wife talked about their departed daughter.

"Yes, Doña Dolores, she was very brave. A true comandante, and I know she was highly respected. She saved my life, and for that I am truly grateful and a little troubled. I have always felt somehow responsible. It is a guilt I feel every day."

"My dear Marc, war is war. It causes many heart aches. We must accept the consequences of war and make peace within ourselves. My husband and I take great comfort in knowing that Adriana was in part responsible for the removal of the tyranny of the Sandinistas. Our people are free. We have had elections. I believe she knows that. Would you like to visit Adriana's grave?"

"Very much. Here at the finca?"

"Of course. Adriana was first buried at the church in Altagracia on Ometepe Island under another name. We were able to have her body brought here a few months later. We sent five men from our finca. They had to tell the Sandinista soldiers on their return trip to Matagalpa that they were bringing the body of a Sandinista soldier. That I regret. She should have come back to us with the honor she deserved."

"I hope she appreciated the irony of that. I believe that would have brought a smile to her face."

Doña Dolores and Don Luis both nodded in agreement. It even brought the trace of a smile to Don Luis' face.

A table on the porch was set by the maid, and Doña Dolores rose, announcing it was time for lunch. A simple fare of roasted chicken, fried maduro platano, beans and rice with a tomato and cucumber salad was served. A refreshing light breeze blew into the porch, enhancing the serenity of the moment.

"Adriana must have loved it here," Marc said.

"As a girl Adriana loved the bosque, the forest. She liked to hike up on the hill above the house, where the forest is thick. She was forever seeking the quetzals, and when she would see one, she would run back to the house very excited. As you know, Marc, the Resplendant Quetzal has become very rare. But Adriana hiked up to where there were many aguacate canelo trees. The quetzals favor the fruit of these trees, which is most abundant in March, April, and May."

"She also liked the forest animals," Don Luis interjected.

"This is true. We have sloths, ocelots, pumas, margays, peccaries and many others. Adriana would sit for hours, cross-legged on the ground, watching a sloth move through the trees so incredibly slow. She would talk to it, and often gave it a name, and urge it to move faster. And then she would laugh and laugh!"

Marc felt the tension that Adriana's name brought begin to ebb. He had had doubts about this visit. He knew it was therapeutic for him and hoped it helped to ease the pain for Doña Dolores and Don Luis. It also fulfilled his promise to

Adriana that he would go to Matagalpa and visit with her parents after the war. At the time they both understood that the visit would lead him to Adriana. Of course it had, but not in the way the two could have foreseen.

The lunch was ended with a simple rice pudding sweetened with coconut milk and topped with powdered cinnamon.

"Perhaps we should go visit Adriana now," Don Luis said.

"Yes, of course. It should be cool there. Come, Marc," Doña Dolores said as she stood. The three walked down the steps to the lawn, and Doña Dolores took Marc's arm.

"Over here," she said, gently nudging Marc to the right. Not far from an old oak tree was a gravesite enclosed with a low wrought iron fence painted white. Ten feet away was a white wrought iron bench. As they walked closer, Marc could see the small simple headstone in the enclosure. It read in four lines:

Adriana María Kupper Vorwald
24 Set. 1964 – 25 Jul. 1986
Nuestra Querida Hija
Descansa en Paz

Doña Dolores directed Marc to the bench, and she sat down. Marc walked back to the gravesite, which was meticulously maintained. Again he looked at the headstone, and read silently to himself the English translation: Our Beloved Daughter, Rest in Peace. Small orchid plants had been affixed to the wrought iron enclosure, and each one of the several varieties had one or more blooms.

"This is very pretty and peaceful," Marc said, looking from the gravesite out across the valley. Don Luis had sat down next to Doña Dolores. "This was one of Adriana's favorite places to play as a little girl. There used to be a swing from the branches up above," Don Luis said.

Marc looked up. The girth of the lower branch was larger than the trunks of most trees. The trunk and lower branches were covered in green moss.

"This oak will be here long after we are gone," Marc said. He stood motionless near the headstone. "I have come to Matagalpa as I promised, my Adriana," he murmured aloud as if she might hear. He thanked her for her friendship, her courage, and her love. He remembered very well Adriana's words at the Palacio Episcopal as the two had pondered their inevitable separation when they arrived at Ometepe Island: "Mi amor, there is a Nicaraguan saying. Amor y dar son lo que dan valor a la vida. Love and giving are what makes life worth living. Your escape to Costa Rica, your freedom, is my gift to you. I give it without reservation. Your gift will come later, when you return to Nicaragua to find me." Tears welled up in his eyes, and he dabbed them with the back of his hand. An arm came around his waist from behind.

"We all loved her very much, Marc. Our daughter brought us much joy. Thank you for your visit here," Doña Dolores María said. Marc turned, and kissed Doña Dolores on the cheek.

"Thank you for allowing me to come. I will never forget this, and with your permission, I would like to return some day."

"You will always be welcome here," Doña Dolores said, turning and starting for the house. "Come Luis," she said to her husband, who got up slowly from the bench, startling Marc with a frailty he had not noticed before.

"Would Don José be able to take me back to the hotel now?" Marc asked.

"Yes, certainly, but you are welcome to stay for dinner."

"I appreciate that. It's been a long day, and I would hate to be rude and fall asleep in the middle of dinner," Marc said with a smile.

"Then you must go and rest. As we say in Spanish, nuestra casa es su casa. We will hope to see you soon, querido." Doña Dolores gave Marc a kiss on both cheeks and Don Luis followed with a handshake and embrace. Marc left with Don José, retracing the road down to the valley. There had been nothing more to say. In truth he was tired, both emotionally and physically.

Roast chicken had been recommended as a specialty at the Restaurante La Posada across the street from the hotel. Marc had two Victoria's with his chicken dinner and was content to dine alone and ponder what the next few days would bring. The next morning he nibbled at the continental breakfast at the hotel with little enthusiasm. He paid the hotel bill and carried his small suitcase to the guarded parking lot on the corner. He easily found the Matagalpa-Jinotega road several blocks west of the hotel and headed south. He had looked at his map and knew he would have to make a decision in about an hour before he arrived at San Benito. He could either turn left at San Benito to the road that lead to Juigalpa and the river port beyond, Rama. Or he would continue straight into Tipitapa and then on to Masaya and Granada. There was little chance Ellen would be at Comalapa. And if she were, would their meeting be just another emotionally draining experience? Yes, he owed Ellen too. She had put her life on the line for him, no small gift from a woman he had not known. And, of course, he thought, I did know her and I loved her for a short time as if she were the only person in the world who mattered to me. Yes, I was dependent upon her, he reflected, maybe it was some sort of twist of the "Stockholm syndrome." She was not my captor but rather my savior. Marc's mind was going in circles, and he forced himself to concentrate on the road. The brown barren fields on either side of the car marked his descent from the mountains to the plains east of Lake Managua.

The Sentra was less than a kilometer from San Benito and Marc still had not made up his mind. Within a few minutes he saw the intersection ahead and the sign that pointed left to Juigalpa. The two lane road was very wide at this point, and a left turn lane began just before the intersection. Without making a conscious decision, Marc moved into the left lane, signaled a left turn though there was no traffic in sight in either direction, and turned onto the Juigalpa road leading southwest to the Boaco and Chontales Departments, and the little village of Comalapa. He pulled to the side of the road and stopped, and looked at his map. It was 79 kilometers to the turnoff to Comalapa, then another 12 heading east into the foothills of the village. He drove on, finding little traffic except some slow buses which hogged the curvy road and were difficult to pass safely. He was getting hungry, but he was doubtful he would find even a basic restaurant he would be comfortable with in any of the towns before Juiglapa. As if ordained, he passed a sign that proclaimed "Los Bosques, Platillos Exoticos del Campo, Juigalpa." He decided to go to Juigalpa in search of food, knowing that it wouldn't be more than 20 kilometers or 20 minutes past the turnoff to Comalapa. Before noon Marc arrived in Juigalpa, and spotted the Restaurante Los Bosques on the left side of the road just as he entered the outskirts. The restaurant sat well back off the road, surrounded by grass and driveways on both sides, the property enclosed on three sides by a ten foot high concrete block fence. Large mango trees shaded the restaurant. Marc pulled in between a 1988 Mitsubishi Montero and a 1990 Toyota Land Cruiser in the parking area behind the restaurant. If the high-end clientele were any indication, he had made the right decision. He was famished. Marc found a table on the large porch under a ceiling fan. There were even table cloths, he noted. He took the menu and ordered a Victoria, which was served to him immediately along with a frozen mug. Marc looked over the menu, but could not translate many of the menu items. Marc considered his Spanish fair, and a menu in Spanish was not usually a challenge. Marc called the waiter over.

"Cual es eso?" Marc asked the waiter, hoping for an explanation of the menu item.

"Boa" came the reply.

"Boa?" Marc echoed.

"Si, Señor."

"A gentleman in his forties was sitting at the table next to Marc. He got up and walked over.

"Can I help you with the menu?" he asked in good English with a heavy Spanish accent. Marc looked up at the man, who he assumed to be a rancher. The man was dressed in jeans, western boots, white short- sleeved shirt, and a white straw rancher's hat typical for the area. He sported a pencil thin mustache.

"I would appreciate that. I'm really not familiar with the items on the menu."

"Your waiter was telling you the Boa is Boa. The serpiente. The snake. Here on the menu it says Boa Desmenuzada. The meat is cooked, crumbled, mixed with spices, pepper, and achiote. It is served with rice, toasted corn tortillas, a lettuce salad, and red beans. The boa tastes just like chicken. It is my favorite meal here," the stranger said.

"I suppose I should try something new," Marc said with little conviction.

"There are some other meals you might like," the rancher said. "Here," he said, pointing to the menu, "is barbecued venison, and here is barbecued rabbit. The barbecued garrobo is what you would call iguana tail. It also tastes like chicken. The armadillo on the menu speaks for itself, and the guardatinaja is similar to the armadillo. I also recommend the cascabel or rattlesnake, which is served barbecued with a sauce of onion, chiles, and fresh tomatoes."

"Thank you very much," Marc said, and the rancher returned to his table. Marc flipped the menu over. He was relieved to see there were other menu items. He looked up at the waiter who was standing patiently by, and ordered a quesoburgesa. The cheeseburger came with fries, and as far as Marc was concerned, went perfectly with the ice cold Victoria. When the quesoburgesa was served, his rancher friend at the next table laughed.

Marc backtracked to the Comalapa turnoff, and began the slow ascent up the washboard gravel road to the village. It would be only a matter of a few minutes until he was there, and he would know. It occurred to him he really didn't know the little village at all, only what he had seen from Ellen's window.

The little village of Comalapa was spread out on either side of the road. Homes and small businesses were built in either wood, brick or concrete block, but uniformly roofed in zinc sheeting. They were set back from the road, perhaps as protection from the rolling clouds of dust generated by passing vehicles. Marc saw a Coca Cola sign ahead to the right that said "Pulpería Margarita." He pulled off the road and stopped in front of it. The dark little notions store was crammed with racks of packaged snack foods, unwrapped loaves of bread stacked on the counter, shelves of lotions, soap, toilet paper, canned goods, and an array of over-the-counter medicines displayed in the case below the counter. A dark skinned heavy-set young woman greeted him. She was holding a baby with a runny nose.

"Buenos Días. Busco la casa de Elena, la gringa enfermera. Usted la conoce?" Marc asked. He saw the perplexed look on the shopkeeper's face that meant either she did not understand his Spanish or she did not comprehend why he would be looking for the house of the gringa nurse.

"Elena, Elena, de Asamblea de Díos iglesia," Marc said, giving it another try.

Suddenly the woman's face brightened to a broad smile. "Sí, sí, la Señorita Elena," she said. Marc was relieved. She did know Ellen.

"Donde vive?" Marc asked, hoping she could tell him where Ellen lived.

"No está aqui, no mas," she said. Marc's hopes were dashed, but it was the answer he had expected. Ellen was no longer in Comalapa.

At this moment a slender young woman with long hair reaching down her back walked into the pulpería.

"Hola señor. What you want?" she asked, in heavily accented broken English.

"I am looking for Elena, the gringa nurse who lived in Comalapa four years ago. I know her house was near here."

"Sí, señor. Her house was there, about 500 meters, más o menos," the young woman said, pointing through the back wall of the pulpería.

"Does she live there now?" Marc asked. The proprietor of the pulpería had already answered this question and he knew the answer. But maybe he could get a clearer answer with this young lady who spoke some English.

"No señor. It is three years she leaves Comalapa."

"Is there another gringa or gringo here with the Asamblea de Díos church?"

"No señor. The Sandinistas close the church when they take Señorita Elena away."

Marc had always feared that Ellen's safety had been compromised because she aided his escape. Now he guessed his foreboding was justified. Had he also caused Ellen's death? He thanked the young woman. Moments before he was elated that he might see Ellen again. Now he felt emptiness and the haunting thought that he might have asked too much. Once again he considered, had concern for his own safety unfairly targeted those who came to his rescue?

It would be dark by the time he got to Granada. He retraced his route to Tipitapa, and from there drove to Masaya and on into Granada. He passed the large baseball stadium, home of the "Tiburons" - the sharks - a sign proclaimed. Pete's map delivered him to the Alhambra Hotel.

Marc pulled the Sentra up to the curb. It was already 6:20 p.m., and dark. Wide steps led up to a deep covered porch that extended the full width of the hotel. To the left were tables and chairs occupied by casually-dressed restaurant diners. To the right of the stairs, wicker rocking chairs faced the now-quiet park across the street. Tall multi-globed turn-of-the-century lamp posts cast shadows into the tree canopies. A light breeze rustled their branches. The faint sound of a marimba group wafted along with the wind. Lively conversation from the hotel porch competed with the more distant sounds. Completing his survey, Marc allowed a uniformed doorman to take his small suitcase.

The veranda was softly lit by wall lamps that reflected an elegant air to the old hotel. Marc strode past the diners on his left and toward the lobby inside. He would ask for Pete Givens at the hotel desk. A small group of guests to his right, sitting in white wicker rocking chairs around a low round wicker table, were chatting and laughing as he walked by.

"Hey Marc, about time you got here," a familiar voice said, coming from the group. Marc turned around, and saw Pete in one of the rockers.

"Hey, Pete, I was just going to ask for you at the desk."

"Pull up a chair. I've reserved your room. You can register later. I want to introduce you to some friends." Marc saw that there were two empty rockers. One had a glass of wine in front of it, and Marc sat in the other. He didn't see Father Pablo, but guessed he was in the men's room. Pete introduced Tom Bell, a business associate, and Rita, Tom's wife.

"What will you have to drink, Marc?" Pete asked.

"A rum and coke sounds good for now." Pete waved a bar waiter to the table and ordered for Marc.

Marc had begun to recount for the Bell's how he and Pete had met for the first time when he felt a pair of hands on his shoulders, and then a soft cheek brushed his followed by a lingering kiss and a hug from behind. He turned in his chair and all he could do was stare in astonishment.

"Hello Marc. It has been too long," Ellen said. The soft deliberate Texas drawl hit him like a sledge hammer. Marc was speechless for more than a few seconds. Pete laughed.

"Ellen, for God's sake, I thought you might be dead. I was at Comalapa today trying to track you down. They said you had been arrested by the Sandinistas and taken away more than three years ago."

"Marc, it's a long story. I think Pete should have told you I would be here. He let you go on a wild goose chase. But I am touched that you took the trouble."

"It was too good an opportunity to surprise Marc," Pete interjected. "I didn't imagine that he would go to Comalapa."

"I'm just relieved that you're okay, Ellen. I had imagined all sorts of horrible things on my drive from Comalapa."

"I'm glad you came through your ordeal safe and sound. I have thought of you often. Pete has told me you are living in Costa Rica now." Ellen sat down in the rocking chair next to Marc. He impulsively put his hand on her arm, and she responded, covering his hand with her own.

"Ellen, just so you know, I have thought of you many times as well. I have never forgotten the evening when you started down the mountain from the cave. It was the last time I saw you. You turned around in the saddle, and blew a kiss up to me. Do you remember?"

"Yes, quite well. It has been a sweet moment for me to remember. You were standing so alone at the cave entrance, and I hated to leave you. Marc, when you finish your drink, we can go across the street and find a park bench. Then we can catch up on each other."

"I like that idea."

Marc and Ellen joined in the light conversation with Pete and his friends. But each kept glancing at the other as though neither one could believe they were reunited. Marc waved off the waiter who asked if he wanted another drink.

"Ready, Ellen?" he asked.

"Yes," she replied, draining the last of a white Chilean wine from the glass and setting it down on the table.

"Please excuse us," Marc said, and added with a mischievous smile, "Pete, thanks for the drinks."

"Anytime, amigo. The next one's on you," he said, waving the two to go.

Frank Gallo

Marc and Ellen walked down the steps and crossed the street. Ellen took Marc's hand, as they walked into the park and found a bench near the fountain. A three-quarter moon shone down through the palms. The fronds yielded a gentle swishing sound as the light wind from the lake made its way west. The marimba group, closer now, was playing Malagueña.

"I have always loved the marimba," Ellen said as they sat down.

"I have never tired of them, I can say," Marc replied. "Ellen, what happened when you left Comalapa? Did the Sandinistas arrest you? And where have you been all these years?"

"I can understand why the villagers in Comalapa thought I had been arrested. In fact, almost all the missionaries, at least in the rural areas, were rounded up and taken to Managua. We weren't badly treated. I guess you would call it a "house arrest." Though we were at the Inter-Continental, the Sandinistas took our passports and there were two days of interrogations at the Department of Internal Security. I think the State Security agents believed I was a spy or at the minimum a Contra supporter. But they had no evidence. I was worried that one of the village informers had spoken against me. At the end of the second day of interrogation they handed me my passport and told me I had to be out of the country in three days. And I was! The head of our evangelical mission was very sympathetic to the Sandinistas, and I think that was a positive factor. I returned to Texas, and worked at a hospital in Ft. Worth. Whenever I had time off, I would go to my parent's ranch to help out. Dad had developed a heart condition and had to undergo a triple bypass, and Mom began losing her eyesight. They had to move into town. A year ago I left Ft. Worth to run the ranch. I was able to hire a reliable foreman and now I can have some time away. It was a seven days a week job. I always laugh when someone tells me that when they retire they want to have a small ranch."

"When did you get to Granada?" Marc asked.

"Two weeks ago. I really loved Nicaragua and the people when I was here, even though it was a stressful time. So with the Sandinistas defeated in the elections and Violeta in office, I felt it was safe to return. Now it's your turn to fill me in on your adventures."

"Okay. When I was up at the cave I was looking forward to seeing you that evening. Unfortunately, I awoke that afternoon with an AK-47 muzzle in my face. When I was rescued by Pete's commando unit, he said that Contra intelligence had told him I would be at the cave. You must have had pretty good communications with the Contras."

Ellen said nothing. Marc continued the story of his escape, the boat ride across the lake, his stay at the Archbishop's Palace in Granada, the voyage to Ometepe Island, and the firefight there. He omitted the intimate times he and Adriana shared, knowing it would be extremely awkward. As he felt the warmth of her hand, he did not want to douse the flame that he felt was being rekindled between them. He did tell Ellen that he had just visited Adriana's parents and her grave.

"That was very kind of you, Marc. I am sure that your visit helped them to accept their daughter's death."

"I hope so. It helped me. I have always felt that I was responsible for her death, and they were kind enough to relieve me of that guilt."

Ellen took his right hand in hers, brought it up to her lips, and kissed the back of it softly. There were no questions. For a time Marc said nothing, content to accept the welcome solace of Ellen's presence. He took each of Ellen's hands in his, squeezed gently, and looked into those searching brown eyes.

"Ellen, since my escape back to Costa Rica after the airplane crash, I have replayed the whole incident a thousand times. Not everything that happened makes sense."

"It was a confusing time, Marc. Not much made sense then."

"Perhaps. But there were too many coincidences. It seemed quite coincidental that your boys with the ox cart were at the airstrip at the time of the crash. Then these three young campesinos knew to gather up all the baggage, make it appear that Fernando was the pilot, set the plane on fire, and bring me straight to you and not to the village. As if they were expecting me to arrive. Maybe someone else – even you – were with them? While you couldn't have taken better care of me after the crash, you didn't seem totally surprised by the situation. Your communication with the Contra forces seemed quite normal, as though you must have had regular contacts. I think there's more to this than I know. I'm not complaining, Ellen. You stuck your neck way out for me. But, I repeat, I think there is more to the story."

Ellen took a deep breath. "Marc, I suppose you will always think that unless I explain. It's important to me that there is nothing between us. I feel that we are good friends."

"At least that, Ellen. I think we may be destined for more than that, if you don't mind me saying. And it's not just the moon, the palms, the marimba and the fountain that causes me to say that. Though I can't think of a more romantic spot to speak our thoughts."

"You are a romantic, Marc. I like that. Let me get over this hurdle between us. You're right, there were too many coincidences. After a year in-country, I went to a quarterly meeting of the field missionaries in Managua. At this point I was thoroughly disillusioned by the Sandinista movement. They divided our local population into two categories, as they did all over the country. People were either thought of as working class or anti-working class. Then Peoples' Tribunals were set up, to deal with the enemies of the working class, in other words, enemies of the Sandinistas. The conviction rate of anyone charged as anti-revolutionary was nearly one hundred percent. I was disgusted. My missionary friend from Chinandega invited me to dinner, and told me a friend of his would join us. That friend was an Embassy employee who used the name Byron Smith. That should tell you something. He was, in fact, a CIA officer. He asked me to be the eyes and ears in Chontales. I accepted his offer, and I was debriefed every time I went to Managua for a quarterly meeting.

Later, a courier brought me word that a small airplane would be landing at the agricultural strip the same morning you crashed, and an agent would be dropped off. I was told it was essential that he arrive in Managua that same day. A farm work truck was to come to my little house and take him to the Comalapa and Managua road intersection. There he was to be met by a car with East German markings and taken to Managua. The courier also had a high powered rifle with scope in a black aluminum case that I was to give to your passenger. The courier told me more than he should have. He said that Fidel Castro had arrived in Managua and was addressing a Sandinista rally that evening in the Plaza de Revolución. It was not hard to put two and two together and see what Fernando's mission was."

"Were you with the boys and the ox cart when I landed and hit the ditch?"

"Yes. I took care of all the arrangements with the boy's help. Once I determined that Fernando was dead, it seemed best to leave him there as if he were the pilot. Then we set fire to the plane. I left immediately for my house on horseback, and sent the truck driver away with a note about the crash. The boys returned with the ox cart which we had hidden you in."

"You've got a lot of guts, lady!"

"I was scared to death to be perfectly honest. When the Sandinistas came for me later, I was sure they knew I was working for the Contras."

Marc leaned over, and gave Ellen a hug, which she seemed to need at the moment. A horse carriage passed along the street between them and the hotel. The lanterns on each side of the driver's seat and the two at the rear softly outlined the carriage as it passed. The carriage and the sound of the two horses' hooves against the pavement vanished as the carriage turned left and proceeded west on Calle Libertad.

A young girl, no more than ten years old, walked up to them through the evening shadows with a large tray of roasted cashews balanced on her head. She lowered the tray carefully, and Marc paid for two small packages.

"Pobrecita" Ellen whispered as the child walked away. They watched her disappear into the night.

"Marc, I'm so glad you're here."

"And so am I, my beautiful Elena." The heaviness of spirit that had enveloped Marc was lifting. His loss of Adriana, deepened with his visit to Matagalpa, was now tempered by the unexpected appearance of Ellen. Adriana, he knew, would always be with him. But there was more than enough room for Ellen. They had a bond few men and women could share.

"A penny for your thoughts."

"I'm just thinking how lucky I was to find you again."

"What are your plans?" Ellen asked.

"My plans are to stay in Granada the rest of the week, if you will be here. I have to fly my clients back to San José in five days. How long will you be in Granada?"

"I had planned a month."

"I've got an extra seat. Why not come to San José with me? Then we can fly back and spend some time looking around. I love Granada, but the Pacific beaches are appealing too. I'd like to visit the little Pacific port of San Juan del Sur," Marc said.

"I'd like that too."

"Can you stay longer than a month, or am I going to have to fly all the way to Texas to see you?"

"Longer I can do. I have a very good ranch manager," Ellen said matter-of-factly, but then added softly, "Marc, I have missed you." She snuggled into Marc's shoulder, and he put his arm around her and bent down and kissed her lightly on the top of her head.

The moon shone down through the palms as if to favor them and little moon beams danced about their feet as the palm fronds swayed in the light lake breeze. Perhaps by more than chance, the marimba group across the park began to play the hauntingly romantic song "La Novia", and the tune was carried softly to them.

It had been a long time since Marc had felt so at peace. It had been a long journey to get here, with many unexplained and unexpected detours, but now he suddenly felt at home.

"Shall we walk back and join Pete and his friends?" Marc asked.

"Yes, but let's not stay too long."

THE END

ABOUT THE AUTHOR

Frank Gallo is a retired Air Force pilot and current private pilot who has lived in Costa Rica, Nicaragua, and Panama. He has flown his Cessna 182 throughout most of Central America, and has visited most of the locations in which the story takes place. These include in Nicaragua: Granada, where he had a home for 8 years, Matagalpa, Managua, Rivas, Leon, Chinandega, Ometepe Island, the Río San Juan and the Río Sábalos as well as many other areas of Nicaragua; In Costa Rica, where he had a home for 9 years, he had visited the Santa Rosa National Park where the Point West airstrip was located, as well as other Costa Rica locations mentioned in the book such as Liberia and San José. Frank's library has nearly a dozen books related to his research on the period of the 1980's when the Contra-Sandinista conflict took place. Frank's published work includes articles in multinational publications on the topics of aviation, Central American living and technology. He lives in Aurora, Colorado.

More than two years of research has led to the completion of this book, which though fiction, details many of the true events that took place during the uprising against the dictator Somoza and the subsequent conflict that took place between the FSLN Marxist/Communist regime and the US supported Contras.

www.ingramcontent.com/pod-product-compliance
Lightning Source LLC
Chambersburg PA
CBHW072218170626
46813CB00003B/994